PRAISE FOR RACH

"*The Consequence of Loving Colton* is a must-read friends-to-lovers story that's as passionate and sexy as it is hilarious!"
——Melissa Foster, *New York Times* bestselling author

"Just when you think Van Dyken can't possibly get any better, she goes and delivers *The Consequence of Loving Colton*. Full of longing and breathless moments, this is what romance is about."
——Lauren Layne, *USA Today* bestselling author

"The tension between Milo and Colton made this story impossible to put down. Quick, sexy, witty—easily one of my favorite books from Rachel Van Dyken."
——R. S. Grey, *USA Today* bestselling author, on
The Consequence of Loving Colton

"Hot, funny, and will leave you wishing you could get marked by one of the immortals!"
——Molly McAdams, *New York Times* bestselling author, on
The Dark Ones

"Laugh-out-loud fun! Rachel Van Dyken is on my auto-buy list."
——Jill Shalvis, *New York Times* bestselling author, on *The Wager*

"*The Dare* is a laugh-out-loud read that I could not put down. Brilliant. Just brilliant."
——Cathryn Fox, *New York Times* bestselling author

Cheater

Elicit
Bang Bang
Enforce
Ember
Elude
Empire

The Seaside Series

Tear
Pull
Shatter
Forever
Fall
Eternal
Strung
Capture

The Renwick House Series

The Ugly Duckling Debutante
The Seduction of Sebastian St. James
The Redemption of Lord Rawlings
An Unlikely Alliance
The Devil Duke Takes a Bride

The London Fairy Tales Series

Upon a Midnight Dream
Whispered Music
The Wolf's Pursuit
When Ash Falls

The Seasons of Paleo Series

Savage Winter

Feral Spring

The Wallflower Series (with Leah Sanders)

Waltzing with the Wallflower

Beguiling Bridget

Taming Wilde

The Dark Ones Saga

The Dark Ones

Untouchable Darkness

Dark Surrender

Stand-Alones

Hurt: A Collection (with Kristin Vayden and Elise Faber)

RIP

Compromising Kessen

Every Girl Does It

The Parting Gift (with Leah Sanders)

Divine Uprising

Cheater

CURIOUS LIAISONS, BOOK 1

RACHEL
VAN DYKEN

DISCARD

SKYSCAPE

SKYSCAPE

Published by Skyscape, New York

www.apub.com

Amazon, the Amazon logo, and Skyscape are trademarks of Amazon.com, Inc., or its affiliates.

ISBN-13: 9781503942097
ISBN-10: 1503942090

Cover design by Damonza

Cover photography by Regina Wamba of MaeIDesign.com

Printed in the United States of America

To my husband, who forced me to leave the house when I needed to write and edit this book—it's finished because of you!

Prologue

Nobody ever tells this side of the story—but it's important. Cheaters aren't born, they're made. Never forget that. You don't wake up one day and decide to cheat, you don't make a career out of it, and you sure as hell don't want to end up hurting an endless number of people for your own psychotic reasons.

Sometimes.

Things.

Just.

Happen.

And other times.

What should happen, doesn't, and what shouldn't happen, does.

Such is life.

The life of a cheater.

This is my story.

You will hate it.

You will hate me.

You will laugh.

You will cry.

And in the end, you will understand.

You will.

I swear.

Because I wasn't born this way—I became a cheater.

But there's redemption for all of us. I have to believe that, or what the hell am I doing?

◆ ◆ ◆

May 2012 Rehearsal Dinner Night

Reddish-brown hair slid through my fingers like silk. A shudder ran through me as the rightness of finally being with her hit me square in the chest. A warm thigh brushed across my leg and then moved, straddling me, holding me captive.

Morally trapping me.

Imprisoning me with each squeeze.

In a hazy distant fog, I realized something felt slightly off.

Her hair had never been that red.

Her thigh that warm.

And her laugh . . .

"I knew you wanted me," she whispered in a coy voice that tried too hard to be innocent.

Huh?

Then all at once the lights came on.

Shit.

Shit.

Shit!

I wasn't in my bed.

Or hers.

It was a mistake, a horrible mistake.

One I wouldn't ever repeat if I could just make it out alive.

But luck had never been on my side.

Never.

So when the door jerked open, I already knew who it was, just like I already knew how it would end.

2

Either in tears or bloodshed. Maybe both? Kayla's hazel eyes locked on mine, then very visibly shut down.

"No," I whispered, my mouth moving, but nothing coming through my lips. They were numb—maybe with grief, drunkenness.

Yell! My body screamed—demanded I do something.

Fight like hell, MOVE!

But I was completely paralyzed with the actual realization that one false step had done this.

They say every man has a story.

Mine started the night I was found in bed with my fiancée's sister.

Chapter One

Lucas

"Lucas Thorn." Jessica said my name the way all girls said my name—in exasperation with a hint of lust and a hell of a lot of breathiness—and always my full name, never Luke, or just Lucas.

I was Lucas Thorn.

The one time a girl tried nicknaming me, I laughed in her face and very quickly sent her on her way.

Then again, I'd been getting tired of her anyway, which wasn't a big deal since I had an ongoing list of women—each of them was comfortable with the fact that she wasn't the only one in my lineup of weekly screws.

Mondays were Molly, because, well, both started with an *M*, and with so many women in my life, my memory was absolute shit.

Tuesdays were either Tabatha or Cary, depending on which one wasn't busy traveling with the airline they both worked for. They rarely flew on the same day. The good news? They were roommates, so I never had to get a substitute if one of them was flying. Because who the hell wanted that?

Jessica's lips pressed into a pink pout, her shiny lip gloss giving me an involuntary shudder as I stepped away and lightly pressed my hand against hers. I was a noncommittal hand-holder, the way I was a noncommittal boyfriend.

Holding hands? Making out? Too intimate.

Sex was sex.

Anything beyond that was asking too much, and they were lucky enough to be with me in the first place.

Hell, maybe I *was* arrogant, but I had a waiting list. And I didn't have time for a stage-five clinger in my life. Been there, done that, burned the T-shirt, only to have it happen one more time before I learned to do a very extensive background check on each chick I allowed into my private life.

"What's up, Jess?" I said casually, pulling my hand away from hers slowly enough not to startle her into thinking I was jerking away from her touch. I waited for her to say something.

Jessica wasn't typically a talker. She made her living as an inspirational speaker, so when we were together it was quiet time, which was fine by me. Most women talked too much in my opinion, and when you wanted good sex, talking had a way of ruining all the rest of the things I'd rather be doing with my mouth.

She took a deep breath. "I'm unhappy."

I sighed. She'd been one of my girls for the past three months, and considering that the typical end date to any of my relationships was around month four, I'd known it was coming. I'd always sensed Jess was different. She wanted the American dream: happy husband, two kids, small dog named Bingo, and the minivan with soccer ball stickers on the back window.

"Should we talk about our agreement?" I motioned for her to sit and give me a second while I went to get our coffee. Only hers was ready, so I snatched it and brought it back to the table.

She took the cup and swallowed a large gulp, with her big blue eyes locking on mine for longer than necessary. "I think I'm ready to be done."

"Alright." I said it softly, as if it didn't bother me that women used me just as much as I used them. "Today?"

"Yes." She nodded and then shook her blonde hair. "I mean, no." Her lower lip trembled. "Lucas, maybe we can—"

My coffee order was called out.

"Hold that thought." I went over to grab my macchiato. Anna was working; she was my Thursday.

"Lucas Thorn." She shook her cropped hair and sighed, placing her hands on her wide hips. "As I live and breathe." She had a teasing Southern accent that got me hard in all the right places.

"Gorgeous." I smirked and leaned in to press a hungry kiss to her mouth. She returned it but then gave me a slight shove. "What?"

"I'm at work." She blushed brightly.

"Green looks good on you." I meant it. She was beautiful, not model thin, but with curves for days. Shorter than most women I typically dated, but a hell of a beautiful mind, and those eyes, I loved them. She deserved someone incredible. It just wasn't me.

"I, uh . . ." She bit down on her bottom lip, then nearly ran into another customer. "Should get back to work. Are we still on for next week?"

"Of course." I hated her insecurity. Then again, I wasn't exactly helping that situation, now, was I? "We'll do dinner. How's that sound?"

"Good." Her smile was bright. "Really good. Have a nice day, Lucas Thorn."

I tried not to laugh out loud. Always both names.

Lucas?

I should have picked up on the seriousness of Jess's tone; she'd called me by just my first name.

And she'd used it again for the first time since we'd met at a bar a few months back.

6

I turned around just in time to see Jess wipe away a tear and look down at her coffee.

She'd seen the kiss.

But she knew the rules.

I refused to feel guilty about the way I dated—the life I lived.

"So . . ." I sat down. "You were saying."

"How can you do it?" She didn't make eye contact, just stared down at her coffee again, then grabbed a green straw and started twisting it tightly between her fingers. "You have seven girls for seven days. And you've never fallen in love with one of them? Not ever?"

"Jess . . ." Honestly, I didn't want to have this conversation with her. She'd been one of my favorites, always positive, exuberant in bed, willing to try anything, and I do mean *anything*, but sometimes, you need to cut the apron strings. "When we started dating, I told you, if you weren't comfortable with my lifestyle that you always had an option to leave. It's not like you signed some sort of psychotic ironclad contract that says I own you."

She stared me down, eyebrows both arched. "You do realize that sounds exactly like something you would do, right?"

"Very funny." She didn't need to know that I once went to a lawyer and asked if I needed some sort of contract so I couldn't get sued if one of the girls got pissed or something.

But as long as I had a verbal agreement from every girl that she fully understood I was dating a plethora of women and that she was one of many, I was good to go. Lucky me! Lucky them.

"Go." I grabbed her hand and kissed it. "You know, Fridays always were my favorite," I said, laying it on thick.

"Oh please." She snorted out a laugh. "I've seen your Monday, remember?"

"Ah, Molly." I laughed. "You're all beautiful."

"I think that's the problem." Jess frowned. "We're all interchangeable. We may look different, have different body types, represent various races and demographics, but in the end, we're just another way for you to please yourself. Not that you don't please us, or me, I just . . ." She shook her head. "It's too confusing, like being on *The Bachelor* without the possibility of getting you in the end."

"Trust me, you don't want me all to yourself. Done that once, it didn't end well. I can't be trusted, and that's the truth."

"That," she said, standing, "makes me sad."

"It shouldn't." I shrugged it off. "It's life, Jess."

"Life is more than sleeping with a different woman every day, Lucas."

"Are you sure about that?" I winked, then eyed her up and down. "Because I'm pretty sure I love it."

"Pig."

"Love you too, beautiful." I pulled her into my arms and kissed her temple. "Don't be a stranger."

"Hah!" She swatted me on the chest. "You'll have a new Friday by lunch."

"Maybe, maybe not." I pulled my sunglasses from my pocket and put them on before grabbing my coffee. "Let me walk you out."

"And there it is."

"What?" I opened the door for her and followed. "There *what* is?"

The Seattle morning was perfect; sun peeked through the thin clouds, causing a pretty glow to land across Jess's face. "You're a total asshole yet a complete gentleman at the same time. What's worse is I can't hate you. Even when I saw you kiss another woman five minutes ago, my only thought was, 'She seems nice—I see what he sees in her.' That's the Lucas Thorn effect." She stabbed at my chest with a finger. "You make cheating okay."

"If you know about it—and all parties agree to it—it's okay."

"That's where you're wrong." She shrugged. "Because I got you Fridays, but every other day? You belonged to someone else. That is never okay, no matter how charming you are."

"A compliment—I'm touched." I shoved a hand in my pocket. "So what will you do now? Get married? Have a ton of kids? Buy a house?"

Her smile was warm. "Maybe."

"Good. Don't forget to invite me to the wedding."

She burst out laughing. "You know? I just might."

"They all do."

Her laughter stopped, and she stared at me, her eyes sad. "I hope one day you find what you're looking for."

"Bye, Jess." I turned and didn't look back.

I *never* did.

Chapter Two

AVERY

"Just one more time," I pleaded, my eyes filled with tears. I seriously needed this internship since the last company I worked for—an Internet start-up—had to let go of ten of its lower-level employees.

Which meant.

Since I was just out of college and had only worked there for a few months.

I was shown the door.

At least it was a nice door.

Red.

And big enough to fit at least three of us side by side as they quite literally pushed us out of the building.

The celebratory *Hey, you got a job!* plant my parents had given me— also the first one I'd managed to keep alive—fell out of my hands from the bluntness of the shove.

My cubicle partner cried.

It had been a sad day for everyone.

Now a pregnant lady was supposed to be showing me the ropes for my new internship position under one of the VPs of the company. Her name was Sharon . . . or maybe Sharie? I'd been so flipping nervous when she'd introduced herself that I couldn't remember which it was. Anyway, she was saying words I didn't understand and looked about two minutes away from popping. It was a miserable start, and she didn't have much time to train me on all my actual duties and responsibilities.

Her giant belly had grazed the front of the desk as she made her way around to me. "Look, Avery, it's not that hard. You get coffee, you fix the copy machine, and you make sure his dry cleaning is delivered every morning. He's one of the easiest of the VPs to work with. Hell, most days he gets his own damn dry cleaning and brings me coffee, so believe me when I say you'll be just fine. You'll work closely with him on every project." She let out a rough exhale. "And at the end of the eight-week internship, he'll grade you on your work. If you do well, you'll get offered a permanent position." Her face contorted a bit as she bent over and gripped the counter.

Oh my hell.

Was she going into labor?

Now?

In the office?

I didn't know CPR.

Not that she would need CPR, or that the baby would. Ahh! I was a nervous wreck. "Are you okay?"

I patted her awkwardly on the back.

She quickly straightened and let out a little sigh. "The baby's trying to move, and space is limited in there."

"You don't say." I smiled through my teeth. The woman was tiny; I was surprised she'd made it this far without popping. "Are you having twins?"

Her glare said it all.

"I was kidding," I said quickly.

"Don't lie," she fired back. "Now, I'd like to enjoy the rest of my leave in peace, so if you have any questions you can always ask Lucas."

"Lucas?" I tried to keep the shudder to myself. I hated that name. It conjured up images of complete and utter loathing, and I almost always associated the name with the horrible things in life, like Ebola. Actually, the two things were interchangeable, Lucas and Ebola.

"Your boss." She rolled her eyes. "Tell me you at least know who you're working for."

No. Because when the job agency called and said that Grant Learning had an opening in their paid internship program, I jumped at it as fast as I could. The only thing I did was a quick Google search about the company.

I was desperate and needed the money so I could pay rent and stave off homelessness and starvation.

Okay, so it wasn't that bad, but it was close. And the last thing I wanted to do was move back home. My family lived in Marysville, and because I'd lived in downtown Seattle for several months, the thought of going home to that had me ready to walk the streets handing out my résumé.

I was quite possibly willing to sleep with a creepy old man to get a job.

So maybe not creepy.

Old?

Maybe.

My mom would kill me if she could hear my thoughts right now.

But my parents had this nasty habit of oversharing every single detail about their lives, and they expected me to return the favor. When my dad got a hangnail last week, he texted me a picture of it and asked if he should go to a doctor.

When I didn't answer, he texted the pic again with the message: I don't think you got this.

The good news? The picture was bigger that time.

My parents were—special.

And my bedroom? Still filled with stuffed animals from my childhood, and with plush pink carpeting.

Sometimes I had nightmares of returning to that room as a grown adult. My dolls came to life and choked me to death while I screamed for help, only to have the captain of the football team, now with a beer gut, tell me he'd only save me if I married him and had ten children.

He'd tried to reconnect with me over Facebook.

And then Snapchat.

He was *nice*.

So nice he now made impromptu visits in my nightmares.

The very idea of having to go back home after I had been hired right out of college with a killer salary and an amazing job title—it burned.

The fact that I was starting back at the bottom?

Made me want to strangle something.

This internship was everything. Going home was not an option. And "failure"? Well, that wasn't a word I was familiar with.

"Alright." Sharon, Shannon, Sharie, whatever . . . clasped her hands together. "He just texted that he's on his way in. Apparently, he had some sort of meeting that I didn't have on my normal calendar."

I shrugged; the guy had more than one calendar? Well, he was a VP, so I guess it made sense.

"Oh, and . . ." She slammed a hand against her forehead. "Don't become one of the girls. If he asks, say no. You listened to those drug talks in school, right? Or the really important ones about not joining gangs and falling to peer pressure?"

"I was homeschooled."

Her mouth dropped open, and a chewed wad of pink gum plopped onto the table before she could stop it.

I pointed with my pencil. "I think that's yours, and I was kidding."

"Oh thank God!" She fanned herself as if my being homeschooled was the equivalent of being in a cult. "Is it hot? I feel hot." She looked from left to right as though she was a few seconds from launching herself toward the closest window.

Well, she *was* growing a human. Hell, what did I know? I'd probably be roasting. "You can go." I stood and ushered her out. "I'm sure I'll be fine."

"Just"—she wagged a finger at me—"if he talks about you becoming one of his girls, say no. Curiosity kills the cat and all that. Besides, he's your boss, so no sleeping your way up. Not only would that kill your chances with the intern program, but he reviews you in the end. You want to be reviewed on your actual performance." She blushed. "In the office."

I wasn't sure if I should be offended or scandalized. By the time she left, the office was just starting to buzz with excitement.

The job was nine to five Monday through Friday and sounded pretty easy. From what I could tell, the company basically ran itself. The department I worked for was in charge of reaching out to local schools and helping assign tutors to kids who needed them. The company was a private learning and tutoring center that had franchises all over the country.

Grant Learning helped high school students with college prep and testing, but its niche, it seemed, was helping elementary students with phonics and reading.

I might have had too much wine the night I looked up the company because some of the testimonials made me cry. It was astonishing how many kids couldn't read and how many of them were just passed through the system because schools were overcrowded.

I sat down at my desk and made sure that I had all the passwords I'd need where I could grab them.

A few curious people walked by.

One dropped some papers on my desk and marched off.

Maybe that was my cue?

I grabbed the stack and shrugged. The papers had my boss's first name on them, and I did remember that . . . Sharon—Or Sharie? Ugh, I really needed to get her name—had mentioned that it was okay to drop off stuff for Lucas in his office.

And since he wasn't there yet, it couldn't hurt to get an early start.

I walked the few feet into his corner office. Geez, I figured VP of marketing and outreach must pay well. His office was more like a studio apartment; he had a conference table in the corner, a plush black-leather couch, and a small bar near the floor-to-ceiling windows overlooking downtown Seattle.

I was just ready to drop the papers on his desk when a smooth, velvety voice asked, "May I help you?"

My gaze lowered to his desk, I don't know why. Maybe because I felt guilty for standing there gaping at the awesomeness that was his office, but a picture on his desk caught my eye.

The angle was off—I couldn't quite catch the face, but it looked familiar.

"Miss?" he said.

With a sigh, I quickly turned around and said the first thing that came to mind when one lays eyes on Lucas Thorn, the one who shall not be named. "Oh, hell no."

Chapter Three

Lucas

She looked nothing like her two sisters, but I'd have recognized her strawberry-blonde hair anywhere.

After all, I'd had to cut gum out of it more times than I wanted to count.

I'd put Band-Aids on her scraped knees.

I'd hugged her when her date for homecoming dumped her because she wouldn't put out.

But it was her expression on the eve of my ill-fated marriage to her oldest sister, Kayla, that I remembered most. The one that said I was no longer her hero and, in the span of minutes, I'd turned into the villain people always suspected I was. Because no one ever believed that the star quarterback, who had simultaneously lost his virginity with the girl he was going to marry, was going to stay true to his first love his whole life. But I was dedicated, loyal to Kayla. I loved her, she was my friend, and we'd been inseparable throughout high school. And when I finally fell— it was epic and expected because how was it possible that I was actually such a good guy? I'd always been considered a "golden boy." People told me I was attractive, charming, a natural leader. Really, I had nowhere to go but down. But what sucked about falling from the pedestal I was put on was that nobody, and I do mean *nobody*, was there to catch me. They were all too busy saying "I told you he was too good to be true."

My own parents abandoned me after that night.

Oh, they still called.

We visited when it was absolutely necessary.

But our relationship was so damn strained, it hurt to even think about it. I'd "ruined" their lifelong friendship with the Blacks. And it sure didn't help that my sister was Kayla's best friend.

Her eyes, those green eyes, were the last thing I'd seen when I walked away.

And at night.

They haunted me still.

◆ ◆ ◆

I swallowed past some dryness in my throat as I waited for her to say something that wasn't a four-letter word.

"You done?" My eyebrows shot up. "Because I'm getting a late start this morning, and the last thing I need is to sit here and have an impromptu therapy session."

Avery glared at me, crossing her arms, making me want to choke on my tongue as her breasts strained against a simple black V-neck blouse that was tucked into leather pants. Her open-toed high heels were blue, making me think of how much bruising one of those shoes might be capable of if she whipped it off and beat me with it.

Her toenails were painted black.

Why the hell was I looking at her toes?

I'd left Marysville right before she started college—and believe me, back then she'd looked nothing like she did now. She'd still been a slim high schooler. Now she was all woman. Shit.

I quickly sidestepped her and made my way to my desk. "To what do I owe the pleasure?"

Her eyes darted between me and the door like she was going to make a run for it, but then her shoulders slumped. "I got laid off from the last company I was with—they grew too fast, let the young ones go—and my parents gave me exactly two months to find a new job or else they'd force me to move home, into my old bedroom, which just so happens to be next to my sister's bedroom. You remember the one?"

I opened my mouth to speak.

She wasn't going to let me. "I mean, of course you do, Lucas." She said my name like a curse. "It was the same room you stumbled into. I think the bed was replaced, or if I remember correctly, *burned* while Grandpa made us swear over a Bible never to utter your name again in his presence lest our souls go to hell."

"Avery—"

"Yup, I'd be next door to that." Her eyes narrowed. "So I took this internship, but believe me when I say I think I'd rather face starvation than work for such a jackass." She gulped. "Even if my future career is in your dirty little hands."

I grinned. "Are you done?"

"No." She huffed, crossed her arms again, then sighed. "Maybe." Her green eyes narrowed. "I have more mean things to say, but I'm saving them for later."

"So much to look forward to," I said dryly. "Look, I can keep this professional if you can. It's the least I can do to keep you from starving your ass off." I peered around the desk and checked her out. "Because that really would be a shame."

With a gasp, she pointed her finger at me. Damn, she was still a little spitfire—I thought I'd like getting scolded by her. "Listen here, you—you whore of a man!"

"That's the best you can come up with? Really?" My grin widened at her nervous hand gestures. Either she was trying to flip me off or she was batting away flying spiders.

"Keep it in your pants!" She huffed once more. "And if you ever check me out again, I'm going to staple your—your penis"—fiery red crept into her cheeks—"to your desk and pull the fire alarm!"

"The threat would work better if you could actually say 'penis' without blushing. You can't even say it, let alone touch one, can you?"

"You're a bad man." She licked her lips about a billion times before turning around in a full circle, locating the door, and stomping out of my office.

Avery Black.

Well, I'd be damned.

My smirk was still present when I leaned back in my chair a few minutes later, trying not to stare at the girl who'd most definitely filled out and turned into a woman.

I was ten years older than her.

She'd been the surprise of her parents' lives, and up until four years ago, I'd all but thought of her as my little sister.

Until I didn't.

My chest sliced with pain as I shoved the memories back into the recesses of my mind. They didn't matter anymore.

In fact, my greatest mistake ended up being my greatest accomplishment.

By sleeping with the wrong sister, I'd done everyone a favor.

I would have never made Kayla happy. She was the type of girl who lived in the same house her whole life, married some sort of football coach, had four kids, drank wine on special occasions, and got a mom haircut because it was easy.

At one point, I thought I wanted that.

That life.

Maybe that's why I'd gotten so damn drunk out of my mind that night. I knew I would ruin Kayla if I went through with our marriage because the relationship was no longer about her, and it hadn't been for a while.

I just didn't expect my own ruin to happen so swiftly.

I'd always been smarter than that when it came to women.

Or so I thought.

A nagging feeling made me want to scratch at my chest where my heart should have been. I ignored it. Like I ignored every single memory of that night. It was all too painful, too stupid, and honestly, it was what had propelled me into the perfect life—so why start thinking about my one regret?

Or the girl responsible for it?

"Are you going to answer that?" Avery was back in my office, cheeks flushed as she pointed at my phone. "It's literally been ringing for the past five minutes."

"Exaggeration. It would have gone to voice mail," I said in a bored voice. "Now, why don't you go do a coffee run?"

She frowned. I could tell she wanted to argue, but I was her boss, so I pointed to the door and waited for her to leave.

With a long sigh, she turned around and left, only to then walk backward toward my office and call over her shoulder, "Still drink macchiatos?"

"Yeah." I was too surprised that she'd remembered to elaborate.

She gave a quick nod and started walking out the door again, only to come back, still refusing to make eye contact, and hold out her hand.

"Cash." She coughed. "Remember? Almost homeless? Starving?"

"You never said 'homeless.'"

"I have to survive off my severance for the next few weeks. That includes rent, food, and any sort of transportation to the office."

I dug into my pocket and pulled out a hundred. "Then keep the change."

She hesitated, staring at Benjamin Franklin's face like the money was a moral dilemma rather than me just doing something nice, as her boss, as her ex-friend.

"Nope." She licked her lips. "I'll bring back your bribe money. Don't worry. I'll count your change to the very cent. In fact, I should ask for nothing but pennies."

I drowned out her incessant chatter and grabbed my phone.

Jess had called twice.

Damn, they always had regrets.

I quickly texted her to say she had done the right thing. Hell, I had every woman pegged. Like I was a freaking mind reader.

She didn't miss me.

She missed the *idea* of me.

Jess: I didn't realize how lonely being alone was. How do I even start dating again after you?

Me: It's natural to be nervous. Why don't you try happy hour and see how that goes? You're a great woman.

Just not *my* woman.

After sending the text, I followed up with another text saying lamely that I had to go to a meeting and was running late.

I didn't and I wasn't.

But she didn't know that.

In fact, other than reading the marketing reports from each school we'd just done outreach with, I had shit to do until Monday.

But it was Friday.

And I no longer had a girl to take home.

Or a girl to go home to.

Jess had loved cooking, so every Friday night I'd go to her house. We'd eat, drink, have amazing sex, and I'd leave in the middle of the night. It worked perfectly.

Except now—now I was irritated.

Because I needed sex.

Like some men needed water.

It was what I did when I felt nervous—actually, it was what I did when I felt anything—sex was my yoga.

And now I had nothing.

I tapped my pen against the report I'd been reading.

Ten minutes later I was *still* tapping, still staring at the same page, when Avery came bustling back into my office like a bat out of hell. Damn, the woman had too much energy.

I was torn between wanting to put a sleeping pill in her coffee or watch her turn in circles until she tuckered herself out.

"Here." She shoved a cup in my face and then dropped the change onto my desk. "I got myself something too for my efforts. Is there anything else, or do you want me to work on the project list I was given?"

Oh shit. I'd been staring at her lips, and I totally spaced what she'd just asked me.

"Do I need to talk slower?" With an irritated frown, she spoke with care, enunciating every word as though speaking a foreign language. "It's not really my thing, but if you'd rather I make smoke signals from my desk or learn sign language, I think I can manage."

"You know, for someone who's trying to get a good review from a VP, you're not really starting off on the right foot. 'Professional,' remember?"

Her expression fell.

"That's what I thought." I smirked. "And sorry, but I had someone"—I searched for the word—"*quit* on me this morning, and it's put me in a bit of a bind."

"Who?" She tilted her head and took a sip of her giant coffee. "Did they do something important?"

"Very"—I tugged the collar of my shirt as she sucked in her bottom lip—"important."

"Well, maybe I can help. And I mean that in a strictly 'I'll take on more work if you pay me more' way, not an 'I want to dig you out of the hole you're in because I'm a nice person and I remember the way you used to hold my hand when we went to the fair' way."

"You were scared of Ferris wheels. It was the least I could do."

Her blush ran from her cheeks all the way down her neck. "They're . . . tall."

"I'm tall. Are you afraid of me?" I leaned forward, placing my hands flat against my desk, ready to pounce.

She paused, and then a loud "Nope!" came out of those pink lips before she leaned forward. "Now, do you need my help?"

I chuckled. "Oh, Avery, I don't think you want to help me in that . . . way."

"What? Is it . . . hard?"

"Very." I coughed. "And often."

"Well, maybe I can make it easier. Maybe I'm better than the last person who did it." She was back to sucking the life out of her coffee cup, and I could almost imagine that mouth on me—or her killing me, more likely. "I'll do anything, Lucas, *anything.*"

"I'd believe it," I said in a hoarse tone. "Now, why don't you go check my schedule and see if the reports from Bellevue Elementary have come in."

"So I don't get to help?"

"That's you helping." I seriously needed her to drop the subject before I entertained the idea. Her family wouldn't just kill me; they'd burn me alive and invite the entire city of Seattle to watch.

"But—"

"Avery." I stood. "Go. I'll call you in if I need you."

"Fine." She stood too and hurried out of my office, and like a damn teenager, I watched her ass move back and forth until she sat down at her desk in the open space across from the door to my office.

I immediately gripped the edge of my desk as a familiar awareness washed over me.

It had been four years since I'd last seen her, but it felt like yesterday.

She should have zero effect on me.

And yet. She did.

More than any of the women I was currently seeing. And she'd done nothing but threaten and yell since she walked in.

I was in deep shit.

I needed to get laid. Tonight.

Avery stretched her arms over her head. Apple-sized breasts pushed forward, stretching her blouse's neckline and revealing an enticing amount of cleavage.

The hell with that—I needed to get laid over my lunch break. And I wasn't even a breast man per se.

I quickly grabbed my phone and scrolled through the options. I typically weighed the pros and cons and had a very strategic way in which I picked girls, but I was desperate.

I chose one I'd enjoyed a few times—she was technically a substitute, and I hadn't decided if I wanted her in the regular lineup. Avery leaned over to pick up something off the floor, the leather pants tightening across her ass.

I couldn't call fast enough.

Nadia answered on the second ring. "Lucas Thorn."

Yeah, yeah, yeah—Lucas Thorn, whatever. "Hey, what are you doing for lunch?"

"You," she whispered.

"That's all I needed to hear."

Chapter Four

Avery

Lucas Thorn was a sickness.

A darkness that never left.

He was a rutting bastard.

He was still—unfortunately—gorgeous.

With big hazel eyes and chocolate-brown hair that curled around his ears, a strong chin with a cleft in it, and a wicked smile that probably killed nice little old ladies with heart conditions—he was the devil himself.

My stomach clenched.

It sucked, watching your hero turn into someone you hated all within the span of minutes—seconds, really.

Four years ago, he'd walked out of our lives. He hadn't just dated my older sister—he'd been a part of our family. A *huge* part.

They were high school sweethearts. Homecoming king and queen, prom royalty, the quarterback who won state and the cheerleader who held his hand afterward.

It made someone like me—a more bookish, slightly nerdy girl—insanely jealous, because if you looked up "American dream" in the dictionary, Lucas Thorn and Kayla Black would have been the definition.

Until the day which shall not be spoken of.

With the estranged jealous psycho sister who I only saw on holidays.

He'd destroyed my family.

And I hated him for it.

Almost as much as I hated Brooke for allowing it. I'd wanted so badly to blame her instead of him.

He'd been so protective of me. Seemed so . . . perfect, in every way.

And now I was angry, not just uncomfortable and nervous but so angry that energy poured out of me. I channeled that anger into my work. I answered emails, called the schools that Lucas needed to visit in the week ahead, and went over the new marketing brochures.

And it wasn't even lunchtime yet.

Coffee was helping—but I imagined that my productivity was generated more by the adrenaline coursing through my veins because Lucas was mere feet away. As if sensing his presence, my heart rate sped up like I'd just taken a shot of caffeine through an IV.

If anything, I expected to start hovering over my desk Red Bull–style, any minute, and I'd sprout legit wings and have to explain to everyone why the new girl didn't use chairs.

"Hello." A heavily accented feminine voice interrupted my psychotic daydream. I wiped my mouth, just in case I had coffee dripping down to my chin, and glanced up.

She had long, wavy hair that went on for miles; it was brown and silky, and I had the sudden urge to cut it all off and superglue it to my own head—yeah, I needed to lay off the coffee. I scooted my cup away and folded my hands on my desk.

"Hi, how may I help you?"

"You." She pointed at me and giggled. "You are so young and small to be working at big office."

"Oh, well, it's Bring Your Daughter to Work Day." I winked. "You know, Daddy's so proud and all."

"Oh, this makes so sense!" I think she meant to say "so much sense," but her English wasn't that great. Alrighty then, moving on. "I need to see Lucas Thorn."

The way she said his name made me want to throw my coffee in her face. She was dreamy and seductive, everything I wasn't, not that I could even try to compare myself to someone like her.

"Who should I say is asking?"

"One of his girls." Of course, now she would wink—it was a condescending wink, one that made my hands twitch. "He'll let me right in."

Alarm bells went off in my head as my stomach clenched. "One of his girls," huh? Sharon? Sharie? The pregnant lady had warned me, but I was afraid to ask for details—and now I was too curious for my own good. With shaking hands, I picked up the phone just in time to see Lucas stroll out of his office, give the woman a smirk, and hold out his hand.

"Lucas Thorn." She said his full name. Again. Like he wasn't aware he had a last and a first. "You're looking good."

"So are you, gorgeous." He winked. "Shall we?" He led her into his office and then, much to my dismay, closed the blinds and shut the door.

Well, that's completely not helpful.

I tapped my pen against the desk while I waited for them to finish. Ten minutes later . . . and nothing.

Though I did see movement—not enough to know what was going on but enough to be even more curious about why the door needed to be shut.

After thirty minutes I'd come up with at least ten different scenarios. Maybe she was from a school in a foreign country? Maybe the kids there needed help reading too! Maybe he was saving children! Or maybe he was a self-serving man whore who was taking advantage of her like he'd done to my family.

Forty-five minutes, they were still in his office.

Should I send in a search party? I wondered.

He did have a meeting that I'd forgotten to tell him about in like fifteen minutes, so did it make sense for me to knock? Call?

Just when I stood, the door to his office opened. His shirt was torn open, its buttons basically hanging by their threads as the woman dabbed her lips with her hand and again winked at me. Her makeup was spread across her cheeks, and her beautiful hair was a complete mess. My mouth dropped open when she limped—yes, *limped*—to the elevator and then turned to blow him a kiss. "Until next Friday, Lucas Thorn." She pulled out a compact and began fixing her face.

"I'll put you down for every Friday."

"Thank you." She grinned. The snap of the compact shutting closed made me jump in my seat. "For allowing me to take the open position."

"You proved your worth!" he called back. His smile was so shameless, I didn't know what to do—with my body or with my hands.

The elevator doors closed.

I was still staring at them when Lucas whispered over my shoulder, "You gonna be okay?"

I jerked away from him. He smelled like perfume. Lipstick and bite marks marred the golden skin around his neck. I wanted to cry.

And I had no right to be upset.

He wasn't my problem.

Or my boyfriend.

He wasn't anything but my boss.

But the lipstick hurt—just like the bite marks did and the scent of another woman, a woman who wasn't my sister or, if I was being really honest, me.

Any girl would have crushed on him.

Hero worship sucked—he'd fallen so far.

And now? What? Quickies in his office?

"Good meeting?" I licked my lips, sat down, and tried to look busy by stacking papers that I'd already reviewed.

"Great." He patted my back. "I should probably go over my other schedule with you when we have time." He paused as if he was reading his own schedule over my shoulder. "But it looks like you forgot to tell me about a meeting, so I'm just going to go change shirts, and we'll continue this discussion later."

"Looking forward to it," I said through clenched teeth.

"You blush when you lie," he called over his shoulder. "Also, those papers are upside down." Then he shut the door to his office.

And I blew out a frustrated huff of air. *Bastard.*

Chapter Five

LUCAS

After my real meeting, I had a few hours to kill and managed to get ahead of schedule for the following week. By the time five o'clock that evening rolled around, I was ready to shut down and leave earlier than normal.

Avery was still at her desk, staring at the computer in awe like she'd never seen one before.

Thank God I'd been smart enough to call Nadia and release the pent-up tension that had still somehow crept back into my shoulders.

She had been a welcome distraction.

Someone who knew exactly what I needed the minute I closed the blinds.

And for some reason, with a completely available and gorgeous woman sucking me off in my office—I'd felt guilty.

Guilty because Avery was a few feet away.

Guilty because I blamed her for so many things.

I freaking hated guilt.

Hated it.

Which meant, by extension, that I hated her.

That's what four years of fucked up got you.

Hate.

"Am I interrupting?" I pointed to the computer. "Or are you just seeing if you can turn it on with your thoughts?"

"Very funny," she grumbled. "It froze."

"You were looking at porn, weren't you?" It was easier for me to be around her since Nadia had taken the edge off, and I knew teasing her would get under her skin. She was way too comfortable taking digs at me while still being one of the sexiest females I'd ever met.

And that thought right there?

Didn't sit well with me.

She looked horrified. "N-no, I just—"

And mission accomplished. "Relax, I was joking."

Avery's wide eyes told me she didn't give a flying rat's ass if I was joking or not—the crack wasn't funny.

"Alright then." I leaned over her body, trying not to laugh as her chair squeaked with the effort it took for her to push away from me. I tapped a few keys, forcing the applications to quit, and then rebooted the computer. "Done."

"So, Lucas Thorn." She said my name breathlessly, but it was all for show. She was making fun of the way Nadia had said it. "You're a computer genius too?"

"Stop batting your eyelashes," I scolded. "It's creepy as hell, and no, I'm not a computer genius—I just know not to have twenty different tabs open at once while I'm trying to listen to Pandora."

She thoughtfully tapped her chin with her fingertips. "I knew I shouldn't have created that One Direction station."

"Please tell me that was your attempt at a joke."

She started to hum the tune to "What Makes You Beautiful."

I covered her mouth with my hand. "Please. Just. No."

She shoved my hand away. The gesture between us was so familiar, I didn't know whether to laugh, or remind her how often we used to tease one another, or just walk away and flip her off for making me remember in the first place.

"So"—she grabbed her purse—"should we go over your mysterious 'other schedule'?"

I narrowed my eyes. "Think you could hate me any more?"

"I'm sure I can find more hate, absolutely." She grinned as though the idea made her downright cheerful.

"Then we probably need alcohol. Good thing you're twenty-two."

"Yes, my life has just begun. Did you know I can ride a bike and everything? Daddy took the training wheels off last week, but the streamers stayed." She gave an exaggerated wink. "Girls gotta have streamers."

Sighing, I braced her shoulders. "If I stop reminding you of your age, will you stop being so damn defensive?"

"No." She shook her head. "Sorry, my defense mechanism is like a giant wall. The Great Wall of China, for example. It separates me from you, and the only way it's getting broken down is with a nuclear bomb."

"Well, that's encouraging," I grumbled. "Let's go."

◆ ◆ ◆

Happy hour was in full swing by the time we made it down to the bar. When I finally located a table I was hit with an irrational desire to pull her chair as close to mine as possible. "So . . ." Avery sipped her Chardonnay and leaned her arms on the table. She wore bracelets that wrapped along both arms a few dozen times, which suited her. She had always been edgier than her sisters, more outspoken. She just *looked* like the kind of girl who was up for anything, which was a far cry from the bookworm I remembered from her high school days. The girl who, back then, refused to touch a drop of alcohol and liked staying in on the weekends.

Go figure.

I sipped my Jack and Coke and tried to think of the best way to explain my dating schedule. It wasn't necessary that she know every painful detail, but I did need her to understand that when the girls came to my office, unless I'd invited them, they weren't welcome.

Some of the ones that I'd broken up with hadn't accepted that our time had come to an end, meaning I'd had a few stalkers. The last thing I wanted was to have any of them in my office, or anywhere for that matter.

I didn't do well with that type of confrontation, and who would? Every one of them cried and then, in a last-ditch effort, confessed love.

The last one said she was pregnant.

That was my breaking point—especially when I found out she was lying.

"So here's the deal with my other"—I coughed into my hand—"schedule."

Avery pulled her strawberry-blonde hair back into a low, messy bun and sighed. "Is it top secret or something?"

"Sort of." Hell, how did I even start this conversation? Awkward didn't even begin to cover it.

"Lucas Thorn!" A familiar voice said my name.

Oh hell.

I turned to the left. Jess was standing with a man at her side, but at least she looked happy.

"Told ya you'd have a Friday replacement by lunch." She winked at me and then turned her attention to Avery.

"Oh, no, she's—"

"Hi!" Avery and her damn manners! "I'm Avery, and you are?"

"Jess!" Oh God. She seemed so thrilled to meet the girl she thought was her replacement. "Can I just say, I'm so glad he found someone so quick. I know that it left him in a bad spot with the rest of the girls and, well, he's a man with a plan, you know? A creature of habit."

"Um, yes." Avery glanced at me out of the corner of her eye.

My mind was blank.

I had nothing.

"Anyway, just remember you only get him for one day, and then everyone else gets a shot. It's really not so bad, it just takes some getting used to—you know, like sharing a boyfriend. Basically that's what you're doing, and it works. I know it sounds crazy, but just give it a chance."

Why the hell was she giving Avery pointers?

Jess's eyes welled with tears as she glanced over at me. "I'll always miss your touch."

Fuck me.

The guy next to her stiffened.

"Oh, sorry, guys. This is my brother, Peter."

Great, nothing like getting buried on a Friday. The look he gave me said to drop dead and wait for a semi to run me over.

"Anyway." She wiped her cheeks. "Those months with Lucas Thorn were some of the best of my life. I'm sure you'll think so too! Good luck!" She patted Avery's hand and walked off.

I opened my mouth to speak but was interrupted by Avery slicing the air with one hand while the other reached for her Chardonnay. She chugged every last drop.

When the waiter walked by, she jerked him by the shirt, nearly causing him to stumble into our table. "Two shots of Knob Creek."

I opened my mouth again, but she made a little noise, shook her head, and clamped my lips together with her fingertips.

And she stayed that way.

For the next three minutes.

Until her shots arrived.

She downed both of them. Yeah, she was definitely not the teenager I'd left back in Marysville four years ago. After a deep breath, she locked eyes with me. "Please tell me my assumptions are wrong."

I cleared my throat. "Maybe they are?"

"Tell me you don't have a woman for every day of the week. Tell me you don't sleep with them and change them around like you would your socks. Tell me that she didn't just assume I was . . . FRIDAY!" Her voice rose an octave, grabbing the attention of those at the table next to us.

"You're wrong." I grinned.

She let out a rough exhale.

"I sleep with a different girl every day of the week—except Sunday. That's God's day, so I hang out with my sister, Erin." I smiled again for the effect. "When she answers the phone, that is."

Avery glared at me.

And then slapped the shit out of my right cheek.

"What the hell, Avery?" I held my cheek and swore again. "I think you cracked my back molar."

She raised her hand once more.

"What? You want the other cheek too?" I turned to avoid another slap in the same spot.

Avery stole my drink and started chugging.

"Okay, no more alcohol for you." I pried the glass from her fingers while she was still drinking out of it. Amber and black liquid sloshed over our table. "You're literally a menace to society."

"Nope, only to you." She wiped her mouth. "So you have, what, maybe six girlfriends—and you cheat on them all?"

I shrugged. "I wouldn't exactly call it cheating if they all know about one another."

"You're like the male component of the sister wives scenario, aren't you?"

"We aren't married." I laughed. "God, can you imagine?"

Her look said, *No, I can't. Because I would strangle you in your sleep or smother your face with a pillow until your poor, pathetic body went limp.*

"Look, Avery, all you need to know is what girls I'm dating so that you don't let in a clinger."

"'Clinger,'" she repeated, her teeth clenching so hard that her cheeks twitched. "So you don't want me to let in the crazy ones who still want you?"

"Stop smiling," I grumbled. "It's creepy with your teeth clenched. And no, don't let them in, or I'll tell the CEO that you can't even turn on your computer."

I smugly sat back in my chair and crossed my arms.

She glared at me. "That's . . . extortion."

"Call it what you want. I'm your boss, and the girls are part of my schedule. Shannon never had any problem with it."

"I KNEW it was an *S* name!" She slammed her fist onto the table.

My eyebrows shot up. "What?"

"Nothing." She waved me off. "So keep the skanks straight. Kind of sounds like a sick sort of board game."

"In a way it is." I licked my lips and leaned forward, ignoring the fact that she was insulting the women. "Keep names straight, locations, likes and dislikes, in and out of bed."

Her mouth dropped open.

I took that as an opportunity to touch her chin and nudge her mouth closed. Her skin was soft, like velvet.

Just like I'd remembered.

My fingertips lingered longer than necessary.

And my thoughts went into dangerous territory.

Because I was losing my mind. That's the only reason my finger trailed down the side of her jaw, back and forth, until her eyelids lowered like I was putting her in a trance.

"No!" She jerked back. "I refuse to fall victim to the Lucas Thorn effect."

"I kind of like the sound of that." I crossed my arms and grinned.

"I'm sure you do." She snorted and hopped off the barstool. "Alright then, I'll need pictures and names to go with them. And know that I'm only doing this so I don't have to move back in with my parents and eat Mom's homemade macaroni and cheese."

We both shuddered. "Some of my darkest days involved that macaroni."

"One night, I dreamed it was chasing me. I was so afraid." She shivered and gave me a bleak look. "You're worse than the macaroni, Thorn."

I walked her up to the bar to pay for our bill, my hand naturally resting on the small of her back. The blouse she was wearing had ridden up on her stomach, exposing a patch of skin my fingers itched to feel. Every part of her was warm to the touch, and my fingertips dug into her back with a possessiveness I didn't even know I felt until a guy near us started checking her out.

Memories immediately transported me back to the past.

❖ ❖ ❖

Driven by alcohol and about one hour of sleep, I made a lame last-ditch effort to talk to her at a local grill. I had to explain why. Even if she didn't listen, I still needed to confess.

"Avery!" A buff jock-type dude I didn't recognize wrapped his arm around her and pulled her close. His mouth was on hers before I could announce my presence, and then his hands pressed against her hips as her shirt rode up past his fingertips.

Jealousy surged through me.

Even though I had no right.

Not at all.

I fisted both hands and gritted my teeth, just as a girl to my right winked and then crooked her finger.

I walked over to her.

I meant to turn away the minute I realized she was drunk and wanted more than just a polite conversation.

She was kissing me before I knew what was happening.
I didn't just like it.
I loved it.
The rush.
The feeling of kissing a stranger a few days after breaking off an engagement, a promise of lifetime commitment that never felt quite right.
It was exciting.
Wild.
And the best part?
There was no chance I would hurt anyone—or anyone would hurt me. It was in that moment that I realized I wasn't the guy who committed—I was the guy . . . who cheated.

◆　◆　◆

Sighing, I pushed the memory away.

My arm moved up and hovered around her shoulders, tugging her body into mine while I used my free hand to reach for my wallet.

"I'm *not* Friday," she said under her breath. "No need to mark your territory."

"I'm just . . . being protective." I shrugged. "Trust me; I'm well aware that hitting on you could get me shot."

"And if there was no chance of bodily harm?" She paused, blinking innocently up at me. "What then?"

"Why do you want to know?"

"Morbid curiosity?"

"Yes." I shrugged. "I'd totally fire my Monday—she's got nothing on you."

Avery wiped away a fake tear. "Gosh, you're such a winner."

"Seven," I whispered in her ear. "Seven women think so. Most men are lucky to get one. So think about that tonight." My lips touched her ear. "When you're alone in your apartment, in your cold bed—I have seven."

"That you cheat on."

"Not cheating if they all know," I said for the second time, sliding a fifty-dollar bill over to the bartender and then leading her out of the bar.

Once we were outside, I had the valet hail a taxi for her.

"I can't afford—"

"Business meeting, I'll pay for it," I interrupted.

"Why?" Avery put her hands on her hips, her green eyes wide. "Why do you do it?"

Nobody had ever asked me that. Maybe nobody had ever cared.

A taxi pulled up to the curb.

"Good night, Avery. I'll see you Monday."

"You aren't going to answer?"

I opened the door for her and almost shoved her in. "Sex, Avery, I do it for really good sex."

She blinked. "I don't believe you."

"Sorry to disappoint." My tone was mean. I should have cared that I was being harsh with her. I didn't. "Sometimes a guy just needs good sex."

I shut the door in her face and didn't look back.

Chapter Six

AVERY

I dreamed of the devil, also known as Lucas Thorn, all night long. In my dreams, he appeared beautiful, like an angel. He even wore white, and then he tied me to a chair and force-fed me my mom's horrible macaroni.

Things got a little dicey when his body turned into a snake wearing a football uniform and a helmet, and then he handed me an apple and told me to take a bite.

Once I bit, his clothes disappeared.

Pretty sure I was having an actual flashback of the Garden of Eden.

To say I'd slept horribly would be putting it mildly, and the worst part was that I didn't really have the extra money to spend on coffee.

I thought about Lucas's stupid schedule during the entire walk to work. Right along with his aggravating midnight text that demanded I come in on a freaking Saturday morning.

I was about five blocks away when my phone rang.

It was Kayla.

Of course, it had to be Kayla. I chewed my bottom lip and stared at the phone. Whenever she called, a picture of us flashed across the screen. We were happy in that picture.

We were always happy unless someone mentioned weddings, dogs, football, cheerleading, or white gowns. Okay, so she was basically happy if you walked on eggshells around her and pretended like everything was totally fine and that life was superawesome and fun!

UGH!

I swiped to accept the call and answered with a bubbly "Hello!"

"I'm so glad you answered!" Kayla shouted way louder than necessary for my sensitive morning ears. "So, listen, I was thinking of visiting this weekend."

"Um . . ." I quickly tried to think of an excuse. "I can't, Kayla. I got a new job, and I may have to work." Total lie, but the last thing I needed was her breathing down my neck while her ex-fiancé texted me instructions about how to keep the clingers away from his regular sister wives.

"Oh." Her voice deflated. "Well, how about next weekend?"

I crossed the street, almost got hit by what I assumed was a poorly rated Uber driver, and managed to make it to the sidewalk in one piece. "Yeah, let's maybe talk about it tomorrow? I'm on my way to work, and my boss is a complete jackass." HAH! That part was true. "I don't want to be late."

"Aw, honey, I'm sorry. Is he at least young and hot?"

"No. Horrible looking. Ancient. Ugly—has two broken teeth and halitosis, which is really unfortunate when he breathes down my neck. I held my breath twice yesterday. He loves his coffee." I grinned wider and wider as I kept imagining all the things I wished Lucas was but wasn't.

"He sounds awful!" She made a gagging noise and laughed. "Well, look at it this way—once you put your time in, you'll get noticed, and then you'll be the boss."

My shoulders slumped. Just the idea that I had to spend time with Lucas to get the position with the company had my stomach clenching with anxiety and my palms sweating. The phone was slipping out of my hands. Great. "Yeah, you're right."

"I'll call later. Love you, Avery Bug."

For some reason, my eyes welled up with tears, maybe because she was the only one who still called me that. Lucas used to, but that was before the incident.

The aftermath changed everything.

Not that I'd ever been able to live up to my sisters' standards, even before that. Kayla was perfect. Brooke was dramatic and wild.

And then there was me.

"Love you," I choked out, then hung up before she could ask if I was okay.

"Halitosis, huh?" a voice said behind me.

A male voice.

A raspy one.

A horrible one.

Slowly I turned, praying in those few seconds that I was wrong and that a superhot Channing Tatum look-alike had been watching me and wanted to take me out on a really nice date and buy me steak. My mouth watered.

I would make that steak my bitch.

See? Starvation! I needed this job!

"Thorn in my side." I managed to say his last name without adding an expletive at the end of it. Such progress. "Didn't see you there."

"Cute." He rolled his eyes and smirked. "Is that my new nickname?"

"If the pitchfork fits . . ." I batted my eyelashes.

"Take it back, or I won't give you this." He dangled a venti caffè mocha in front of my wide, shame-filled eyes. "It's your favorite. I even had them add extra whipped cream."

"You. Are. Satan," I whispered hoarsely. "That coffee may as well be an apple. Take a sip, Avery, just one little taste—and boom!" I clapped my hands. "Clothes gone, I'm naked!"

Lucas's frown deepened, his smirk disappeared.

"I think I'm hallucinating from lack of sleep." I grabbed the coffee from his hands. "And I'm sorry I said you were the devil, and that you had halitosis, and cracked teeth—and for stabbing you with that knife."

"When did you stab me?"

"Oh, sorry." I shrugged. "Sometimes I confuse the really cheerful, happy daydreams with regular life."

He took a wide step away from me. "Just out of morbid curiosity, did you stab me in the chest or the back?"

"The back." I glared at him. "You know, that's where you stab people who betray you, thus the term backstabber—"

He raised his hand. "I get it—don't make me take back the coffee, Avery Bug."

I choked on my next sip and nearly spit it out onto his nice white shirt.

He patted my back a few times, then rubbed it. "Are you okay?"

"Yup," I wheezed. "Wrong tube."

"Geez, you need the opposite of caffeine."

"Why are you on the street? In front of Starbucks, and—oh, this is our building. I got turned around." I frowned. "Huh, imagine that. I'm a total power walker."

"I'm not high-fiving you"—he shook his head at my elevated hand—"for walking on two legs, even though for you I'm sure it's a huge accomplishment." He pointed to his briefcase. "I have something for you to review before our meeting with the rest of the execs."

I hunched my shoulders and followed him into the building.

We were the only two people on the elevator.

Which was really unfortunate, but what would I have expected on a Saturday morning?

The annoying classical elevator music just made everything that much more irritating, grating on my already-frazzled nerves.

"Who were you talking to?" he asked without looking directly at me.

I licked my lips. "My boyfriend."

He froze. "Your *boyfriend*?"

It was a total lie, but I couldn't just say I was talking to the ex-fiancée he'd cheated on, now, could I?

"Yup . . . C-Carl." Oh good, a stutter—that was new. Thanks, Thorn, for adding that to my already awesome conversational prowess.

"C-Carl?" He smirked. "With two *C*s"?

"Laugh it up, jackass." I shrugged. "He's a . . . professional, um, dancer."

"So you're dating a male stripper?"

Of course, that would be the exact moment when the elevator doors opened and two nice elderly ladies with cute purses and tight chignons stepped on.

The company employed a lot of teachers to help with the online tutoring, and I was sure, by the horrified looks on their faces, the two ladies taught first grade and were just itching to red card me.

Not like I hadn't spent most of my elementary-school days having my yellow card replaced with a red one for speaking out of turn.

"Good morning," I said in my most cheerful voice.

They ignored me.

Lucas covered a laugh with a cough behind his hand. I raised my foot and stomped down on his nice shoes.

He bit out a curse, causing the two ladies to stiffen.

"Language, Thorn," I said in a serious tone just as the chime announced a stop and the doors slid open.

"Bite me, Avery."

A gasp was heard, and then both old ladies scurried off the elevator, nearly colliding with one of the company mail clerks. The doors closed and we were alone again.

"All in all, a really solid start to my Saturday. Why are we here again? I thought interns only work Monday through Friday."

"Impromptu meeting."

"Gee, I hope that doesn't throw off your Saturday plans."

Lucas's lips twisted into a seductive smile. "My Saturday is a very patient woman . . ."

I took two sips of coffee, then a third. The elevator doors opened again. "Who's your Saturday?"

Ugh, I hated that I was curious by nature.

"Funny you should ask." He led the way to his office, set his brief-case on his desk, then pulled out a stack of papers and held them out to me.

On the first page was Monday, or Molly.

She had a short pixie haircut that looked killer on her, and with tattoos down her arms and a nose ring—well, she so did *not* look like a Molly to me, but she was absolutely stunning. Her tattoos added to her beauty, and her smile was wide. She looked normal, too good for him. The bastard.

I turned to the next page. Tuesday, or Tabatha and Cary. "Wait." I frowned. "Why *two* girls?"

Lucas glanced over my shoulder. His breath, which unfortunately didn't smell like an old man's, kissed the top of my neck. "They're roommates."

I took a few soothing breaths. "And they're okay with this?" I seri-ously wanted to rip up the paper, set it on fire, and shove it down his pants. What a complete ass!

Lucas's voice was calm, gentle. I dared not look at him. "They're flight attendants, they travel a lot, and neither can seem to find time to date regularly. The arrangement works for them because it's convenient."

I snorted. "What? So you screw them, and they say thank you?"

"No. Actually, we don't have sex every time. If you must know, sometimes they just want to relax and hang out, so I make them dinner, rub their feet, and sometimes just please them."

Had it just gotten really hot in that office?

My face heated to a painful degree. "You . . . please them."

"Why is that so hard to believe?" He walked around me. I chose to stare down at the paper so I wouldn't look at his gorgeous hazel eyes.

"It's just—" Both girls had brown ombré-style hair coloring and seemed to love pink lipstick. "I thought it was all about sex, that's all."

"Believe me, pleasing them pleases me." His voice was gruff. "And in the end, they want to make me happy in bed because of it."

I took a cautious step back and quickly glanced at the next page. "Wednesday looks . . . way too normal."

He laughed. "Chelsea's a teacher."

I almost dropped the stack of papers again. "But that's so . . ."

"What?" He placed his hand on the paper and lowered it so I had no choice but to look at him. "Normal?"

"I was going to say typical, that you'd sleep with the help." I grinned wide. "Let me guess, she works here?"

"No, she works at the low-income school down the road, earns below the poverty line, and volunteers at a soup kitchen every Saturday."

Well then. Who was the ass now? "Sorry." It literally hurt my body to apologize to the man.

"You didn't know."

"So I've already met the new Friday." I tried not to get jealous as I glanced at Nadia's picture and moved along to Saturday.

"Whoa." I stared at the picture. Hard. "She's . . . um, different."

"Forty." Lucas answered quickly. "And yes, Amy's special, but then each of the ladies has something unique. She's fascinating, irresistible, loves going for long walks, has three dogs, works at Starbucks headquarters."

"I hope she gives you free coffee," I joked.

"Sex in exchange for coffee would be wrong. Where are your morals?"

"MY MORALS!" I yelled.

Lucas burst out laughing. "Don't get your panties in a twist—I was kidding. Stop looking at me like you want to stab me in the testicles."

"The idea has so much merit." I sighed dreamily, holding the papers to my chest. "So these are the chicks you . . ." I waved a hand flippantly in the air.

"Screw," he answered helpfully. "Yes."

"And cheat on."

"They're well aware of the arrangement."

"And Sundays?" Not staring at him was too hard; therefore, I focused on the cleft in his chin so I wouldn't look at his perfect lips . . . or the swell of his biceps. When he crossed his arms, I was almost afraid the shirt was going to rip, and it was a nice shirt, soft, white. Okay, Avery, stop staring at the fabric like you want to make babies with it. That's weird—don't be weird.

"Sundays are for my sister, Erin."

He shifted uncomfortably. Was it my imagination, or did those biceps flex beneath the shirt like he was tensing?

As if the tensing wasn't bad enough, he cleared his throat and blinked way too many times for a man who was being completely honest about his sister.

"Huh." His shirt really was nice though—stain-free. How did he manage it with all the sex and lipstick? "So you were being honest about that?"

"Honesty," he said, "is necessary when you casually date seven women, right?"

"Oh please!" I locked eyes with him. "You're excusing horrible behavior by saying the girls are aware, but the whole sex without strings doesn't exist. That's a fantasy like Santa Claus or the Easter bunny."

"Holy shit! Santa's fake?" He winked. "And they're all okay with it. Besides, it's not like I'm sleeping with you."

I hated him for saying it.

Because immediately I had a vision of his mouth on mine, clothes on the floor, and every forbidden fantasy I'd had throughout high school flared to life, fanned by the words that he'd just released into the universe, words that would be impossible to take back.

I sucked in a breath, and he licked his lips, his eyes focusing on my mouth.

It was wrong.

And a small part of me liked that feeling, the wrongness of being in my boss's office, the history, but it was only 1 percent.

Ninety-nine percent of me still wanted to nail him to a wall and use his balls as target practice with a shiny, new aluminum bat.

Lucas took a step toward me. I took a step back.

He stopped approaching, instead shoving his hands into his pockets and offering a lazy smile. "That's rare."

"What?"

"A girl running in the opposite direction."

"I'm not one of your desperate women grateful for little cheap crumbs—plus there are only so many days in a week." I tried to sound cheerful, like it wasn't a big deal that he was a lying, cheating asshole of a man, and not the man I used to know.

"Pity," he whispered.

"Hey, you two, meeting in five." I jumped a foot at the sound of the feminine voice, and then Lucas became all business.

I scurried back to my desk and shoved the papers into my purse just in time for Lucas to lead me to the conference room.

Chapter Seven

LUCAS

I hated Saturday meetings—they threw off my entire week—but this time, I'd looked forward to going to the office on my day off.

And it had everything to do with a certain spitfire currently drawing a horrible stick figure that I could only assume was me, with an arrow going through its head, and then the heart. An airplane was going down in flames in the drawing, and it was about to flatten said stick figure that had my name written above it in giant block letters.

Nice.

"Lucas."

I glanced up, acknowledging the speaker at the head of the table.

Bill was my boss. Hell, he was everyone's boss. He was the founder of Grant Learning. This announcement had to be big for him to call in all the VPs like this. "I know you typically do a four-ten if you can, but I'll need you to move back down to five-eights."

Avery frowned.

"No problem." I suddenly had no issue with being in the office more. Besides, I usually had so much work, it was rare that I could take Fridays off anyway.

"Thank you, everyone, for meeting on your day off. I know this is very last minute, but I have an update on the new tutoring app that I think you should be made aware of."

I leaned forward. The app was my idea. I'd hired the tech team to build an app for students. It worked a lot like Uber. Whenever a student needed help with a homework assignment, he or she could check to see if a tutor was in the area. The tutors were all screened by us and put into our system, and with his or her parents' permission, a student could hire a tutor immediately. That made it easier for students who lived far from our franchises to get help.

"We're out of the beta testing and ready to launch." Bill grinned wide. "Good job heading this up, Lucas. The results have been outstanding."

Pride swelled in my chest. "That's fantastic."

Sure, I was a jackass, I *"cheated"* on women, or just dated multiples, depending on one's perspective, but I loved kids. Adored them. They were still so damn innocent. They had the whole world ahead of them, and I wanted to make sure that they had every opportunity possible. My parents had given me that—I wanted to pay it forward.

Just thinking about Patty and Bill had me itching all over.

God, it had been way too long since we'd talked.

And I only had myself to blame.

Things were still tense—years later. It burned that my own parents still held me responsible for what had happened with the Blacks. Like I single-handedly ruined a twenty-year friendship on purpose.

What? Did they think I *wanted* to destroy lives?

My mood darkened as it usually did when I thought about the mistake, about how and why it happened. Hell, if Kayla and I had gotten married, I would probably have been teaching my own kids now.

The thought was absolutely terrifying. Not the kid part, but the part where I was married to a woman like Kayla.

Maybe that's why I liked the opposite of what she represented.

My eyes focused on Avery.

She glared at me and then made a slicing motion with her finger across her neck. Yeah, message received.

"Your department is going to be in charge of visiting all of the local schools and doing a training tutorial on the app," Bill said. "So for the next few weeks, you'll be very busy." Ah, that's why he needed me to work Fridays. "And because Shannon's taking maternity leave, we'll need your new intern . . ." His eyes searched for Avery. "There you are. Avery Black, you'll be assisting Lucas with his school visits and keeping his schedule straight during the launch."

Avery swallowed and gave him a very strong nod, as if to say, *I've got this, can do it in my sleep and won't let you down.*

That was her attitude about life—about everything.

I envied her that.

Even if it was a front. Her confidence had always been impressive. At such a young age, it was rare.

Especially considering how much shit she took from her sisters growing up. She'd always been a tomboy.

And now?

Now she had curves for days. She surpassed her sisters in ways that were astonishing.

And there I went again.

Staring at her.

Lusting.

Wanting.

Isn't that what got me screwed in the first place?

Her strawberry-blonde hair was pulled into a high ponytail that kissed the back of her neck. Her white silk shirt hung loosely tucked into black-satin shorts, and she was wearing tall black stilettos.

I was sure Bill was still talking.

But I was too busy lusting after my ex-fiancée's little sister, a tale as old as time—been there, done that—but I couldn't help myself.

Being near Avery made the want that much worse. Whenever she used to give me the silent treatment, it had been torture. She was a talker, and I used to love it when she'd tell me about all the drama in high school while I was busy joining the workforce. Avery had always had a way with words, but not only that, she was animated. So animated that I used to make her sit on her hands when she talked because she made me so dizzy. I don't remember a time when she'd ever sat and folded her hands while having a discussion. She was all action. I was suddenly thankful that hadn't changed.

It would have been a travesty.

"Alright, that's it, guys. Thank you." Bill dismissed us.

Avery ripped the drawing from her notebook and handed it to me. "I made something for your fridge."

"That was thoughtful," I said dryly. "I look forward to glancing at my impending death every time I want some OJ."

"See?" She grinned. "I can be nice."

I grunted.

We walked in silence back to my office. It was nearing ten in the morning. I was supposed to meet Amy for lunch a few blocks over, so I had some time to kill. I went into my office and hit the return key on my computer.

"Do you need me for anything?" Avery popped her head in my office. It was on the tip of my tongue to tell her to bend over my desk.

She was right.

I was a horrible human being.

Would probably rot in hell.

But damn, she was pretty.

Her eyes narrowed. "Stop that."

"What?" I grinned wickedly and shoved a pen in my mouth, sucking on the tip.

Her chest rose and fell a bit faster, her cheeks reddened. "The Lucas Thorn effect doesn't work on me, sorry."

"It does, you just won't admit it."

She stomped into my office and slammed her hands onto my desk, leaning over so far that I could see down her blouse. Hell, she had nice tits. "Look at me like that again and I'm putting Ex-Lax in your coffee, then locking all the bathroom doors."

"Graphic." I licked my lips, craning my neck so I could look into her large green eyes. "Also false."

"Excuse me?" Her teeth clenched, snapping together as if she wanted to take a bite out of my head.

I got a bit closer, my mouth inches from hers. "You wouldn't do that to me. You're too nice."

She grinned and then shoved at least two weeks' worth of files off my desk. "How's that for nice?"

"Mature, Avery." I let out a series of curses.

Avery bit her bottom lip and then sighed. "Okay, so maybe that wasn't the best idea since you're assessing me on this internship."

"Now you think that? After the damage has already been done."

Her eyes filled with tears, and then her nostrils flared as she narrowed her eyes at me and lifted her chin. "It's a business relationship. Check my ass out again, and I'll report you for sexual harassment."

I stared at her in silence for a minute before I pointed down at the files. "Your job is in the palm of my hand, Avery Bug . . . Maybe next time play nice, or who knows what I'll be forced to do. I'd hate to give you a bad review—after all, I know how much you hate not being perfect."

It was a low blow.

She knew it.

I knew it.

All her life she'd been trying to measure up to her older sisters, and I'd just made her aware of it all over again.

I opened my mouth to apologize, but she turned on her heel and left. On her way out of the office, she flipped me off with one hand and waved good-bye with the other.

So much for getting work done. It would take me at least an hour to organize all my files again.

But for some reason, when I got down on my knees and started shuffling them together, I smiled the entire time.

She had fight in her.

I had to give her that.

◆ ◆ ◆

"Hey," Amy mouthed, waving me over to the dimly lit booth. She was wearing a short black dress with capped sleeves, and her hair was pulled back into a low ponytail. Little smile lines formed around her mouth and eyes. She was beautiful in a mature way, a way that Avery would never understand.

Damn it. I needed to get Avery out of my head before I started calling out her name midorgasm or something.

Which had never happened.

But something told me that if I kept thinking about her like that, it would. And while some women would forgive the whole *Hey, I date other women right along with you* thing, I was pretty confident that calling out "Avery!" at the wrong moment would be crossing the line.

"Hey, gorgeous." I kissed her full on the mouth as her arms wrapped around my neck, forcing our bodies to connect and giving me a nice tease until I could get her naked and underneath me. "Mmm, you taste good." Amy was an amazing kisser. In fact, I was pretty sure she was the best I'd ever had, which was saying a lot.

I didn't typically kiss many of the girls I was with.

I made an exception for Amy.

Any living, breathing male would.

"Busy day?" She tilted her head and waved down the waiter.

"Nothing I can't handle." I winked. "So, lunch and then my place?"

"Sounds great." Her hands shook a little as she reached for her water. Frowning, I watched in fascination as she chugged half of it and then nearly spilled the rest onto the table.

"Look." I reached for her right hand and grasped it in mine. "If it makes you nervous, we can just talk." Damn me to hell, I needed sex. I needed Avery out of my head. Fast.

"No, no. You've been so . . ." She nodded way too many times for her words to be believable. "I'm fine, completely fine. You've been so patient with me, and ever since Sam died, I just . . ." Her eyes welled with tears. "I think this is best, like ripping off a Band-Aid."

My chest clenched as I stood and moved to her side of the booth, pulling her into my arms. "Amy, the last thing I want is for you to feel uncomfortable. Not only will it be a horrible experience for both of us, but you'll feel guilty. I want you to be free." I kissed her soft cheek. "I want you to allow me to please you, to bring you pleasure, no-strings-attached pleasure. I'd like to be the first man to do that since his death, but if I'm not the right man for the job, we can end this, no hard feelings." What the hell was in the water? I meant every word, but damn, losing two girls in one week?

"No." Her voice was firmer this time. "No." Her grin was shaky. "I don't want food."

The waiter approached just then, and at Amy's words he hunched his shoulders and walked off.

"I want you." Her eyes lit up with excitement. "But I may be horrible."

"It's been a while." I nodded thoughtfully. "Let's just take it one step at a time, alright? You have the right to feel anxious."

"Lucas Thorn." She breathed my name. "One day you'll tell me what turned you into this, but until then . . . I'm going to be grateful for it, even if it was horrible, because I don't think I could do this with anyone else."

I didn't want to talk about my past. That was another thing I made sure my girls agreed to: they were never allowed to utter the question, *Who hurt you?*

I never talked about it.

And if one of them persisted in asking, I kicked her out of my bed and replaced her, but with Amy, it was different. She needed an emotional connection; hell, she just needed to be needed. Up until her husband's sudden death she'd been a stay-at-home mom. Her new life was scary, and she was used to having a man depend on her for everything. Now she was back in the workforce and the dating field at the same time. I knew it was terrifying for her.

She wasn't my usual.

I'd met her at one of my favorite bars and knew she'd be a great addition to my weekly list. She wasn't pouty, or dramatic—hell, none of my girls were—she was just, nice.

I liked nice.

Needed it just as much as I needed sex.

Besides, I had the roommates for my more unusual tastes.

"Let's go." I held out my hand. Amy stared at it and then took it. I tugged her out the door. My apartment was in a luxury building near the edge of Belltown. The walk would be good for her, good for us, and maybe she'd be able to focus her thoughts more.

Her breathing picked up speed the minute I stopped in front of the Volta building. With an amazing view of Puget Sound, my two-bedroom penthouse was a bachelor's dream come true. And though I had a fantastic salary as a corporate VP, the only reason I had been able to lease one of the top floors was because the owner of the building had been my Wednesday. God, sometimes I missed Monica, but she'd gotten married, moved on, and often emailed me pictures of her baby.

Even after she'd gotten married, I'd been to dinner at her apartment more times than I could count.

I stopped going when she got pregnant. Her husband, while understanding, wasn't really a big fan of my lifestyle. I couldn't blame him.

After all, I'd seen his wife naked and still had the balls to sleep with other women on other days of the week.

"So"—Amy clenched her fists—"this is it?"

"Let's go." I rubbed her back and led her through the lobby and quickly into the elevator, hitting the button for the eighth floor.

Twenty seconds later, the doors opened.

She gulped.

I shoved the key in my door and let her in. She was one of the first women who had actually seen my place, although she'd never been in my bedroom. None of my girls had. And I had a feeling she wasn't going to be staying long anyway.

"Wow." She gasped. "Your floors are incredible. Everything is so modern." Another gasp. "That. Kitchen."

"I love cooking." I smiled.

She returned it, then nervously tucked her hair behind her ears. "Should we . . . go to the bedroom?"

"Nope." I grinned. "I think we should stay in the light, so I can see you."

"But—"

"Amy . . ." I pulled her into my arms. "Let's just kiss."

So we did.

For a half hour, on the couch, and then, on the floor, me on top of her, her legs wrapped around my waist.

I was into it.

Until I started thinking of Avery.

Amy must have felt my hesitation. "We don't have to do this. I know I'm inexperienced, and—"

I silenced her with my mouth and slid my hand up her thigh. "I think I know how to get you to stop thinking."

She fell apart in my arms within two minutes.

Her body was so responsive, starving for a man's attention. And I felt good about it, good about giving her the release she needed, even though I was confused about why I didn't really feel like sex.

Amy yawned.

I let out a low chuckle. "I'll call you a car."

"No, it's okay. I'm just—" Another yawn. "Sleepy."

"Orgasms do that to a woman who's always had to be on top all her life." I winked and pulled her to her feet. "I'll pour you a glass of wine while you wait."

She nodded, her eyes blurry, unfocused.

I pulled up Uber and grabbed her a nice black sedan that was only five minutes away, then poured her a glass of chilled wine.

When I returned to the living room, she was sitting in one of my favorite chairs, legs tucked beneath her, staring out at the Sound.

"Here." I handed her the wine and waited for the inevitable, when she'd tell me that while I was really great, she just couldn't do this.

"You're wonderful." She didn't look at me. "And I'm so thankful that you've been patient with me, giving me weeks to decide what I want—and I think, I think I want something different . . . than this." A tear slid down her cheek.

I caught it with my thumb and pressed a kiss to her neck. "Amy, you're absolutely beautiful, and it's okay to feel that way."

She stared into my eyes. "I don't get it."

"Get what?"

"You." She shook her head. "This, Lucas."—Ah, the expected last-name drop!—"You're better than this."

"That's where you're wrong." I smiled sadly. "I'm not."

"But—"

I stood. "Your car should be here in about one minute. If you change your mind, you know where to find me."

"Thank you." Standing up on her tiptoes, she placed a polite kiss against my cheek. "I hope you find your happy, Lucas—I really do."

She walked away, and I stared as the door clicked shut. I gulped down the rest of her wine and continued staring at the door.

"What the hell is in the water?" I muttered, then reached for my cell and called my best friend, Thatch.

I wasn't interested in any of the substitutes tonight.

Maybe I just needed a guys' night, a night to clear my head of all things work and Avery.

I wanted to blame her.

So I did.

It was, after all, *her* moans I wanted to hear, not Amy's, damn it, and when I'd tried to get in the mood, I couldn't.

Because even though Avery was sometimes a judgmental psycho, all I could imagine was her standing over me with tears in her eyes—like her hero had fallen into the depths of hell, and she had no way of saving him.

"What?" Thatch barked by way of answering his cell. "I'm getting ready to go into the OR."

"You work tonight?"

"Off after this last breast augmentation."

Lucky bastard got to touch tits all day long and get paid for it. "Our spot at seven?"

"Done."

He hung up. Thank God he was free, because for a half a second I had entertained the thought of calling Avery.

Shit.

Chapter Eight

Avery

"I hate him." I sucked my drink down, my lips clamping hard on the straw with a vengeance.

"Eh." Austin arched an eyebrow and grinned. "You've said that like ten times—once on the way over here, twice when we walked in, and every time you take a sip. I'm pretty sure I got the memo."

"Why are we friends?" I wondered aloud.

"You've been stuck with me since second grade. I'm not changing now, even though I'm so busy these days I can barely see straight." She pouted her red-tinged lips and twirled her hair into a low bun, then slumped her shoulders. "I think I may actually decide to become a bum. You know, live off the land."

"You were kicked out of Brownies," I pointed out. "And last time your electricity went out, you asked if I knew how to light a match."

"I was just making sure I was doing it right!" she yelled defensively, her pale skin going red.

I burst out laughing. "Because you're afraid of fire, admit it."

She lifted one shoulder. "It's more of a healthy fear, like *Oh, that shit's hot—let's not burn down the house or a finger off.* Those things happen, you know, with stuff like firecrackers."

"Okay, my little fire-fearing friend." I patted her hand gently.

She scowled. "How much do you hate him again?"

"This much." I held my hands wide, nearly taking out our waitress as she tried to squeeze by us. We were at the bar, drinking away our sorrows. The only reason I was there was because Austin had promised to buy me two drinks. Then again, her parents were rich, so I didn't feel too guilty about saying yes.

She still lived at home.

Of course, if my parents had three pools, a sauna, and a tennis court, I would ask to be buried in their house.

But no. Instead, I had my mom's macaroni and a room filled with stuffed animals that came alive at night. Yay me!

When I was little, I was convinced my teddy bear was real—and all these years later, I still found him in different spots throughout the house, though I was pretty sure my dad moved him around to freak me out, the bastard.

I let out a wide yawn. "Hating people is exhausting."

Austin gave me a funny gaping look, then red flooded her cheeks.

"What? Why are you blushing? Who did you see?" I glanced around the dimly lit bar, hungrily seeking the reason for her reaction, but all I saw were overworked men in poorly fitting suits and a few girls with way too bright lipstick and skirts that barely covered their asses.

Austin gaped again, her gaze tracking right behind me.

"What?" I turned, but she grabbed me by the dress and held me in place.

"If you love me, as a friend, you won't turn around right now."

"Why?" I asked slowly.

"Because the hottest man candy in the entire world just looked our way, and if you look, he'll know I'm talking about him. Quick, lipstick on my teeth? Weird makeup smudges on my cheeks? Tell me straight, sister, because I'm going over."

Austin always looked perfect, even when she was tired from trying to finish her MBA in less than two years.

Her dark brown hair was wavy and messy but gorgeous, and her blue eyes stood out like giant, dazzling diamonds.

"You look horrible, ugly. How did you even leave the house this morning?"

"Thanks." She kissed the top of my head, hopped off the barstool, and ran off.

I finally turned around when I thought it was safe, but it was too dark to make out the guy she was talking to. Then again, she was taller than most, so her body was blocking the view.

"Move, bitch," I hissed under my breath.

"Well, well, well. Drinking alone I see," a familiar voice said to my left.

I closed my eyes and willed Satan away. That was how those things worked, right? I needed garlic.

Instead, I reached for the salt in front of me and shook a little in Lucas's direction.

When I opened my eyes, he was glancing down at the salt on his pants with a cheerful grin. "I think that only works on vampires. Or is it witches?"

"And here I thought it worked on all of Satan's minions and even the little red man himself—my bad." I smiled wide and took a large drink of my vodka and Coke. "And I'm not drinking alone. Austin found, according to her, the hottest man alive, so she just had to chase after him. Fingers crossed she won't get another restraining order."

He scowled. "You still hang out with *her*?"

It was no secret that he'd never approved of my friendship with the girl who pushed me off the monkey bars in first grade. I have the scars to prove it.

"Yes, Thorn." I nodded. "Because that's what friends do when they don't screw you over and destroy your life by betraying your trust. They stay loyal, friends for life and all that. Duh, we only had like fifteen friendship bracelets in middle school."

"Oh, I know." He stole my drink and gulped it like a caveman. "I'm the one that had to cut them all off when you broke your wrist and it started to swell to the size of a small whale."

"Hey!" I snatched my drink back, only to find the glass was empty. See? He was a complete monster! "It's not my fault I fell off the roof!"

"It was totally your fault!" His voice rose. "You were waiting there to dump water on me!"

"Because you called me stupid!"

"You failed math on purpose to talk to the quarterback!"

We were chest to chest.

I don't know when it happened. When the anger between us sizzled into something else.

But it did.

And I had no graceful way of making it unhappen, so I jerked away, like he was too hot and I'd just burned myself on his perfectly sculpted chest.

He rolled his eyes and motioned at the bartender. "Chill, I don't hit on children."

"I'm *sorry*." I punched him in the shoulder. "Did you just call me a child?"

He eyed me up and down quickly, dismissing me like I wasn't in a really tight purple dress that made my boobs look awesome. "You're twenty-two. Hardly an adult."

At that moment, there were so many immature things I wanted to say and do. Most of the latter involved something sharp—or maybe just a really, really large car that I could steal and run him over with—but instead, I went with a more stupid option, knowing it would cause Lucas to back off. I thrust out my chest and whispered in a low voice, "Funny, I'm pretty sure that's the last thing my boyfriend thinks when we're in bed together."

Lucas spit the drink he'd just ordered all over the bar, slowly turning his head, hazel eyes locked on mine. "No."

"What? What do you mean *no*?"

"You shouldn't be having sex."

I burst out laughing. "You do hear yourself, right? The king of the polygamy colony? Because that's not just the pot calling the kettle black, that's like—you know, I can't even come up with a comparison. It's plain stupid."

"So now I'm stupid?"

"At least I didn't call *you* a child."

He smirked. I didn't like it. I knew that smirk. He believed he had the upper hand, though he clearly didn't. "So you want me to think of you as a woman—is that what you're saying?"

My mouth opened and closed at least twice before I gulped and looked away, then whispered, "You're still stupid."

I was really good at comebacks.

Austin chose that awesome moment in time to charge up to me with a man in tow and yell, "We're going to do shots!"

"Pass."

"Thatch?" Lucas coughed out. "Found yourself a girl, have you?"

I looked back and forth at each of the men. If Thorn knew the dude, that was bad news for Austin. She deserved a good guy, a nice guy, one she could take home to her mansion and make sweet love to while her maid brought her grapes in bed. Not . . . him.

"Oh, hey, Lucas—sorry, didn't see you."

"How was surgery?" Lucas asked, completely ignoring everyone but mainly me, which was dumb. I wanted him to ignore me.

And maybe if I kept repeating that in my head, I'd actually start believing it.

"Typical, boring." Thatch sighed and flashed a sultry smile my way. His wavy blond hair touched his shoulders, making him look like a really hot surfer. "And you are?"

"My best friend," Austin purred. "I begged her to come out tonight and—" Something must have clicked in Austin's brain, because she stopped talking, and her eyes zeroed in on Lucas. "YOU!"

"Oh hell," Lucas muttered. "Hi, Austin, nice to see you've grown into your ears."

"And yet here you are." Austin shook her head. "Years later, and your nose, still big. I bet your good friend Thatch can help you out with that."

Lucas's nostrils flared on cue, while Thatch hid a laugh behind his hand and coughed out, "Well, this is fun! You guys all know each other?"

"I'll give you the short version," I piped in. "Lucas almost married one of my sisters before sleeping with my other sister the night before said wedding that didn't happen. Austin and I were bridesmaids, so she was spending the night. In a drunken attempt to leave the house without getting shanked by my grandfather—who fought in Nam, by the way—Lucas ran into Austin's brand-new Mercedes with his SUV." I grinned. "I skipped the really fun parts, but you get the idea."

Thatch whistled, while Lucas mouthed "Thanks" in my direction.

Austin added a dreamy sigh. "I loved that car."

"I'm sure your parents were more than happy to buy you another," Lucas added with no regret in his smooth voice.

And although he was spot-on, I felt the need to defend my friend. I was just about to when Thatch interrupted.

"Hey, I live just down the road. Why don't we all take the party to my place and order pizza? I'm starving, and as much as I'd love to take Austin out alone, I'm pretty sure that one or both of you will end up dead if left to your own devices—so let's go."

"I like him, so take-charge," I whispered to Austin.

"Good with his hands," Austin added.

"Sexy too. He wears jeans well."

"He can hear you," Lucas said.

"Oh, he was meant to." I winked at Thatch and gave him a little wave while Austin grabbed her purse and jacket.

I followed everyone out of the crowded bar, because at this point going home to my empty apartment meant I'd lose whatever war that was beginning between Lucas and me.

One of my heels caught in a crack in the sidewalk, and I tripped.

Lucas caught my arm and hissed out a curse. "Learn to walk in them or don't wear them at all, Avery."

There would be blood, folks.

There would be blood.

Chapter Nine

Lucas

"What the hell was that?" I was torn between strangling Thatch or hitting him over the head with the pizza box. "They can't be here!"

Thatch yawned behind his hand. "Sorry, man, I'm supertired. Can you repeat?"

I punched him in the shoulder. "The hell, man! That's Avery, little girl Avery, the one that's working for me now. I texted you about her yesterday! And that's her best friend. You can't just screw her best friend and then expect it not to affect my workday! I have to see Avery on a daily basis—you screw her friend over, and she's going to blame me!"

Thatch's eyes narrowed. "And you care why?"

"Because she'll make my life more of a living hell."

Thatch peered around the corner as Avery's laughter trickled into the custom kitchen. "Yeah." His eyebrows rose. "You realize she's like a fourth your size, right? You could sit on her, and she'd probably puke up her pizza."

"I'm sure that's what I'll do, then. Thanks for the wisdom. When I'm at work, irritated as hell, I'll just sit on my new intern?"

He shrugged.

"Helpful," I snapped.

"Look, Austin's hot." His grin was shameless. "And I haven't gotten laid in a few days. Besides, she doesn't seem to care that I've done nothing but stare at her tits for the past two hours. Get this, she asked to see my bedroom."

"Oh gee, Thatch, maybe while you guys are back there you can show her your comic book collection." I punched him again and swore while he cackled.

Bastard really did have comics, not that it mattered.

"Or . . ." He held up a finger. "I could just screw her sideways into Sunday."

"Solid plan." I exhaled. "I'm just going to go."

"No!" He held out his hands. "You have to take the other one."

"Avery," I said through clenched teeth. "Not a chance in hell. You invited her here—ergo, you *un*invite her so you can get in her best friend's pants. I refuse to help."

"I'll fix your nose." He winked.

"Low blow, you cock-sucking bastard."

He sighed and ran his hands through his overly long, shaggy blond hair. If you didn't know he was a plastic surgeon, you'd think he were a nomad living on the beach with a surfboard as company. "Look, just make up some lame excuse about getting her into bed at a decent hour so she can be fresh for Monday."

"Tomorrow's Sunday."

"Is it?"

"Thatch."

"Dude, you cheat on chicks all the time. Just do what you do best—get her out so I can get in." His chest puffed out like he was proud of his own wordplay.

"It's not cheating." I rolled my eyes. How many times did I have to explain myself? Especially to my best friend.

Avery's laughter caught my attention again.

I'd always loved her laugh.

Now it just reminded me that I'd gone four years without it. Laughs are funny like that; just like scents, they can be attached to memories you'd rather forget.

"Fine." I let out a defeated sigh. "But you owe me, big."

His only answer was to pull out a bottle of Prisoner sweet red wine and shrug.

"Minion!" I yelled, turning the corner and entering the living room. "Time to go."

Avery crossed her arms and leaned back comfortably against the couch, stretching out her legs; they went on for days. I ignored the way they swelled gently into her full hips, just like I didn't curse my best friend to hell when she licked her luscious lips and muffled out, "Yeah, I don't think so."

"Pretty sure"—I stalked toward her—"I didn't ask what you think or thought. It's getting late, and as much as I'm loath to admit it, I need you on your A game next week at work, alright? I would hate for you to get fired, live on the streets with the bums, and end up digging through trash cans for a Twinkie, all because you stayed up too late and refused to go night-night."

Avery's eyes narrowed into tight slits. "You're—you're—"

"Go." Austin shrugged. "Besides, I think Thatch and I"—she grinned and released a happy sigh—"have some really important work to do too."

"Slut," Avery coughed.

"Jealous?" Austin fired back.

"She has a boyfriend," I said smoothly, confidently, looking back and forth at Avery and then Austin. "Right? Male dancer?"

"Um." Austin's cheeks reddened as she slowly nodded. "Y-yes, she does."

I don't know why I did it, why my teenage self suddenly came alive like a vampire at night and decided to launch my adult body across the room and slap a hand over Avery's mouth. "What's his name again?" I said.

Avery tried to bite my hand.

Austin kept mumbling.

Avery kept biting.

Until Austin finally said, "I forget. They've only gone on two dates."

"What?" I roared, pulling my hand back. "You slept with him after two dates?"

Avery groaned and covered her face with her hands. "You have no right to be angry when you sleep with a different girl every single night."

"He doesn't sleep with anyone on Sundays," Thatch piped in as he made his way into the living room, where the third world war was breaking out.

"Thanks," I said through clenched teeth.

He shrugged and offered Austin a glass of wine. "Want to see my comic book collection?"

I moaned, while Avery burst out laughing.

"Is that what the kids call it these days?" Austin stood and let out a sultry laugh. "Tell me you have costumes to go with, and I'm in."

"God, where have you been all my life?"

"I think it's time to go," Avery whispered against my fingers.

Her lips were hot.

Her tongue touched my skin.

And I suddenly didn't want to wash my hand—ever.

Which clearly meant that Avery and Austin were bringing down the average age of the group by their collective immaturity. Great, by next week I'd be twenty-one again, doing Irish car bombs and puking in the streets. Couldn't wait for that fun!

Thatch led Austin to the bedroom, and I held out my hand to Avery. Naturally, she slapped it away because she was an ungrateful pain in my ass, but at least I'd offered.

We started walking out of the apartment in silence.

"Don't forget your purse!" I called out just as she passed it.

With a near stumble and face-plant against the counter, Avery grabbed her purse and hooked her arm around it, then her blurry eyes connected with mine.

"Shit," I muttered. "Are you drunk?"

"No!" She laughed while she said it.

I counted to five.

I was trying to keep myself from dropping enough F bombs to make her sob her eyes out and impale me with the shoes she was still having trouble walking in. If she was drunk, I couldn't just happily send her on her way.

I had to take care of her. Damn me to hell.

"Come on," I said in a gruff voice. I was gentle as I wrapped my arm around her waist and helped her walk toward the elevator.

She clung to me.

I didn't expect to like holding her—or to move a little closer while she nestled her head against my chest and yawned. "I'm tired."

"Well, it's one in the morning."

"That's so early!"

"God, was I ever that young?" I asked, mostly to myself.

Her body slumped heavily against me as the elevator surged down toward the lobby.

"Hey, where do you live? I'll get you a car." I shook her a bit.

She didn't move; instead, she wrapped her arms tighter around my neck and made a little mewling sound that was cute as hell.

Her breath was hot against my neck, her body soft.

"I better get a damn medal for this," I whispered to myself, careful not to wake her as I lifted her into my arms and walked the two blocks to my place.

By the time we reached my apartment, she was full on snoring, and every few minutes she whispered, "Twinkie."

I'd like to think I was the reason she was dreaming of Twinkies chasing her since a Twinkie was one of the last things I'd mentioned to her before she conked out.

She was a strong little thing, clinging to me like she was afraid I was going to put her down.

It had been a long time since I'd let a woman cling to me at all. All arms and legs, wrapped around me, with no sex in the foreseeable future.

Just thinking about sex with her had my body responding when it needed to stay the hell dormant. Like a bear during the winter.

I didn't turn on any lights as I walked into the spare bedroom and laid her across the bed.

I would not take care of her.

I would not put a blanket over her or make sure she had water by the nightstand.

Nope.

She did this to herself.

Not me.

I shrugged and got as far as the door before I stopped, turned, saw her smile in her sleep, and heard her make a quiet sound. With a curse, I banged my forehead against the doorframe a few times before returning to the room, pulling the covers back, and slipping her beneath them, but not before taking off her shoes.

I even went so far as to go into the adjoining bathroom, get a glass of water, and set it by her bedside.

It felt wrong somehow—her being in my apartment.

In one of my bedrooms.

And I had no idea why.

Frowning, I stared down at her small body.

How many times in the past decade had I helped her sneak into her parents' house after a night out with friends? Taught her how to get over a hangover? Or just let her sleep over when her entire family was out of town and she had to stay for softball practice to avoid getting kicked off the team.

That certain night needed to never, ever, never enter back into my consciousness.

Ever.

◆ ◆ ◆

"Thorn!" Avery yelled, barreling toward my house. I was home for the week-end and staying with my parents, who just happened to live across the street from Avery's family. "Open the door!"

"Shhh!" I opened the door and smirked. "Avery Bug, my, my, my, this is a surprise—do you do this often? Go to strange men's homes and ask to be invited in?"

She slugged me in the shoulder. At seventeen, she was still all arms and legs, but her strength was impressive. "I'm scared, let me in."

I pushed the door wide. "Be my guest, little sis."

She stuck her tongue out and skipped into my house, then plopped onto my couch, putting her feet up on the table and sighing happily. "Sorry. I'm alone all weekend, and I heard a noise."

I nodded. "Probably a burglar or an axe murderer. They do seem to know whenever girls are alone in all those horror movies. Good thing you're here."

"Make me popcorn?" Her smile about killed me.

"You do realize some people work for a living, right? And don't often get time off."

She wiped a fake tear. "You're so . . ." She frowned. "Old."

"Why did I let you in again?" I wondered aloud.

Avery laughed and pulled her long strawberry-blonde hair back into a ponytail. "Because you love me?"

"True." I couldn't help but smile. "I do, but not enough to make pop-corn all by myself." I held out my hand.

She jumped up from the couch and took it. "Race ya!"

We stayed up until four in the morning, watching horror movies and eating junk food. I'd been working so much to save for the wedding and honeymoon that I hadn't taken any time for me. Kayla was working as a schoolteacher and trying to get her master's at the same time. So although I loved her, I rarely saw her, especially since I'd taken a job downtown while she was still in Mill Creek. With the traffic snarls and my having to leave really early in the morning, things between us were . . . strained.

"So." Avery laid her head on my shoulder.

I stiffened.

But I had no damn clue why.

It was Avery.

She was like a sister.

Except I swallowed and looked away, careful to pull the blanket up over her bare legs and short-as-hell shorts.

"Thanks." She yawned. "I was cold."

"Wearing shorts like that, I imagine you're lucky you don't have hypothermia."

"Hey!" She slapped a hand over my stomach and left it there. "Not my fault they're in style."

"Whatever you say."

Feelings I didn't understand started pounding through me, blood roaring in my ears. No, no, no, I could NOT be attracted to Avery.

Seventeen.

She was seventeen.

I was such an ass! Marrying her sister in less than a year, and I was lusting after Avery, of all people?

Avery? Who got her braces off two years ago and had yet to grow into her body?

I really was stressed, overworked.

Avery sighed. "I got dumped."

"Sorry, Bug." I wrapped an arm around her tightly. "But he probably didn't deserve you."

"Yeah, that's what I said after I punched him in the face."

I burst out laughing. "Oh, please, please tell me you gave him a bloody nose."

She shrugged. "He shouldn't have messed around with another girl."

My stomach clenched.

Was I capable of that?

Fear paralyzed me.

Because suddenly I wondered, if I had the chance to make out with Avery right then—if I had the chance to do even more than that, no strings attached—without Kayla finding out, would I?

The thought haunted me the rest of the night, including when I brushed a kiss across Avery's cheek and then her lips as she slept against my chest.

I knew, in my gut, I already had my answer.

Chapter Ten

AVERY

I smacked my lips together, my very dry lips. Note to self: hydration saves lives. Ugh, why hadn't I had any water at Thatch's? Maybe because Austin had kept pouring wine and I'd kept drinking it, chugging it more likely.

I blinked, then rubbed my eyes. Awesome, they were almost glued shut with mascara, making it nearly impossible to see.

This was all Thorn's fault! I'd left with everyone because I wasn't about to let my best friend go to some strange man's apartment. And then Thorn had gone and ordered pizza—with my favorite topping—that cheating whore! Okay, so my logic was a bit screwy. It's not like he'd forced me to eat all the pizza and drink all the wine, but still!

It's sad when you start to like a guy based on the fact that he remembers you love pineapple on your pizza even if he picks it off his own piece because he hates pineapple.

I was too spoiled. Too set in my ways!

I would so not survive on the streets.

I groaned again and then finally got one eye open.

The room was pretty dark, which was weird since sunlight woke me up most mornings. My apartment faced east, so I always knew when it was time to get up. It would probably help my attitude in the mornings if I could afford curtains instead of those five-dollar blinds you get at the big-box store and cut to size. I must have failed scissors handling in grade school, because my blinds didn't fit, not even close.

"Why . . . ?" I whispered hoarsely into the silent room, angry that I had let him get to me again, and even angrier that somehow I could still smell him.

All warm, and spicy, but like a hot whiskey spice—or pancakes. I sniffed, wondering. Why it smelled like pancakes. I didn't have a roommate. And I didn't cook.

I pried my other eye open.

My body froze.

Heart stopped beating.

Lungs collapsed.

Not my room.

I shrieked and pulled the covers up to my chin. Not my bed.

And then, the devil himself appeared at the door, sans shirt to cover his ridiculously cut body. Lucas smirked. "Morning. Was it as good for you as it was for me?"

My brain straight up exploded.

Muscles flexed against the doorframe. He held a spatula in one hand and a plate in the other. The aroma of awesomeness drifted to my spot on the bed, and my stomach grumbled.

"Great trick, by the way—you know, that thing with your legs. Though damn, Avery, no need to slap my ass so many times. And I mean, if you want to call me your daddy, that's all you, but since I know your daddy, maybe cut back on all the dirty talk referencing him while orgasming."

My eyes must have been as wide as saucers. I couldn't find my voice, my stupid stomach was now growling, and he was still standing there, like we hadn't just had drunken sex. Sex I couldn't remember.

I quickly peeked under the covers.

I was still dressed.

"Lighten up." He padded over to me and handed me a plate. "You were asleep before I kidnapped you. And since leaving you on the street corner would have been frowned upon, I had no choice but to bring you home."

I frowned down at the plate. "Where's my fork?"

His low-slung jeans and chiseled stomach were inches from my face. It wasn't fair; I cursed fatness on him, his family, his dog, his cow—

"Here you go." He pulled a fork out of his back pocket. "I thought it wise not to give you weapons until I knew without a doubt you wouldn't stab me."

I snatched the fork and smacked him on the hand with it anyway.

"Shit." He jerked back. "I did a nice thing for you last night. You know that, right? *Nice.* Also known as doing a solid for another human without expecting anything in return."

Glaring at him over the giant plate of pancakes, I stabbed a few bites with my fork and stuffed them in my mouth.

"Oh good, the silent treatment." He winked. "Hurry up and finish your pancakes. My sister's on her way over, and I'm pretty sure the last thing she needs is to see Avery Black in my spare bed looking—" He licked his lips.

"Ugh . . ." I swallowed. "Say it. I look like shit."

"No ugh. I was going to say 'looking like she's been thoroughly screwed.'" He didn't smirk, or wink, or do anything that would indicate if he was kidding, being an asshole, or just being plain honest.

"You've got syrup on your nose." He swiped it off with his finger and walked away.

I stared after him like I'd just woken up in some alternate universe—one where somehow I was the Black sister who'd ended up with Lucas Thorn, and he was making me pancakes in bed.

Guilt stabbed me right in the chest. Because how many times had I wanted exactly that? How many times had I measured myself against Kayla? And come up short?

Did God hate me that much? To dangle crack-filled pancakes in front of me along with the man who got away? The same man who broke my sister's heart? And damaged countless lives?

I entertained that conundrum for possibly thirty seconds before I shoved it away and finished my pancakes. He'd always been a good cook, which was just another thing that I hated about him.

Assholes weren't allowed to be good cooks. Or rich. Damn it, he should have been poor! With a beer belly and adult acne!

With no choice but to do the semiwalk of shame into the living room, I gathered my hair into a low ponytail, located my shoes, and shuffled barefoot into the light.

Like a loser.

"Thanks." I dropped my shoes onto the hardwood floor and washed off my plate, then found the dishwasher and loaded it. "For the pancakes."

Lucas was staring at me over his coffee as though I'd grown five heads.

"What?" I shrugged. "What's that look for?"

"Did you just clean a dish?"

"Bite me."

"You *never* do dishes."

"Lucas, as much as I'd like to shove our history up your ass and light you on fire, I can't, you know, because I wouldn't survive prison, and they don't have Starbucks there . . . But four years is a long time. I've changed." I sighed. "I mean, both of us have. I'm a mildly successful college graduate discovering what I want to do with my life, paying my own electricity bill and you"—I pointed to him—"you . . ."

"I what?"

He took a long sip of coffee. I didn't wait for him to swallow.

"You're a lying, cheating whore." I said it sweetly, even batted my eyes at him. That made it better, right?

"It isn't cheating if—"

"Right, I get it—to you it's not cheating if they know. To me it just seems like a really solid way to get an STD or get a girl pregnant that you don't even like, making it so you have to fire Monday, Tuesday, Wednesday, Thursday, and Saturday!"

"I do like them, and why not Friday?"

"Oh, I had a good feeling about her." I smirked. "She had nice lipstick. I can see it now: an unplanned pregnancy, little Nadia moving into this chic apartment, putting her stuff all over, and you finding tampons in the bathroom, only to come out to her sobbing on the couch while the baby cries . . ." I sighed cheerfully. "The perfect family."

Lucas went from vibrant to pale, all within the span of a minute.

"Something bothering you, Thorn?"

"Other than your voice?" He shook his head. "Nope, can't think of a thing."

A knock sounded at the door. Lucas nearly dropped his coffee, then stared at the door. "Shit, she's early."

"So." I located my purse, tossed on the couch, and snagged it. "Just let her in, what's the big deal? It's not like anything happened, and your sister loves me."

He gave me the most irritated look ever. "You're right. I can't think of one solid reason why it would be weird, my sister walking in, seeing you for the first time in years, looking the way you do, walking the walk of shame out of my apartment . . . her thinking that I've plowed my way through every Black sister. You're right—why am I so worried?"

My heart clenched. It shouldn't have, but that's the thing about hearts; even when you think yours is solidly on lockdown, it still manages to twinge when someone says something hurtful, especially when they don't even realize it is.

Then again, Lucas had gone from promising something he had no business promising a girl of seventeen—to landing in her older sister's bed. Drunk off his ass.

I took a deep breath and paused to think. "We'll lie."

"No shit. Why hadn't I thought of that?" He glared at me.

"I'm storing this conversation for later, when I throw it back in your face and give you a big fat giant 'I told you so.'" I stomped over to the door and threw it wide open. "ERIN!" I might have said her name a smidge too loud, considering she took a cautious step back like I was about to launch myself onto her. "Long time no s-see." Oh hell, the stutter—that wasn't what was needed in this situation. Confidence, Avery!

Erin's eyes narrowed, and then she shoved past me, grabbed the closest weapon, which just so happened to be the spatula, and started reaming on Lucas.

It was a really great show. Where was popcorn when I needed it?

"A little help!" he screamed in my direction while covering his head with one hand and his man parts with the other.

I yawned, checked my fingernails, entertained the thought of busting out some yoga, then very slowly raced an imaginary snail over to their location and said, "Stop, it's okay, Erin."

"IT'S NOT OKAY! HE SWORE HE WOULD NEVER REPLACE ME ON A SUNDAY." Swat. "What's WORSE!" Two swats. "He did it with you!" Swat, swat, swat . . . "How dare you, Lucas! This is going to disappoint Mom and Dad all over again! I can't believe you! And with her? She's completely innocent! Do you want Mom to cry over you again?" She swatted him a few more times.

Laughter gurgled in my throat, though I struggled to hold it back. Oh man, that spatula was getting some action.

"Well, um, actually . . ." I moved to stand in front of him and then wrapped my arm around his neck, squeezing as tightly as I could without bruising him. "We're seeing each other, er . . . exclusively."

"You are?" "We are?" Erin and Lucas asked in unison.

"Yeah, you know, our little Thorn is going straight, aren't you, baby?"

She dropped the spatula, and tears filled her eyes. "Are you serious? You're not whoring around anymore? Cheating on poor innocent women and giving them the bullshit line that if they know—"

"—it's not cheating," I finished for her. "Stupid, right?"

"Stupid doesn't even begin to cover it." She smiled brightly through her tears. "I'm just—I don't think I've ever been this happy." She ran a shaky hand through her hair. "God, Mom and Dad have been so worried about you with all of this weird dating going on, and you know how things have never been the same with our families after . . . This could literally fix everything!" She beamed at Lucas. "I mean, clearly you're over everything now? You can move on from all this serial cheating or dating or whatever it is? I swear if Mom and Dad actually knew what you'd been up to, they'd kill you." Her eyes filled with more tears. "My baby brother's settling down!"

I felt slightly guilty as I squeezed him harder and said, "Kind of feels like we just took the first real steps on the moon, right?" Curse words flew under his breath as he tensed beneath my touch.

"Lucas!" She smiled. "Stop being such a baby. I won't tell Mom and Dad. I'm just, I'm so proud that you've found your heart."

"Imagine—it was in my hands this whole time! And to think we nearly sold it to Satan!" We both burst out laughing.

Lucas flinched and mumbled, "Excuse me."

Which wasn't like him.

I mean, he was usually polite.

But he was the type to play into schemes like that, or at least make me pay for what I just did, but hey, at least I'd made him look awesome in front of his sister and protected both of us from shaming in the process.

Instead, he walked from the room without another word.

"Maybe you should go check on him?" She frowned like she was concerned his feelings were hurt. Sorry, honey, that ship sailed long ago. The man had no feelings; he was like an emotionally neutral Switzerland.

But I went anyway—to save face.

What I didn't expect to find was Lucas Thorn having a full-fledged panic attack in his master bathroom, or for him to be bleeding as pieces of mirror spread across the sink and onto the floor, as though he'd just tried to rip it from the wall, got frustrated, and punched it instead.

"Lucas?" I stepped around the glass to where he huddled in the corner, blood trickling down his arm and onto his jeans. "Holy crap, you're bleeding! Are you okay?"

"Leave."

"Lucas—"

"I don't need your help." He glanced up, and his eyes were unfocused. "Tell my sister I fell, tell her I saw the devil in my reflection and was fighting my own demons. But I want you out of this apartment in two minutes, or I'm going to fire your ass."

"What?" I hissed. "I just saved you!"

"No," he barked out. "You saved *you*. That wasn't saving me—that was screwing me over, so thank you very much for ruining my life."

"Well," I snorted. "Payback's a bitch."

He eyed me up and down and whispered, "You have no idea."

Chapter Eleven

LUCAS

I was able to convince my sister that I'd accidentally slipped and hit the mirror—it was a lame-ass excuse, but she seemed to buy it.

I thought things were cool until she texted me links to a few websites for anger management.

The very last thing I needed was for the Marysville gossip ring to start its chatter. Or for my parents to call Avery's parents out of concern that a repeat was taking place—God, I could only imagine. I was a man on borrowed time, because even though I loved my sister, she couldn't keep a secret to save her life.

Which meant.

I was completely screwed in every single way that mattered.

I couldn't win.

Either I said I was with Avery and finally make everyone happy by fixing the four-year divide between our parents—or history would repeat itself: my dad's heart would fail out of disappointment for his only son; my mother would cry herself to sleep every night; and Avery's parents, who I loved almost as much as my own, would be angry yet again.

The worst part? My sister had cried. Again. After brunch.

I blamed her pregnancy.

She said it wasn't about the baby but because I'd finally grown up and decided to think about someone and something other than myself and my own personal feelings. Funny, because I thought I was already there. I had a solid job, a nice apartment, a fantastic life, and I enjoyed a different girl every day of the week.

That was grown up.

Unlike taking home a drunk Avery Black and helping her nurse a stupid wine hangover that should never have happened in the first place.

My head hurt. The whole situation was going to end up coming back and biting me in the ass. I couldn't shake the feeling that bad things were coming.

Chapter Twelve

Lucas

Three hours later, and I still couldn't shake the headache or the onslaught of memories I'd kept locked away. They thumped around in my brain like a bad movie on repeat.

Avery didn't know.

Nobody did.

Avery knew what I wanted her to know, which was enough.

I stared out the window of my apartment. I had to face her at work tomorrow, and I had to make sure that she didn't get under my skin, or ever find out the truth about that night.

My phone rang.

It was my mom.

Son of a bitch.

Let the games begin.

"Hello?" I always answered my mom's calls. If I didn't, she called the police. In her mind I lived in the big, bad, scary city, and even though I was only about an hour away, I basically lived "in hell." Her words, not mine.

"Honey, don't freak out." Her tone was way too elated for this to be a normal check-in. "But I just got off the phone with Erin."

A rock the size of Texas settled in my stomach as my heart started rapidly thudding against my chest.

"Of course you did." What were the chances of a meteor hitting the earth? Scratch that, landing smack dab in Belltown, only to take out one single room in an apartment building?

"And don't be angry with her, but some interesting news just . . . slipped out."

"Naturally."

"Because you know Erin."

"I know Erin." I sighed and pinched the bridge of my nose.

"I mean, really, it wasn't her fault at all—I think it's the baby."

Damn it! Unfair! You can't blame an unborn child for her inability to keep her trap shut! Hell, damn, shit, ahhhhhhhhhhhhhhhhh. With shaking hands, I poured some whiskey into a glass, then stared at the bottle and brought it to my lips.

"Are you drinking?"

"No." Hell yes.

"Honey, think of your liver."

HAH! My liver was the least of my worries. If God were just, he'd kill me now, right now. I closed my eyes tight. We were going to have the conversation. The one I always swore I'd never have. Where my mom dug up the past, made me feel like shit, and cried.

"Anyways . . ." She chuckled. "The youngest Black girl? I mean, do you think that's a good idea? Things are just starting to get back to normal between us and the Blacks. We act like neighbors again, we wave at one another. Why, just the other day your father said hello to them and didn't get ignored!" She sighed, maybe realizing that it had taken four years simply to exchange a hello. "Well, it doesn't matter I guess. What's done is done. And honestly, this may help heal what happened between us." She started sniffing. "I miss them so much. You know I went to high school with Tess and Stewart." Yes, I knew. Everyone knew that the minute I'd fucked up, I hadn't just done it to myself but to a friendship that was known throughout our town. For shit's sake, our parents used to plan block parties together. Avery's mom was my godmother! Guilt kicked me over and over again until I thought I was going to puke. "Your father and I are so proud!"

Thud, thud. My heart strained to a painful degree. And there it was. Proud.

They were proud.

"You're proud," I repeated. "The last time you said that I was graduating college with honors. You've said that twice to me in my life." The other time was when I asked Kayla to marry me.

"Oh, don't be so dramatic." She paused. "Honey, are you sure you're not drinking? Erin said you had a little incident with your mirror."

"Thought I saw a spider." I sighed and took another heavy drink. "You know how I get."

"Use the little spider thingy I got you from the airline catalog! Remember, it saves them so you can set them free in the wild."

Of what? Downtown Seattle?

Parents. Why? Just. I had nothing.

"So when can we do dinner?"

That was better. Change the subject. Though dinner with my parents after the Avery news probably wouldn't be the wisest course of action.

They were proud.

Proud.

I had no choice.

"I think I'm free Tuesday night." Both Cary and Tabatha were on a flight that evening, so I wouldn't get the much-needed and deserved sex I'd been looking forward to ever since Avery Black had blasted back into my life like an atom bomb.

"Boom!" I made a little exploding motion with my hand that held the bottle. *Kids, this is your brain, this is your brain on drugs—note it looks exactly like what happens to Lucas when he and Avery are in the same room. Fascinating!*

"Tuesday," she whispered to herself. "Tuesday." Another long pause. "Tuesday."

"In two days, Mom!"

"Don't raise your voice at your mother!" my father bellowed, and I jerked the phone away from my ear.

"Oh good, you're on speakerphone." I made a gun shape with my hand, motioning toward my head, and took another swig from the bottle.

"Son, are you drinking?"

"Nope." I took another long drink.

"Tuesday!" my mother shouted. "Perfect. We'll text you the name of the restaurant. Now, make sure to bring Avery." When my parents and I went out to dinner, they always picked the restaurant and I always paid. It was kind of how it worked—it was the least I could do after all the pain I'd caused. Wait, did she just say "Avery"?

"The hell?"

"Language!" my father boomed.

"Sorry—I meant, she's busy." I rolled my eyes.

"Can she cancel her plans?" my mom pleaded and then started sniffling.

"Son, don't make your mother cry. She's had an emotional day, what with Fluffy dying."

"Fluffy's been dead FOR A YEAR!"

"Still . . ." She sniffled loudly. "Hurts, you know that the Blacks gave me Fluffy before . . ."

Before I screwed up.

Before I ruined my parents' lives.

Before I moved away.

So I did what idiots always did when cornered—I damned Avery Black to hell and said, "I'm sure she can make it."

The conversation ended when my mother asked when we were having kids.

I carried the bottle to bed.

Chapter Thirteen

Avery

It wasn't a big deal. Just a Monday. I was making it worse than it really was, anxiety building up in my stomach so much that I'd almost puked twice that morning.

He'd actually threatened to fire me—or at least give me such a bad review, I wouldn't be able to work for the company, the one that had a six-figure starting salary with my name on it and a really shiny company card that would let me charge things like lunch.

Steak.

Business trips!

It was like my imminent homelessness meant nothing to him!

I was exaggerating.

But still!

He was an ass!

But it wasn't his threat that had been the last straw—it was the look on his face while he'd said it, like he'd just seen a ghost or maybe he was spooked to see a demon when he looked into the mirror. God only knew how many of those he had hanging off his body, what with all the sin he invited. Because I had to face the truth—he was a down and dirty cheater.

I don't know why I had such a hard time believing it when it slapped me in the face on a daily basis—via his updated calendar notifications on my cell.

There was no way that heaven was smiling down on Lucas Thorn and offering up top-notch guardian angels to do protection duty.

I wasn't going to get paid for another week, so extras like coffee were out of the question, which just made my anxiety that much worse because I was completely exhausted.

Especially since Kayla had decided to call—again—to ask if she could visit. It wasn't like Kayla lived in the wilds of Alaska, but she did live in Bellingham, which was a good two-hour drive from downtown. And since Kayla was a horrible driver and had road rage like something you'd see on *Cops*, it was probably better for everyone in Seattle for her to stay in Bellingham every weekend instead of visiting me.

A nagging voice reminded me that it wasn't necessarily her driving skills that gave me anxiety—but the fact that I'd have to see her.

Face-to-face.

The girl I could never live up to.

The one who used to make it painfully obvious that I never would.

And the one with a boyfriend she had cheerfully dangled in front of my face. The hard part was she was always so sickeningly sweet, I was never sure if she was malicious or just plain ignorant of the fact that I'd had a thing for him.

Ugh. Four years later. And it still haunted me.

Seeing her just reminded me of all the things I'd tried to forget and put behind me. She was always so passive-aggressive that by the time we were done hanging out, I was emotionally spent.

The office building loomed ahead of me. I squinted up at it, covering my face with part of my hand as the sun cast its glare against the glass.

"What are we looking at?" Lucas whispered in my ear.

I let out a little yelp and jumped away from him, and I would have run into a passing biker if Lucas hadn't pulled me out of the way with his coffee-free hand.

"Must you be such a pain in the ass?"

"Must you try to kill me?" I fired back.

He rolled his eyes. "Let's go." He started walking, hauling me with him. We weren't walking in the direction of the office.

"Um, Thorn—"

"I will seriously shove this Starbucks up that skinny ass if you don't stop talking and just listen for once in your life."

I shut up and followed, but only because he'd said "Starbucks" and was very purposefully moving in the nearest outpost's general direction. If I looked pathetic enough, would he buy me coffee?

That was what my life was coming to.

Pity coffee.

My shoulders slumped at the thought when we walked into the building. The smell of fresh baked goods hit me with full force, and my stomach growled loudly, saying to everyone, *I'm a hungry bear and may eat my young. Out of the way, please!*

I followed Lucas to the line, still tempted to speak, but I figured if he wanted noise from me, he'd say something like, "You may grace me with your voice now, Avery."

Even though I wasn't talking, every time I heard someone order pumpkin bread I sighed, loudly, so loudly that the barista eyed me cautiously. *Chill, Starbucks, I'm not going to steal a piece of pumpkin bread.*

My mouth watered.

I mean, I wasn't that desperate.

But if I took two, maybe three, steps toward her, yelled "Fire!" and then screamed nonsense about a bee attacking me, the pumpkin bread she had in hand would probably fall to the ground, and it would be wasteful if I didn't rescue it from the ants.

All creatures deserve food—but pumpkin bread was too good for ants, too rich, and they'd explode all over the floor from the richness and it would be my fault—for saving the barista's life, right? From the bee?

I think I just confused myself.

"Why are you breathing so heavy?" Lucas asked from my right.

I snapped out of my pumpkin-bread daydream and shrugged. "Sorry, low on sleep."

He gave a noncommittal nod and then it was his turn. Greedy little bastard already had one coffee—now he was getting another one! "A venti macchiato and a large coffee with room for cream, two slices—"

I elbowed him hard in the ribs.

"Sorry, um, three slices of pumpkin bread, thanks."

He handed the barista his card, while my greedy eyes locked on the pumpkin bread as the barista placed it into a bag and gave it to him.

With an exasperated sigh, he shoved the bag into my hands. "Just leave me one bite."

"No promises." I was already digging into the bag, my mouth watering as I followed him around the counter with a little pep in my step.

Lucas grabbed our drinks and motioned toward one of the tables. I sat, stuffed more pumpkin goodness into my mouth, and managed to chug some coffee almost all at once.

Lucas shook his head. "I always forget how seriously you take your pumpkin bread."

I moaned and took another huge bite. "My theory is this."

He leaned forward, a smile curving around his gorgeous mouth. "Alright, out with it."

More pumpkin bread found its way into my mouth as I talked—I didn't even care if I looked like a starved animal. "Pumpkin bread has the same addictive properties as cocaine."

"That's your theory? That it's a drug?"

"Right." I sighed and leaned back. "Except it doesn't make you skinny, unfortunately."

His smile widened, and he grabbed a small hunk of bread. "Want to know my theory?"

"Yes, that's exactly what I was thinking—I hope Lucas tells me his theory so I can eat his portion of bread."

Lucas scooted the bag toward me and whispered, "Merry Christmas."

"Oh, pumpkin gods." I moaned again.

His eyes darted to my mouth.

"What?" I wiped my lips. "Is something on my face?"

"No." He looked away. "So my theory is this . . . pumpkin flavoring is a conspiracy by the government to see how many ways we can market a flavor and make money off it."

"Boo." I gave him a thumbs-down. "Thanks, grinch. Oh, and stop ruining holidays."

He smirked. "You've known forever that Santa isn't real. Still doesn't stop you from leaving him cookies every Christmas Eve, then sneaking downstairs and eating them all by yourself."

"One"—I held up a finger—"it's genius because nobody will touch them for fear that I'll get mad. Two"—I held up a second finger—"when everyone else is sad about the Christmas cookies being gone, I know I'll have them all to myself. It's like . . ." I sighed, ". . . a Christmas present. To myself."

"Except for that one time." He smirked.

"Cruel man." I glared at him. "How dare you eat my cookies?"

He shrugged. "They were sweet."

Was it hot? In this little Starbucks? By the window where the sun was searing me alive like I was under a magnifying glass?

I tugged at my sleeveless blouse.

"About Saturday . . ."

Uncomfortable conversation, here we come! I strapped in and waited for the inevitable. And then realized, to my dismay, that he'd just bought me coffee and food without letting me go to the office.

My eyes filling with tears, I shook my head a few times. "Lucas, I may give you crap, but I really need this job."

He frowned, like he was confused.

"Don't say another word." I held out my hands. "I'll do anything, Lucas—and I mean *anything*—to keep this job. I wasn't kidding when I said my parents were chomping at the bit to get me to move home, and I don't want to. It's not just about me being defiant; they want me to take over the family business."

Lucas burst out laughing and then sobered. "Oh, you're serious."

"I can't sell chicken, Thorn."

"I mean, to be fair, Avery, your parents own a very lucrative organic meats company. I'm sure they could offer you at least five figures." His smile was way too smug, but I still had to be nice to him rather than throw him off a cliff, because he could fire me.

"Look"—I tried a different tactic—"Mom and Dad are great, I love them, but Brooke lives at home . . ."

"What? Brooke?" He frowned. "I thought she went off to LA to try acting or something."

I gulped. "Or something."

"Avery?"

"She slept with the wrong person, made the wrong friends, and is now very happily hanging out in her old bedroom and doing the books for my parents' business. She hates life, and she's grumpy, and she's not a nice person. So, no, I don't want to move home, and, yes, I do need this job. If you're going to fire me, fine, but at least give me two weeks' notice so I can build a nice shack by the water. All the good street corners are taken, and I refuse to be confused with a prostitute!"

"You done yet?"

"Yes." I sighed, feeling slightly better but still shaky, like he was just waiting for me to calm down so he could run me over with a motorized vehicle, only to apologize and do it again, such were the ways of Lucas Thorn.

"You said you'd do anything?" I didn't like that look, that look with his eyebrows arching a bit, exposing more of his hypnotic eyes and damn cleft chin!

"I—"

"You said, and I quote, 'I'll do anything, Lucas . . .'"

"I don't sound that shrill," I snapped.

"Eh, pretty sure you do." He took a long, smug sip of his coffee and then shrugged.

"So you need me—am I hearing this correctly?"

I shifted in my seat, avoiding eye contact. Napkins littered the floor by my feet and—oh look, a green straw. Maybe I could save it for later and use it to help build my shack by the water. Homelessness wouldn't be so bad—I mean, I could bathe in the ocean, live off the land.

I once heard that grasshoppers taste like chicken.

"Avery, look at me." His voice was smooth. Slowly I lifted my gaze to his stupidly beautiful face. "Dinner. Tuesday. Those are my terms, take them or leave them."

I jerked back in response. "Dinner? That's it? Lucas, is this your idea of a sick joke? You know one of my favorite things to do is eat. I take food very seriously."

"Don't I know it."

Okay, so it's entirely possible that I once fell asleep at his house and woke up screaming, "Hamburger!"

But in my defense, I'd forgotten to eat after soccer practice, and the parents had been gone again, which meant I got scared and went to Lucas's house, because, well, he had bigger muscles and was strategic in all his monster-fighting ability. The man had fake ninja stars.

"Just dinner," I said, my eyes narrowing.

It was his turn to look uncomfortable. "Dinner and polite conversation."

I pointed my finger at him. "I don't trust you, Thorn."

"Oh, I'm sorry. Are you under the impression I want your trust?"

Okay, well, that was unnecessarily mean.

"Look, dinner with me Tuesday and you won't get a bad assessment. In fact, I may just give you a perfect review when the internship is over."

"Fine," I snapped, narrowing my eyes at him. "Where are we going?"

"El Gaucho."

I gasped.

His smile was huge. "What? Mouth already watering?"

"No, I just—too much pumpkin bread."

"Right."

We stared at each other in silence.

Until two really pretty girls in Delta Air Lines uniforms approached our table.

"Lucas," they said in unison. "We've only got a few hours left because of the weird schedule. You ready to go?"

"Yup." Lucas stood and greeted both girls with a full-fledged kiss on the mouth.

My mouth dropped open at the attention he paid both of them, in front of one another, like it was completely okay to swap spit with two people on a Monday morning.

In Starbucks.

In front of me.

I quickly glanced away when Lucas looked down at me. "Avery, meet Tabatha and Cary."

"Hi." I forced a pained cheerful smile that I really didn't feel like offering. Why were they okay with this? How? They were both really cute girls, dark hair, dark eyes—just normal girl-next-door types. I didn't get it. At all.

One was maybe a size twelve or fourteen, and had curves that would make most girls feel extremely inadequate. The other—I wasn't sure if she was Tabatha or Cary—was a little bit smaller but not by much. They both resembled a guy's fantasy girl, at least in my mind.

I looked down at my own frame and frowned.

Maybe that's what he meant when he said he didn't date children. I realized how young I must have seemed to him; with my hip leather pants and sleeveless shirt, I might as well have been a boy.

My boobs were nowhere near as big as theirs.

Honestly, I hadn't wanted to involve myself in his weird bedroom shenanigans; they made my chest feel too tight. Emotionless detachment was the only way to go where Lucas Thorn was concerned. But now, now he had me, because I was curious.

Cary and Tabatha had a little something to hang on to, and they wore their confidence well.

Story of my life: I think Lucas and I are back in friendship territory, only to discover there's another girl (or two) standing in the way.

Not that I'd ever admit that to him. Ever.

It was hard enough admitting the truth to myself.

◆ ◆ ◆

"Lucas, you've been drinking," I reminded him. A lot. It was the night before Kayla and his wedding. I'd never seen him drink so much.

"So wrong," he whispered. "So, so wrong."

"What's wrong?" I asked, wrapping my arm around his waist while we walked back toward the house. The party was still in full swing, but he'd been done a few shots of tequila ago.

"You." I stumbled with him toward the house and nearly slammed into the side of the garage as he barreled into me.

"Lucas?" I touched his cheek. "Are you okay?"

His eyes focused on me, and he cupped my face with both hands. It was dark outside, and I could barely see the outline of his mouth. He was always smiling.

Except now.

"Lucas, is it Kayla?"

He snorted. "Kayla? You think this is about Kayla?"

"You are marrying her tomorrow."

"You think I don't know that?" he sneered. "You think I'm not fully aware that I'm supposed to be her husband?"

"But—"

"I know," Lucas snapped. "I know I'm getting married, just like I know that for the past year, the only girl I've wanted to kiss is you."

My knees buckled. "Lucas."

My eyes filled with tears.

Because I'd loved him longer than forever.

And he'd just said he wanted to kiss me.

But he was engaged to my sister.

My older, much prettier, much more stable and confident sister.

"Wrong," he whispered. "But just once—God, just once I want to do the wrong thing. Do you think I'm a bad person?"

"No." *I shook my head.* "I think you're drunk and confused."

"I'm drunk." *His forehead touched mine.* "Not confused."

"Lucas . . . you should sleep it off."

He nodded and then, without warning, crushed his mouth against mine, his hips pinning me against the wall.

I didn't know what to do except kiss him back and then very politely—because I was always polite—push him away.

"Sorry." *He hung his head.* "I just . . . I wanted wrong."

"And did it feel right?"

His smile returned. "Yeah, it did."

My heart flipped. "Lucas, if you aren't ready for marriage . . ."

"I'm not ready for marriage," *he said quickly.*

He swayed on his feet. I let out a sigh, trying to play off that I was annoyed instead of completely frazzled, heartbroken, upset, excited. I was too many mixed-up things. I didn't want that future for him, and I hated myself for even contemplating helping him get over his nerves about marrying Kayla, though I knew it was all wrong. It had been for a while.

"Fine, stay here, hold up the wall, and I'll go get my room ready for you, okay? I'll sleep on the couch. That way you won't be in the same room as Kayla, and you can decide what you want to do, alright? The last thing you need is to go back to your parents' house and grab keys to one of the cars or start confessing to your dad that you won't go through with it."

He nodded, his eyes completely unfocused. "Avery."

"What, Lucas?"

"You always were my favorite Black sister."

What was I supposed to say to that? Especially since I wasn't the Black sister who had the ring on her finger. Guilt stabbed me all over until I felt numb.

Because he'd said exactly what I'd always wanted him to say.

But he was completely wasted. And marrying my sister.

◆ ◆ ◆

"So I'll see you at work this afternoon?" Lucas softly knocked on my head with his knuckles. "You home, Avery?"

"Ugh." I shook my head. "Yes. Sorry. Home. Work. Dinner Tuesday. Thanks."

I left Starbucks so fast that I almost ran into a poor old man trying to order a cup of Pike Place Roast.

Lucas Thorn was the devil.

I just sometimes wished that he'd stayed where he belonged—in hell.

Chapter Fourteen

LUCAS

We didn't have time for sex. Okay, that's not true. We had time. But I wasn't interested. But admitting that meant too many awful things. Maybe it was the universe telling me to stop sticking my dick in multiple women—or maybe it was just bad luck.

Hell, at this point, everything pointed to the day Avery Black came crashing back into my life, all strawberry-blonde hair and judgmental eyes, with tall heels and kissable lips.

Tabatha kissed my neck while Cary slid her hand up my thigh. We were at brunch.

When Cary's fingers grazed me, I had no choice but to either let her take it further or shove her away and tell her I was feeling . . . sick.

Tabatha kept kissing.

What the hell type of dude told two girls to stop while he was getting this kind of attention during mealtime?

"Lucas Thorn," Cary breathed in my right ear while Tabatha kissed the other, her hands staying firmly planted at her sides while her roommate and best friend continued trying her best to get me off under the table.

A vision of Avery flashed through my mind.

Her eyes mostly.

Not even her body.

Her eyes, that was what did it. They had me jerking away from both girls like they had the plague.

"Whoa." Cary stifled a laugh. "I didn't pinch that hard."

She pinched my business? Seriously? Who did that?

Tabatha's tongue grazed my ear again.

"You know what?" I tossed down a few twenties and stood. "I have a meeting in a few." When I turned, they were both flushed and ready, yet there I was, staring at them like a moron rather than taking them into the bathroom and allowing myself to get made into a Lucas Thorn sandwich. Damn it. Was I broken?

Tabatha shrugged. "That's okay. We should probably get going anyways. Next week at the regular time? Cary's working. You can come over—I'll make your favorite homemade macaroni."

I groaned and patted my stomach. "Sounds amazing."

"Why do I get the feeling that sometimes you'd choose my macaroni over sex?" Her eyebrows arched up.

"Probably because you've never had bad macaroni, which means you don't know how to appreciate the good kind."

"Hmm . . ." She stood and kissed me on the cheek while Cary kissed the other and swatted my ass.

"Later, sexy," Cary cackled, and both of them walked out, in matching uniforms, arms linked.

Shaking, I ran my hands through my hair and was about ready to have a nervous breakdown when my phone rang.

"Yeah?" I grabbed my coat and headed out of the restaurant.

"She's a clinger." That's all Thatch had to say before I burst out laughing. "She asked for my phone number."

"How else is she supposed to have another booty call with the good doctor?" I grinned like a smug bastard, enjoying his panic, and then I warned him to stay away. "You know this is your fault, right? You know that inviting a woman to your apartment usually means that she'll start envisioning her shit all over the place—and next thing you know, she's about to have your baby."

"SHE'S NOT PREGNANT!" He started cursing again. "Look, you know I have commitment issues."

"No." I rolled my eyes. "Shocker."

"Like you should talk, you selfish bastard." Thatch sighed loudly. "Break up with her for me?"

"Not a chance in hell."

"But—"

"Nope."

"Lucas Thorn."

"Maybe if you had tits, and even then, that just makes shit weird, Thatch."

I hit the elevator button and waited while Thatch started complaining about why sex can't just be sex.

"You're telling me." I snorted into the phone. "Look, I gotta go. Just remember Austin and Avery are best friends, meaning, you screw her, her friend is most likely going to try to find a way to screw me. Girls go to the bathroom together. If they do the nonserious stuff in teams, you bet your ass they're going to treat a breakup the same way."

"That really wasn't helpful, not at all, Lucas."

"Or"—I shrugged and hit the button for my floor—"you could just make the sex really, really bad next time, say, finishing in like thirty seconds and screaming 'Porcupine!' or something."

He was quiet, then said, "I can't decide if that's genius or stupid."

"You never know until you try. Think of Christopher Columbus. Everyone thought he was stupid for sailing toward the New World, and look! He proved them wrong. The earth was in fact round, my friend."

"Did you just compare yourself to someone who discovered an actual continent? Because it seems like you did, and this is after you told me to yell 'Porcupine!' when I orgasm."

"Well, when you repeat it back like that . . ." I grumbled as the elevator doors opened to my floor. "Look, I gotta go. Leave me out of it though."

"No promises," he said just as I ended the conversation and greedily searched for Avery.

She wasn't behind her desk.

Nor was she under it—I had to check because hiding and pouncing was exactly the kind of thing I could imagine her doing, just so she could scare the shit out of me and get it on camera or something. Then again, she wasn't seventeen anymore, but this was still Avery we were talking about. Ergo, I still looked.

Frowning, I turned around in an effort to casually strut into my office and slammed right into Avery, knocking her backward onto her ass.

Folders went everywhere.

Papers scattered across the floor.

And her wedged heels somehow managed to fall from her feet, though they still dangled around her ankles.

"Are you okay?" I leaned down to grab her hand, but she didn't take mine.

"Yeah." Her cheeks reddened. "Sorry, I was just dropping off some files, and then I saw that these were addressed to another department and thought I could drop them off and . . ." Her voice trailed off as she flashed me a worried look, like I was going to fire her any minute.

Instantly feeling like an ass, I grabbed her by the waist and hoisted her into the air. "I'm not going to fire you."

"Okay," she huffed, tears welling in her eyes.

"Shit, Avery." Earlier I'd been taking out my frustration with my family on her. Apparently, the distance and years hadn't changed this aspect of our relationship, because this was a familiar pattern. I made her feel bad or guilty about something that wasn't her fault—something she had no control over.

Especially the fact that I was extremely attracted to her—and knew it was wrong then, just like it was wrong now.

I jerked my hands away; they felt too comfortable around her waist. "Seriously, are you okay?"

"Yes." She nodded and took a step back, then bent over right in front of me to grab the papers she'd dropped.

I gaped at her, and my mouth instantly went dry at the sight of her ass in the air; my fingers were inches from grabbing her waist and tugging her against me, unzipping my pants and—

Well, there it was.

Lucas Thorn? Complete asshole.

We were at work—at work!

A small, guilty voice reminded me that I'd done several girls at work before, but it was never sex, only kissing, some heavy petting, hand jobs, and occasional blow jobs—nothing that would take too long or look overly suspicious. So why the hell was I daydreaming about a girl who would be more likely to shank me in my sleep than kiss me?

And she was . . . Hell, did she need to move her ass back and forth while picking up all the folders?

"You know what?" I said in a hoarse voice. "Why don't I just grab the last few papers and—"

She peered over her shoulder. "It's my job, I've got it—"

"Avery, I'm warning you, pick up one more piece of paper and I'm going to pull that pencil skirt down to your ankles and toss you over my very sturdy, very new desk."

She jerked to attention, smoothing her skirt down with her hands before giving me a nasty look and storming off.

And they say honesty is always the best policy.

Her shoes slammed against the hardwood floor as she walked unsteadily back to her desk. I covered my mouth with my hand and tried not to make a sound as I watched her flushed neck turn a little redder.

I'd affected her.

And by the look on her face, she was pissed about it.

Her back was ramrod straight as she sat at her desk.

The phone rang.

She dropped the receiver four times before finally being able to hold it near her ear.

"Yes." Her eyes roamed over to where I was leaning against the doorway to my office. "Yes, I'll let him know."

When she hung up, my eyes narrowed. "What's that look mean?"

"Oh, it's just—" She sighed. "Nothing, we have school visits at one and three o'clock now. Both high schools want to implement the app, but they want you to teach the teachers so they can go teach the—"

"—students." I nodded, all business. "Got it." I checked my watch. "We leave in fifteen, alright?"

"Yup." She looked at her computer while I picked up the rest of the papers.

I quickly checked my email, turned off the lights in my office, and then headed out; the school visits would take the rest of the afternoon.

Avery shot up from her desk, grabbed her jacket and purse, and followed me to the elevator.

It was empty.

Why was it always empty when I was with Avery?

The private space gave a man ideas.

It gave *me* ideas.

"So"—she cleared her throat—"I thought the roommates were Tuesday."

I frowned in her direction and shrugged. "Not that it matters since it's my schedule, not yours." She flinched. "But they fly out tonight, so I don't get them tomorrow."

"Okay." She drew out the word and stared straight ahead. "But you still have Monday tonight, right?"

"Right." Though I hadn't texted Molly yet, which wasn't my typical MO. Normally, I texted her first thing in the morning and made plans.

"Oh."

I groaned. "Avery, out with it. Just say what you want to say."

"By midnight you'll have slept with, what? Three girls? All within a twelve-hour period?"

"Not that it's any of your business, but no, I'll have slept with zero, especially if this elevator keeps moving at the pace of a snail." I checked my watch again. "And not that I think you had a high opinion of me in the first place, but I try not to screw girls at brunch. It upsets the other patrons, makes them stare at their sausage a little too hard, if you get my meaning." It was a bit of a white lie, but it had the desired effect. The last thing I wanted to admit was that it bothered me for Avery to know all the gory details of my sex life.

She gasped.

"Oh, I'm sorry. Did I scandalize your virgin little ears?" I teased.

"I'm NOT a virgin!" She finally looked at me, thank God. "Not that it's any of *your* business, but I have loads of sex, all the time."

"Really?" I crossed my arms. "All the time, huh?"

"All the time." She confirmed that with a serious nod. "In fact, I'm having sex tonight."

"Are you?"

"Yes."

"With Carl?"

"Who?"

"Fess up, he's not real."

"He's ABSOLUTELY real!" She scowled as the elevator doors opened. "In fact, we're meeting for drinks later."

"Where at?"

"Not telling you." She stormed out of the elevator and into the hallway.

"Fine." I held up my hands. "Let's call a truce. Besides, we have a lot of ground to cover this afternoon. Now give me your phone."

Her eyes narrowed. "Why would I give you my phone?"

I sighed and looked heavenward. "So I can give you my number just in case this jackass is real and I have to hunt him down. Why else?"

She hesitantly handed her phone over to me. "No funny business?"

"Nope." I held the phone in the air to prove I was doing something simple, like typing in my number.

While also turning on her GPS and Find My Friends app.

Harmless.

Right?

"Here you go." I handed it back.

"That took too long." Her eyes narrowed.

"Usually that's a bonus, when things take longer." I shifted toward her, almost pinning her to the wall of the hallway. Her perfume floated around me.

She pointed her cell at me. "No more sex talk."

"Stop being paranoid." I placed my hand on her lower back. "Now, let's go save the children."

"Ughhhhhh." She groaned and jerked away from me. "God really did a number on you, Thorn."

"What?" I smiled brightly. "Because I love kids?"

She eyed me up and down and smiled wickedly. "I cursed you yesterday."

Well, that was wonderful. "Um, thank you?"

"I cursed your cow too."

"I don't believe I own a cow."

"Because I cursed you." She nodded. "But beware if one suddenly appears in your life. It'll probably be cursed, just like your cat."

"You cursed a poor, helpless imaginary cat?"

"Of course! I had to include all animals in your foreseeable future. Oh, also, I prayed you'd develop adult acne and get in a car accident where you'd be forced to walk into the light, but let's be honest—the darkness calls you way more."

I groaned. "Business. Professional. Why don't you try that for, say, three hours?"

"Fine." She pulled on her jacket while I called an Uber.

"So, save the children time?" She peered up at me with hopeful green eyes.

"Exactly," I whispered.

Chapter Fifteen

Avery

I opened up an IPA and chugged half of it before I slammed it down onto my small kitchen table and contemplated making friends with the spider in a corner of the room.

No matter how many times I sprayed for spiders, one always found a way in.

And they *never* ran away from me, just stared me down, waiting for me to make my move so that they could yawn, wave, and then slowly crawl back into the hellhole they'd come out of.

Spiders and Lucas Thorn had a lot in common.

Interesting.

I played with the green label on the beer bottle and yawned.

It had been a long afternoon at the schools. Not only did I suddenly appreciate the fact that I was out of high school and free of the smell of books, lockers, and puberty—but luckily for me and Lucas, one of our school visits had been the very high school we'd attended.

At different times of course.

But it didn't help that when we walked by the trophy case, there was still a picture of him and Kayla in their homecoming garb.

Causing long-buried memories to flood to the surface.

Memories of Kayla holding his hand and winking at me behind his back.

Being obsessed with him, lusting after his stupid body when I was a freshman. And the night he held me in his arms, his lips brushing my seventeen-year-old skin.

I wasn't sure if I should block the glass case with my body or pull the fire alarm to distract him. I mean, was he over Kayla? The situation? I had no clue, but I did know that we needed to focus. To his credit Lucas completely ignored it. He put his professionalism first. I could learn a lot from him—loath as I was to admit it.

When he needed to be all business, he was.

Whereas I was having a minor anxiety attack, pitting out my shirt while my old principal sat a few rows in front of us and took notes about the new app.

I almost tripped on my heels when Lucas asked me a question, one that I had to answer out loud—like I was in class—in front of at least half of the teachers who had taught me four years ago.

Four years ago, when I'd graduated with bags under my eyes and a swollen face from crying.

He was supposed to be at my graduation.

He'd never made it.

Then again, understandable since Grandpa had said he'd wait in the truck just in case he spotted Lucas—maybe he could run him over without getting caught.

But still.

"Um . . ." Lucas smiled brightly at me.

I cleared my throat. "The stats show that if we give free access to the students, they're ninety percent more likely to use the app to get homework done on time. Our research discovered that most high school students don't complete their homework because they're so busy with after-school activities that they don't get started until pretty late at night or they're too tired to finish."

"Thanks, Avery." Lucas smiled again and addressed the teachers. "We're ready to move beyond the beta phase, so with your permission we'd like to implement this program immediately and see how the students react."

The rest of the meeting went great.

But I was completely drained by the time I made it home. Maybe it was because I'd had to keep my emotions in check around Lucas. Or maybe it was because those halls reminded me of how lost I had felt when I no longer had him as my rock.

I slumped further into my kitchen chair, then snatched my beer, walked over to my living room—you know, like two feet away—and sat cross-legged on the floor in front of my laptop.

It was too late to go out—not that I had plans or anything. I'd lied about Carl. Who the hell was named Carl? And a dancer? What had I been thinking? Good call, Avery, bragging about dating a ballerino in front of Lucas. That would show him.

A man in tights.

Well, superheroes wore tights, so it was kind of the same thing, right?

My phone buzzed.

And the name Lucas Thorn popped up on my screen.

I stuck out my tongue, then finally answered. "Minion here."

"Satan calling," he snapped right back.

"Good one."

"So how's the date? You know, the one with all the sex?"

"It's . . ." I looked around my empty apartment. Peeling paint clung desperately to the east wall near my bed, and my place smelled like old Chinese food and french fries. My stomach growled.

I had one beer left.

And leftover chow mein.

Just under a hundred dollars, and I still had five days before I'd get paid.

"Did you just sigh?" he asked.

"No." I sighed again.

"Avery."

"Thorn."

"Be honest. Are you really out with Carl?"

"He, uh, had a recital." I slapped my hand against my forehead. Great, Avery, because grown men had recitals?

Lucas was quiet for a moment. "Oh, so he teaches children, then?"

Thank God one of us was logical. "YES!"

"No need to shout it, Avery."

"Oh, sorry, I just, um, got excited. You know, about the kids."

"I bet." He chuckled. "So, I was thinking . . ."

"Good for you, Thorn."

He ignored me and pressed on. "Are you hungry?"

"Is this a trick?"

"Maybe. Maybe not."

The spider in the corner continued to make itself at home while I made myself comfortable in the middle of the floor. "I'm always hungry." There, that sounded good, not like the starving human I was. More like, *oh cool, I could eat*, when really my brain was screaming I would destroy an entire elephant right now, sorry not sorry.

"Answer your door."

I gasped. "Did you order me PIZZA?"

"Why are you always yelling at me?"

"Sister. Wrong bed. Broken engagement. Whore—"

"I'm sorry, did you want food?"

"Yes!" I jumped to my feet and ran over to the door and pulled it open, then fumbled with my phone as I nearly dropped it onto the floor.

"Thorn."

"I was in the neighborhood." He grinned.

"What? Fighting crime?" Just then a loud scream erupted down the hall.

With a gasp, I grabbed his shirt and jerked him into the living room, then proceeded to lock every lock on my door.

The screaming got louder.

With a yawn, I turned around and took in Lucas's wide-eyed expression.

"Are you sure you're safe here?"

"Oh that?" I pointed at the door. "That's nothing. Mr. Thompson just gets confused sometimes and walks into the wrong apartment while women are changing. His timing is impeccable."

"So . . ." Lucas clutched two bags, and I couldn't take my eyes off them. "Mr. Thompson is a peeping Tom who just randomly breaks into people's apartments?"

"He doesn't break in—I mean, not really. He opens the door, takes a step in, says he's lost, and walks right back out. Harmless really."

"Which is why you lock your door."

"I refuse to let him become the only man to see me naked in a year." I laughed and then smacked my hand against my forehead. "I mean—"

"Noooooo, you mean Carl's not real? How are the dancing children by the way? Invisible?"

"Hey! That's an actual *real* nonprofit."

Lucas's cleft just made his stupid smile look bigger, and more . . . mocking, and sexy, but I refused to find him sexy, so I forced myself to think his smile was stupid and ugly. "I know—I give to the cause."

"Of course you do."

"What's that supposed to mean?"

I couldn't take it anymore. I marched over to where he was standing, which was like a foot away from me, given how small my apartment was, and snagged the take-out bag from his hands. "What do you have?"

"Easy." He pried my hands from the bags. "You get food, but you have to do something for me first."

"Nope." I shook my head. "That's cruel. You know how much I love food. How dare you use it as a way to get me to do you a favor! I have to work with you, isn't that favor enough?"

Lucas sighed, his shoulders moving up and down with each exhale like he was so irritated with me his body couldn't help but *show* it. "More like I have to put up with you and you have to put up with me."

"Wait"—I held up my hand—"where's Monday?"

"You mean Molly?" His smile was so smug, I wanted to punch him in the throat and then send him out to Mr. Thompson for some playtime.

"Yes." I tried reaching for the bag again. "Molly."

"You look great by the way, very shabby chic."

It was then that I realized my attire. I was wearing ratty red shorts from high school and a white T-shirt with "I'm a Unicorn" scrawled across the front.

My socks had at least two holes in them.

Summary—I looked homeless.

I quickly touched my hair. At least it was pulled back into a bun, out of my face.

I groaned. In a scrunchie. I actually had a scrunchie in my hair.

"Those making a comeback?" He pointed at the scrunchie and burst out laughing. "Because I have to say, I'm a huge fan."

"Out!" I gestured toward the door.

"What?" He set the bags on the table and turned toward me. "You're just going to kick me and the food out?"

"The food can stay. It's done nothing offensive."

"And I have?"

"You are breathing."

"So violent and jaded for someone so young."

"Molly?"

"Her parents are in town, and she figured it would be too hard to explain that the guy she's seeing is also seeing other women and, no, would not in fact be proposing marriage anytime soon. They're very strict Catholics."

"So?"

"So they want her to have children. Loads of children."

"The last thing this world needs is carbon copies of Lucas Thorn running around, wreaking havoc on this city. The police have enough trouble with Mr. Thompson."

"Cute." He sighed and turned in a circle, then finally pulled out my one chair and pointed to it. "Sit."

"I think it's better that I—"

"Now."

I slumped over to the chair and sat, crossing my arms over my chest while he started pulling out box after box of Thai food.

My mouth watering, I stared until my vision blurred as steam from the chicken pad Thai wafted into the air, tickling my nose.

I let out a moan; I couldn't help it.

Lucas stopped with the food, his body stiffened.

"What?" I swallowed and glanced up at his gorgeous face.

His eyes locked on mine. "I forgot."

"Forgot what?"

"That when you're hungry you eat like a hyena." His eyes zeroed in on my full mouth. "Or a shark during Shark Week."

His sleeves were pushed up to his elbows, exposing gorgeous tan forearms. I tried not to stare, but it was hard. This was why Lucas Thorn was a menace to society, and a very bad man. He was too good-looking to be real. It was unfair that he had such a horrible personality to go with those good looks.

Not that he'd always been such an unfortunate human being.

But still.

He slapped my wrist with one of the plastic forks and shook his head. "Not yet."

"But—"

"Patience. Tomorrow night." He licked his lips, suddenly appearing more nervous than I'd ever seen him look. "I need you to be . . . nice."

"That's what this is about? You want me to be nice to you? During dinner?"

He nodded slowly. "Yes . . . nice to me during dinner. And not the fake nice that makes me want to strangle you within an inch of your life, but the nice where your smile actually reaches your eyes—and your laugh makes a man forget himself. That kind of nice." He turned away and looked toward the spider. The lucky bastard was probably never going to leave now that it had experienced the Lucas Thorn effect. "Think you can handle that?"

I slowly pried the fork from his now-clenched fist, and then maybe insanity took hold, because I placed my hand on his and squeezed. "I promise; I'll be nice."

"Swear." His eyes narrowed as he peered down at our hands. "Over your Thai food."

"You're serious?"

"Deathly." His voice lowered as he leaned down so we were inches from each other, our bodies almost touching.

"Fine." I took a deep breath. "I swear over this Thai food that I'll be nice to you tomorrow night, the real nice that you want."

"Or so help me God I will never eat another bite of Thai food again." His eyebrows shot up. "Say it or no food."

The temptation of my favorite dishes was too much to bear, so I gritted my teeth and repeated. "Or so help me God I will never eat another bite of Thai food again."

"Great!" He smiled brightly. "Because my parents are coming."

Chapter Sixteen

Lucas

My parents were great. I took a long sip of bourbon.

Fantastic, extremely supportive, loving. This time I chugged half my drink and slammed it down onto the bar, then checked my watch.

Correction. They *were* great until I ruined their relationship with the Blacks and solidified our family as the one that nobody waved to during the annual neighborhood Fourth of July celebration.

People had taken sides.

It didn't take a rocket scientist to discover who ended up in camp Thorn.

Crickets.

And my parents.

My sister was solid middle ground.

Which meant that my entire family was probably ready to throw a damn parade over the fact that somehow I was making a wrong right again.

There wasn't enough whiskey in the world to calm the nerves I was feeling. Letting Avery loose on them without prompting her just seemed like the worst sort of idea I could possibly come up with.

Then again, the only other option was to admit the lie.

Admit my lifestyle.

And let them down all over again.

Mom would cry.

Dad would yell.

And news would spread of how far good ol' Lucas Thorn had fallen again. But honestly, I didn't give a shit about myself.

But my parents? I loved them.

They'd supported me during one of my darkest times; the least I could do was have dinner with them, play nice with Avery, and let them assume that all had finally been healed. Then later Avery and I could mutually and publicly decide to break off our relationship on good terms.

"Another?" The bartender nodded toward me, already grabbing a clean glass.

My fingers slid against the cold glass as I stared down into the clear brown liquid. How the hell did this happen?

Right. Avery.

Another drink.

Damn it, she just had to try to help. I should have known better. After all, I'd been on the opposite end of her help more times than I could count.

Once she tried to save a cat that I'm 99 percent sure was possessed by an actual demon. It nearly took off one of my testicles and, damn it, I needed those!

The mouse she decided to save when she was twelve almost made it, but my childhood dog grabbed ahold of it; blood went everywhere.

And it wasn't her fault the neighbors were having a birthday party at the time for their four-year-old son—or that all his friends just happened to be in the front yard when it happened.

Who was I kidding? She was absolutely a danger to society and me both.

But I had no choice.

My mom had texted me at least a dozen times to make sure I wasn't backing out. During a moment of pure insanity I even entertained the thought of just hiring someone who looked like Avery, so as not to risk the real Avery slipping up and ruining everything. The restaurant was known for its dark lighting. Hell, El Gaucho gave patrons flashlights for reading the menus! An impersonator could work! Maybe. Okay, probably not.

They knew her too well.

"Okay!" a voice said to my right. "Before you freak out, just know, Austin dressed me. I forgot how nice this place is and—"

My mouth dropped open as Avery crossed her arms—her breasts spilling over the neckline of her red dress.

"Is that whiskey?" She slipped the glass from my fingers and tossed back my entire drink, then slammed the glass onto the counter. "I'll have another." She winked at the bartender. "My dad's paying."

Avery was pointing at me.

"Remember what I said about being nice." I pinched her side.

She gave a little yelp and somehow landed in my lap.

I froze.

She froze.

Our eyes locked.

And maybe I was already half-drunk, because I didn't shove her off onto the floor or start yelling at her to behave.

Maybe it was because of the dress.

I was a sucker for red.

It was a shade darker than her hair. The thick straps tightened over her shoulders into a complicated maze of twists and turns dipping low and kissing her ass.

With a curse, I sucked in a breath and waited for her to move.

But it was Avery.

She never did what I expected her to. Instead, she wiggled her ass and glanced over her shoulder. "This nice enough for you?"

Do not react. Do not react.

Be mature.

The bigger person.

I slapped her ass cheek and shrugged. "You're getting warmer."

Her grin was deadly—I should have known better than to challenge someone who hadn't used training wheels when she was young. Avery rejected anything that made her feel like a kid and went straight to a ten-speed.

She was way out of her league now.

And yet, tonight, she was going to pretend that we were in a relationship, pretend that we didn't have a shitload of history between us—pretend that a few days ago I wasn't in someone else's arms.

"How's it feel, I wonder?"

The bartender placed a napkin in front of her, the drink followed. She slowly lifted it to her lips and sipped.

"Your ass?" I asked with a hoarse voice. "Or having the bartender think I'm the creepiest dad on the planet?"

She burst out laughing, nearly spilling the drink on both of us. "Come on, admit it. It's funny."

"Not so funny."

Avery licked her lips and stared at the bartender out of the corner of her eye. "He's horrified."

"And yet you look so cheerful about it."

She shrugged one shoulder and took another sip. "I like to shock."

I burst out laughing. "Oh, I'm sorry—I thought that was a joke. You're abrasive as hell, but nothing about you could shock me. After all, I've seen you running naked through sprinklers."

Her eyes narrowed.

Oh shit.

Carefully, she set the drink back on the bar and turned around to face me. It was impossible not to react to her lush body, which was pressed against mine. Thank God the bar was dark.

Her arms snaked around my neck and then—with a leg, her right one, I think, propped up on the barstool—she full on straddled me in my seat, her eyebrows rising in a challenge.

I cupped her ass again and waited.

She didn't move.

The bartender's mouth dropped open.

"Congratulations, you've officially given the old bartender a heart attack."

"Not good enough," she whispered.

"Avery," I ground out her name like a curse. "What the hell do you think you're doing?"

The heat of her body was searing me alive. Her breasts pressed up against my chest, rubbing once, twice, the friction so erotic, I stumbled over my next breath.

Do. Not. React.

Her hair fell in a curtain over her shoulder, and then she pressed her lips to my neck.

I gripped her skin, digging my fingers into her flesh, fighting against every instinct I had to plunge my tongue into her mouth and slam her body against the bar, rip her dress off, and lay claim to her.

I was acting like a caveman.

An insane caveman.

An insane. Starving. Caveman.

She winked.

Hell.

"Honey!" A shrill voice interrupted the moment right before the part of the kiss when the lips almost touch, should by all means touch, but instead are cock blocked by a psychopath mother who has no appreciation for personal space.

She poked her head between us and tapped my shoulder. "I thought that was you two!"

"Found us," I said in a lame attempt to buy myself some time, because—fun fact—at some point I was going to have to stand.

Which meant, with my luck, my mom would look down and go, "Oh, honey, shouldn't you take care of that?"

At which point I would be forced to explain to my mom all the reasons why Avery couldn't help me take care of it, only to get worked up again while Avery licked her lips and focused her attention on my dick.

Well, since there was no way out . . . I held up my hand. "One minute, Mom."

Avery's grin was evil, and my mom was still standing a foot away. As I leaned over to whisper in Avery's ear, which also meant I could smell her flowery perfume, I bit down on her earlobe. "You'll pay for that."

"Oh." She winced. "Sorry, but your weekly schedule's booked, and we all know Sunday's God's day." With that, she hopped off my lap, looked down, and quickly turned and hugged my mom. "Why don't we go to the table while Lucas takes care of a little pesky problem . . ." She turned. "Maybe some ice in your next drink will help, sweetie pie."

"Thanks, pumpkin face," I said through clenched teeth. "You're always so smart."

She giggled and waved. "Oh my gosh, stud, that's what I'm here for! To be your brain when all the blood in your head goes south!"

My mom let out a little gasp just as my dad appeared. "Cheapest valet parking in the city." He frowned. "Patty, you look pale." His attention quickly turned to Avery as a huge grin spread across his face. He opened his arms wide, and she basically jumped into them.

"I'm starved." After Avery hugged both of my parents, she patted her stomach. "Aren't you guys starving? Let's go." She maneuvered herself between the two of them and walked away while I downed the rest of my drink and contemplated murdering Avery with a steak knife.

I glanced up. The bartender's judgmental stare wasn't welcome, which was why I needed to make it clear she wasn't my daughter. "She's my date."

He nodded.

"Not my daughter."

"Whatever you say, man."

"No. Seriously. Besides, she's a horrible, vengeful, spiteful woman."

At that moment Avery's laughter floated over to us.

The bartender frowned. "Yeah, she seems horrible."

"She's a damn thorn in my side!"

He held up his hands. "Then maybe you shouldn't have brought her to such a romantic spot."

I tugged at my shirt collar and cursed.

He gave a low whistle, then poured a shot of whiskey and slid it over to me. "On the house, man."

"Thanks." I tossed it back, cracked my neck, and made my way toward the laughter.

I froze midstep when I saw my Mom reach out to hold Avery's hand.

Damn it, I hated memories. They never stayed put, did they? Our parents had always been close. Hell, my parents actually went to Avery's graduation, though I stayed home and got drunk off my ass, all the while staring at her graduation announcement and picture like a wasted loser.

"What's so funny?" I said once I reached them.

"Oh, our Avery." My mother didn't mean to claim her, did she? By proclaiming ownership of Avery, my mother would give her the wrong idea about what she meant to me, and the last thing I needed was to explain to the Blacks why I broke another one of their daughters' hearts . . . over a simple misunderstanding. Then again, it was Avery's fault to begin with. She was the one who had said something to Erin. She was the reason I was even IN this situation.

"Mr. Thorn, we'll seat you now."

The hostess grinned from ear to ear as she eyed me up and down, and she definitely grazed the front of my pants with her fingers when she laid a napkin across my lap.

Avery elbowed me in the chest—hard.

"Oh dear." My mom noticed the jab and covered her mouth. "Is everything okay?"

I grabbed my water glass and took a big gulp so I wouldn't be expected to respond.

"Perfect!" Avery said a little too loudly. "I just have this weird reaction whenever other women try to grope my man." She glared up at the hostess. "Especially in front of my future in-laws."

I spit out the water all over the table.

Avery offered a sugary smile. "Groping is rude, don't you think?"

The woman paled and shook her head. "Your, um, waiter will be with you shortly." She then basically ran off.

And I was pounding my chest, trying not to choke on my own spit while my parents' eyes widened.

Oh shit, was Mom crying? She used the white napkin to dab at the corners of her eyes, not that it helped, because more tears appeared.

This. This was my hell.

Thanks, Avery.

Maybe I should have had her promise not to lie about shit rather than to be nice. Apparently, being too nice was a very real thing. And it was currently staring at me like a deer in headlights, and I had no idea how to fix what she'd just done.

My dad stood just as the waiter approached. "Champagne for the table!"

"Dad." I shook my head. The waiter was grinning ear to ear—of course he was, because I was about to pay out the ass for this dinner. "We don't need champagne."

"Sure we do!" my dad thundered back, his gray bushy eyebrows drawing together like two sexually frustrated caterpillars. Damn it, Avery! My own sexual frustration was playing tricks with my mind. "We're celebrating."

"Oh!" The waiter beamed at us. "What are we celebrating?"

"My son!" My dad wiped a tear from his cheek. "He's getting married to this terrific young woman!"

It was Avery's turn to choke.

There was nothing else I could do—just pat her back and then, when she looked at me with horror-stricken eyes, slide my hand under the table and squeeze her knee with force, all the while smiling through my clenched teeth. "I. Hate. You."

"Feeling's mutual." She grinned and then slapped me lightly on the cheek.

"Oh, Bill, just look at that." Mom sighed dreamily. "Didn't I always tell you they were perfect for each other?"

My dad gave an eloquent grunt and shooed the waiter away, most likely to grab the most expensive champagne on the menu.

"You did." Dad reached for his water. "I believe on several occasions you told Lucas he was marrying the wrong Black sister."

They were being kind.

Helpful.

In their own sick, psychotic way.

Because from their end of the table, everything looked fine—I was finally with the right Black girl, the girl they'd loved all along. The girl whose soccer games they'd cheered at.

Avery finally spoke. "Um, I think you misunderstood." Her eyes were wide with panic. She looked exactly how I felt.

When I had left Marysville for a job in the city, she was left to deal with the ramifications of my actions. She'd suddenly gone from being a part of my family to . . . nothing. Oh, my mom still gave Avery birthday presents every year.

Not that I was supposed to know about it.

But the fact that my parents were even offering that little olive branch made my chest hurt.

I pinched Avery's thigh and shook my head.

My parents were silent.

And because my mom believed herself to be a bit of a psychic, she slammed a hand over her mouth before exclaiming, "YOU'RE HAVING LUCAS'S BABY!"

"Oh dear God." I looked for a quick exit, and at one point even contemplated sliding under the table and pulling all the screws free so it would slam on my face and knock me unconscious.

"NO!" Avery shouted just as loud as my mother had. Shit, I could just see the wheels in her head turning. She always was a fixer, and there was no doubt in my mind she was trying to find a quick way to fix everything while still making me look like the golden son. Avery had to have heard how strained my relationship with my parents had been over the years—it's not like the tension was a secret. Why? Why do that for me? I'd only asked her to dinner, not to save me. And yet there she was, about to do exactly that. Or at least try, anyway. "No, no, no, you, um, see." Yeah, good luck getting out of this one. She looked to me for help.

I shrugged and took a long drink of water.

After all, this scenario existed because she'd opened her big fat mouth in front of my sister, and there was literally nothing I could do other than watch the train wreck.

"Oh, do go on, sweetheart." I winked.

After glaring at me, she snapped her attention back to my parents and stage-whispered. "Sorry, I'm not pregnant. But I do have a question—not to get too personal, but does ED run in the family?"

I choked on an ice cube while she slapped me on the back, then started rubbing.

"She's joking!" My voice was hoarse. "She's kidding, she's—"

"Oh, honey." My mom's voice was grave. "Do you think it's because of . . ." Her voice lowered, as did her head, like she was getting ready to finish the thought under the table. ". . . you know, the accident?" She pointed at my crotch.

I would probably never get an erection again.

Thanks, Avery.

I waved all future sexual encounters good-bye and stomped as hard as I could on Avery's foot.

She burst out laughing and reached for a piece of bread. "It's been so fun catching up, I'm so glad we did this."

"I hope you choke on that bread," I said through clenched teeth, whispering against her neck like I was nuzzling her instead of contemplating wrapping my fingers around her porcelain skin and giving a little squeeze.

"Do I know about this accident, Patty?" Avery just had to ask.

And Mom, being Mom, just had to answer. "Oh, he was such a small boy."

"Still is." Avery said under her breath.

I squeezed her knee again. She gave a little yelp and stole the bread right off my plate.

"Thief," I whispered.

"Liar," she countered.

"Well, it's the damnedest thing," Mom continued, completely oblivious to the war zone across from her. "He just loved that little game where you drop the game pieces down the slots and they line up—you know, the one with the holes." Mom waved her hand in the air.

Our waiter approached.

Thank God.

"Here is our most recent favorite, nominated for its clear taste and . . ."

I tuned him out and shared a look of pure evil with Avery.

"You wanna play, little girl?" I cupped her cheek with my hand, using my thumb to flick her lower lip. "I'll play."

"Bring a cup." She winked.

The waiter filled my champagne glass, and Avery's attention was back on my mom. "Are you talking about Connect Four?"

"He liked the holes." Mom covered her mouth with her hand, but it didn't matter—her voice carried, it always carried. It pained me to admit how often I was the topic of one of her inappropriate conversations.

"You said that." Dad poured himself a glass of champagne and lifted it in the air toward me.

God, I'd need to consume that whole bottle to start forgetting this evening.

"He." She made a motion with her pointer finger. "Loved." Oh, here it came. "The." Another jabbing motion. "Holes." The last was said in the creepiest of whispers.

Avery gasped.

Dad chuckled and belted out, "Never did figure out how he got his little hot dog in there!"

Tears pooled in Avery's eyes, and then she burst out laughing with my parents while I poured myself more champagne.

"Sweetheart"—Avery elbowed me—"why the holes? Do you think it's because you have a fascination with sticking things . . . where they have no business going? And Patty, I ask this with all seriousness . . ."

I swore under my breath.

"Was he an equal-opportunity hole user? You know, sort of like if there was a hole, he just wanted to stick something in it." She briefly pressed her lips together. "I guess you could say, like having a different hole every day of the week, perhaps?"

Mom sighed. "You know, now that I think about it, he did try it more than once, the first time was—"

"Mom!" I yelled. "I need, uh, to excuse us for just a second. Avery hasn't taken her digestive pill for the meal, and I think I left it in the car. We'll be right back."

Avery frowned. "My digestive pill?"

She stood and excused herself. I grabbed her elbow and steered her away from the direction of the ladies' room and into the wine cellar.

"WHAT THE EVER-LOVING HELL WAS THAT!" I roared, my chest heaving as I pressed Avery against the nearest wall. I wasn't sure if I was mostly angry or just embarrassed.

"Equal-opportunity hole user?" She shrugged and then giggled and tugged the collar of my shirt with both hands. "So really, you've always been a whore?"

I let out a growl. "I've never wanted to slap a woman so badly in my entire life."

She made a face. "Look down. My knee would get you in the junk before you ever got the chance, and we don't want your Wednesday getting upset that you can't perform."

"If I can't perform, I'll just spend the day following you around and making sure everyone in your vicinity is fully aware that you didn't comb your hair until you were six and had to chop up your hot dogs until you were seventeen!"

"THEY'RE A CHOKING HAZARD!"

I smirked. "Maybe inform the next guy so he has fair warning."

"You smug bastard!" She tugged my collar tighter, and as our lips grazed, an electrical current of energy zipped between us.

"Shit." I exploded, on the spot, lost my mind, and crushed my mouth against hers.

And then nearly experienced either a mild stroke or an orgasm when her tongue met mine halfway.

Chapter Seventeen

AVERY

Kissing Lucas Thorn was a poor life choice—it had *always* been that way. Why could our kisses never be romantic? Involving situations where we went out on a normal date? Where nobody was pissed or drunk or about to get married?

His hot mouth slid against mine while his fingers dug into my ass, and then he gripped my hips. His thumb was pressed against my skin so hard, I'd probably be able to use the print to unlock his iPhone later—the pressure felt good, too good.

Bad idea.

Bad idea.

Kissing Satan.

Good, Avery, moan, because that makes him want to stop.

My arms, betraying bitches that they were, wrapped around his neck, and then my hands slid down his chest as I deepened the kiss, my body erotically rubbing against his.

Lucas tasted like champagne—his tongue did a weird twirl thing that had my legs nearly collapsing and sent shivers down to my toes and in all the wrong places because this wasn't happening, this couldn't happen! Not only because he was my boss.

He literally slept with other women.

ON PURPOSE.

And they knew about it.

Besides, he cheated on my sister!

I knew what he was capable of.

I would not be that girl.

"Stop!" I jerked away and then leaned in and kissed him again. He kissed me harder and harder, and I pulled back again. "No—I mean, we should stop."

"Yup." His hand cupped my breast.

I let out a little moan. "In like ten seconds, eleven maybe."

"Eleven seconds and we stop." His eyes blazed as his mouth descended again. His hand rubbed against my right breast and then lowered to my ass again as he pinched it and then slapped.

Hard.

"Okay," I hissed, shoving him away. "I can explain this."

His chest rose and then sank, as though he'd just had the workout of his life. "Oh?"

"Family pressure combined with drunkenness and lying makes people do really stupid things. You know, brain cells die because of the . . ." He licked his lower lip. "A-alcohol."

"Mmm." He reached for me again.

I let him.

WEAK!

The next kiss was softer.

It was the way I'd always wanted Lucas Thorn to kiss me—like I was precious, like I mattered—so for good, I pushed him away.

For my good.

For his.

For the sake of the friendship we used to have.

And for whatever future friendship we were trying to build. Everything was too confusing, and the kiss wasn't helping things. Not at all.

"I'm not going to be your new Tuesday."

He grinned. "Of course you won't, Tuesday's taken."

I glared at him.

He grinned harder. "But Saturday just quit, so—"

I slapped him so hard across his right cheek that I'm lucky one of my fingers didn't fly right off and land in someone's wineglass.

"The hell!" he swore loudly, violently, and almost teetered back against one of the expensive bottles of wine.

It would have made my night had he broken the one that was over three grand.

"Listen here, THORN." I got all up in his business, chest to heaving chest. "I will never be one of your whores! I don't care if the only way for you to survive one more day is for me to substitute for your Saturday, I won't do it. I WON'T DO IT!" I stomped my foot. "I won't, I won't, I won't."

"You said that already." He removed his hand and sighed. "Saturday always gets the longest time . . ."

I smacked him on the shoulder. "DO YOU HEAR YOURSELF?"

"DO YOU?" He threw up his arms. "Could you yell any louder?"

I opened my mouth.

He slammed a hand over it and shook his head sternly. "Look, all I'm saying is this—that was a good kiss, a great kiss, we know each other, we like each other. Think about it." Was he actually serious? Did he think I had so little self-respect that I'd just hop into his bed after knowing that he'd cheated on my sister? A small voice whispered that there was more to our past history.

The voice I had ignored the night Kayla cried in my arms.

The voice I ignored whenever I went home and had dinner with the family, only to find the air so strained I wanted to break a dish or yell to relieve the tension.

Lucas stared at me, like his idea had merit, like I was actually thinking about dumbly nodding and going along with it.

Weird, how you could lose so much respect for someone in an instant. The rose-colored glasses I'd so often looked at him through—the ones that I was just starting to brush off and think about wearing again—shattered.

Lucas Thorn wasn't the guy he used to be.

He'd never be that guy again. No matter how many times I wished it. The guy from that photo back in the high school was long gone. The guy I'd been obsessed with.

The guy who had ruined everything with one fatal mistake.

One I still blamed myself for.

I pushed the guilt away.

And I wasn't the girl I used to be—the one he would be willing to give up his serial screwing for. I was like every other girl, like the ones he spent time with during the week—completely and utterly replaceable.

And that hurt.

More than it should have.

Because I'd always come up short when it came to Lucas, just like I always came up short when it came to my sisters, who never let me forget it. I was Avery, the tomboy, the silly one, the one who had more guy friends than girlfriends. The girl who got her first kiss at seventeen and even then couldn't keep that boyfriend.

My sisters meant well. At least I lied to myself and told myself they did. But the damage had been done long ago, and it was hard to replace all my insecurity with confidence when the one guy you'd always wanted was offering a booty call—because he had an open position.

I was letting it hurt me more than it should, probably because somewhere, in my heart, I had hoped that he was just being an insecure jackass that was wounded a long time ago and was dealing with it in any way possible.

"Look," I said, my gravelly voice completely betraying my feelings, "you're just horny and upset because you haven't gotten laid in twelve hours or however long it's been. I'm sure this is a whole new reality for you, dating a woman without a guaranteed happy ending after dessert, but if you ever—and I do mean *ever*—try to kiss me again without my permission while still screwing other girls . . . I will kill you in broad daylight, plead guilty, and cheerfully sit in a jail cell the rest of my life. Got it?"

His face fell. "Avery, I was kidding. You know I would never put you in that position. I'm sorry I took it too far."

"So you're saying that if I wanted to be your Saturday, you'd say no?" I yelled. Why was I upset?

Lucas took a step back. "Wait, what?" He shook his head and walked around in a minicircle before jabbing his finger at my chest. "You were just threatening to kill me with a smile on your face if I ever offered. I told you I was kidding and apologized, and now you're pissed because you don't think I want you?"

"YES!" I threw my hands in the air. "Look, I would NEVER become your Saturday, but that doesn't mean I want you to think I'm not good enough to be ON the list! Stop insulting me!"

"YOU'RE IMPOSSIBLE!"

"I'M A WOMAN!" I raised my voice even more.

We were once again chest to chest.

And once again.

We kissed.

I think I led the next kiss, not that it mattered since we were both guilty—and oh my Honey Nut Cheerios, his tongue.

I was going to build a shrine in honor of his mouth.

Or a . . . What did I just say about his tongue?

No, his hands, his large hands as they moved down my body, sliding against my hips as his erection—

NOOOOOOO!

"STOP!" I slapped him again and tumbled back.

This time I hit his left cheek so . . . at least the redness matched the patch on his right cheek.

He hissed out a curse and glared at me. "Are you serious right now?"

"Sorry." I covered my face with my hands and laughed. "I got carried away."

His face was flushed red.

His lips were swollen.

And damn it, Lucas Thorn still looked like an Armani underwear model.

How was that possible?

"Kids?" Patty's voice echoed in the room.

"Quick!" I jabbed him in the chest. "How's my hair? Is there lipstick on my face?"

He grinned. It was a bad grin, a wicked grin, a grin that promised punishment.

Without any warning, he ran his hands through my hair, fully messing it up, then tore at part of my dress.

When his mom walked into the wine cellar, I knew what she probably saw.

A girl who'd just seduced her perfect son, and tried tearing off her dress to do so.

"Oh!" Patty covered her mouth with her hands. "Oh dear." She did a full circle and then glanced at us again. "I, uh, I didn't mean to intrude—we just need to put our orders in."

"Great." I forced a smile.

Lucas wrapped an arm around me and chuckled. "Oh, Mom, sorry. We just got so carried away with all that baby talk that, well, I think it got Avery excited to start trying, and before I knew what was happening, my pants were already—"

"Okay, pumpkin!" I slammed my hand over his face. "Let's leave the details to the wine in this room . . . and us . . . and the table. No need to share!"

Patty's grin literally could not get any wider. "Oh, grandchildren!"

"I should, um"—I gestured toward the ladies' room behind me—"fix my hair."

Patty nodded.

When I didn't move, Lucas grabbed me by the shoulders and pointed me in the right direction.

Once I finished freshening up, I headed back to the dining room, only to find Lucas waiting for me with a smug grin on his face. "I thought you were fixing your hair?"

I let out a little groan and marched toward the table, with Lucas Thorn slapping my ass, like I was a cow in line for the fair, the entire freaking way.

I was going to kill him before the night was over.

And I would do it with a smile on my face.

Chapter Eighteen

Lucas

Dinner was an absolute disaster, like something you'd see on TV and assume never happens in real life—but it does.

Then again, I grew up with that. The insane mother who talks too loud in the grocery store and mistakes K-Y for cooking oil. The father who buys beer but never drinks it, and just stocks his fridge so that company can be impressed with his ability to pick a good IPA.

When I was in high school, my parents were known as the Thorns, and it wasn't said in an excited, cheerful way. It was whispered behind my back as my oblivious parents marched to the beat of their own drum and hosted Harry Potter costume parties in their front yard and naked bingo on Friday nights, with an Indian dream catcher as the grand prize.

I wasn't sure if they were weird on purpose.

Or just found it entertaining to shock people.

"So . . ." My dad stabbed his last piece of broccoli and shoveled it into his gaping mouth. "When's the wedding?"

Avery pinched my thigh and then gave the flesh a little twist.

My mom, sadly, had seen the entire ending to our last kiss, and wrongly assumed we were so in love we couldn't keep our hands off each other.

Well, she at least had one part right. Since sitting down, we hadn't been able to keep our hands off each other—I had bruising to prove it.

I spent most of the dinner making sure that all steak knives were pushed away from Avery. Knowing her, she'd stab me in front of my parents, then make up some shit about how blood turned me on.

I wouldn't put it past her, bloodthirsty wench.

She finally stopped twisting the flesh on my thigh long enough for me to catch my breath and think of a logical excuse to get out of the predicament we'd found ourselves in. So far the dinner had done nothing but encourage my parents. And it's not like I had another choice; telling them the truth would devastate them all over again.

And as for admitting that my faux engagement to Avery wasn't going to help our families reestablish their broken and then lost relationship—I couldn't even imagine that possibility. Not after seeing their reaction to us as a couple.

I imagined the aftermath: Mom would cry and ask where she went wrong. She'd stop at every table in the restaurant, point and beg to be told why she was getting punished again and why her son felt the need to show his penis to a different woman every day. She'd shout "Penis!" because she never said sexually charged words quietly. And then she'd end up telling the whole god-awful story about when I'd started to go downhill—the night I made a bad choice and ruined their lives forever.

Dad would make the sign of the cross over his chest and stare down at his plate until it either came alive or Mom escorted him from the restaurant.

Nope. The truth would be a disaster.

"Um," I finally found my voice. "You know, right now we're really just enjoying this . . . time." I nodded. "It's nice just"—I waved my hands in the air—"being together."

Mom's eyes narrowed. "Lucas, I hate to tell you this, but you are thirty-two." She leaned forward, though she didn't lower her voice. If anything, she took a deep breath, ready to put every ounce of energy she had into whatever advice she was about to give. "SPERM START DYING AT YOUR AGE!"

"Thanks, Mom," I mumbled. Avery shook with laughter.

"WELL!" Mom threw her hands in the air as if I was a hopeless case. "DO YOU WANT your SPERM to die?"

Trick question? If I said yes, would she slap me? If I said no, would she encourage more sex?

Life choices.

Sometimes they sucked.

"I see what you mean," Avery said. "The last thing this world needs is a man as virile as Lucas Thorn being rendered unable to reproduce."

Okay, laying it on a bit thick, Avery. I refused to look at her, because when I looked at her, I remembered the way her mouth tasted—and that would encourage me to throw the girl over the table and screw her senseless in front of my parents. Hell, my mom would probably cheer us on and make sure that we forgot a condom. She'd make signs that read "Grandchildren Under Construction" and paint her face like she was at one of my old football games.

They'd been great fans at all my sporting events.

Mom reached across the table and met Avery's hand halfway. They squeezed like they were sharing a private moment, but when Avery tried to pull away, Mom held on tighter.

Hah.

Trapped.

I leaned back and crossed my arms. Should I save her?

Nope.

Out of the corner of her eye, Avery glared at me.

I didn't move.

"Avery, dear"—Mom cleared her throat—"I hate to bring this up, but should you be drinking if you're trying to get pregnant?"

"Yeah, Avery?" I jerked away her wine and downed it all, then set her empty glass back in front of her while her nostrils flared.

Alcohol was the only bonus of the dinner.

Other than that last kiss.

But I refused to think about the kiss.

Or where our hands were during the kiss.

Damn it.

Avery opened her mouth.

Mom shushed her. "Now, you just listen, Avery, this is wisdom from the women in the Thorn family, that now I'm passing down to you."

"Should she take notes?" I piped in.

"Oh!" Mom grinned. "I'll email them to her too, just in case you forget. Now, listen carefully." I smirked as Mom geared up. "Thirty minutes, your legs straight up in the air—that way the sperm stays inside your uterus!"

Dad started texting frantically.

Avery's face flashed red.

"And then!" Mom still wasn't letting go of her hand. "Remember, no using the ladies' room for a while. We want those swimmers to reach their destination! Don't we, Bill?"

"Uh-huh." Ten bucks Dad had no clue what Mom had just asked him.

"Now!" Mom's demeanor changed from cheerful to serious. "You have to swear, right now, not to ever use a condom. I imagine you've both been tested."

Avery again tried to pull her hand away. The wide-eyed look she was giving me was hysterical. Clearly, it was lost on my mom that Avery probably wanted to establish herself in her career before she started popping out kids.

"Well?" Mom wasn't letting it go.

"I, um." Avery couldn't have turned any redder if she'd tried. "I, uh, it's been a while since I've been to the doctor, but I mean, I'm totally fine."

"Oh, honey, oh no—oh, that won't do." Her face fell. "I'll take you!"

"NO!" On that I had to intervene, but I was too late. Once an idea hit my mom, it was impossible to change her mind. She was like a politician running for president; no matter how stupid her ideas, she rode them until they fell apart, which most of the time they did.

She was Ralph Nader.

Bless her heart.

"YES!" Mom released Avery's hand, finally, and then pressed both hands to her own cheeks. "I'm not working tomorrow! I'll come downtown! I'll pick you up! We can have a girls' day! We'll have lunch! Oh, oh, oh!" She wiggled in her seat, and then her eyes welled with tears. "I've been waiting for this moment my whole life. The moment I could spend time with the girl my Lucas would settle down with."

"Eh, you spent time with Kayla," Dad interjected. Apparently, he *was* listening. Could this dinner get any worse? At all?

"Oh"—Mom waved him off—"Kayla never counted. After all, a mom knows these things. Our Lucas has had his eye on Avery for a while. Ever since she got breasts!"

And there it was.

Avery choked down her water.

And I prayed for the apocalypse.

We all fell silent as my mom wiped a few tears from under her eyes. "I'm sorry—I know I sound crazy. I can hear myself, you know."

Dad nodded.

"But it's just . . ." She slapped my dad across the chest, and he looked up. "It's been so long since we've truly spent time with your parents, and we've always thought . . . Well, we always thought we'd be a family, you know? And ever since"—she lowered her voice—"the incident." All eyes focused on me. "It's been so strained, and . . ." Mom was full on crying now. "Your mother was my best friend."

Anger surged through me.

It was one thing to blame me and make me feel guilty. After all, it was my fault.

But to pull Avery in, to make her feel like she had no choice.

I had to say something.

Even though I knew it would be the final nail in the coffin of my relationship with my parents.

I bit back a curse. "Listen, guys, I need to tell you something—"

"—A gift!" Avery elbowed me. "We left your gift in the car."

"Do you leave everything in the car?" This from my dad.

"Oh, honey, it's love. You're forgetful. Remember when you and I got engaged and—"

Avery tugged me away from the table, walking at breakneck speed until we were once again in the wine cellar. Ah, memories.

"What the hell are you doing?" she snapped.

"Look"—I ran my hand through my hair—"it's over, I can't . . . As amusing as it is to make you suffer, I'm not going to let you go down with the *Titanic*."

"Are you the *Titanic* in this situation?" she asked in a soft voice.

"Get on the lifeboat." I nodded. "Maybe in your version you can save Jack and live happily ever after." My eyes locked on hers.

Avery sighed and hung her head, then kicked the wooden table. "Grab a bottle of wine, and we'll add it to the tab as our gift—your parents will never know."

"Okay." For some reason I was disappointed. Though I wasn't sure why. Maybe because I half expected her to at least do something.

Then again, I'd cheated on her sister.

I was beyond saving in Avery's book, and knowing that burned like hell.

"It's been hard on my parents too." Avery looked up at me with tear-filled eyes. "Like really, really hard." She swallowed and pressed her hands to her temples. "Maybe . . . Oh God, I can't believe I'm saying this, but maybe if we fake it a little longer at least our moms will talk, and your dad and my dad can go fishing again—"

"   they loved their annual fishing trips."

She smirked. "Remember the trout I hid in your bed?"

"I watched you do it and then threw it at your face."

"I wasn't very sneaky then."

"Hate to break it to you, but you aren't sneaky now."

"So I walk loud." She shrugged and offered me a beautiful smile, a kind smile, and then she reached out to me. "A few more days of pretending won't kill us. In fact, it may be the answer to everything."

"Oh, and how's that?" I grabbed her hand.

"My parents shouldn't have ever pushed yours away. The Blacks and the Thorns are like . . . peanut butter and jelly."

"My mom misses her jelly."

Avery burst out laughing. "Yeah, okay, grab the wine and try not to encourage your mother toward making any more weird appointments."

We walked hand in hand back to the dinner table.

"So what do you say?" All eyes focused on Avery as my mom continued dabbing her eyes with her napkin. Apparently, she'd continued crying while we were gone.

"I, uh, I don't know, boss." Avery looked at me, willing me with her eyes to stick to the plan for a few days. We could do a few days, right? "Can I have tomorrow off?"

"You know what? Wednesdays are always slow. It's totally fine with me. You girls have fun."

With clenched fists at her sides, she gave my mom a curt nod. "Sounds . . . ," she whispered, then took a deep breath. "Well, like it's going to be the best day of my life."

Mom still wasn't keeping her voice down. "Oh, I have just the gyno. He's a gorgeous young thing with—"

"Hell no." I shook my head. "Some young hot doctor isn't going to look at her . . ." I licked my dry lips. "What about Dr. Byrne? Isn't he ninety?"

"Honey, the man can barely see!" Mom laughed loudly. "Can you imagine? He'd need a magnifying glass to—"

"SOUNDS GREAT!" Avery shouted and elbowed me in the side.

Mom tilted her head in my direction, and then a slow smile spread across her face. Oh no. Oh dear God. I knew that smile. I knew it well. My stomach dropped.

"Lucas"—she grabbed her water—"you'll come too."

Note how she didn't ask.

She told.

Like a true mother.

And like a good son, I had no choice but to nod and utter, "Sounds like fun."

Chapter Nineteen

LUCAS

"Riddle me this," she said in a calm voice once we were back in the car. "How did a dinner with your parents turn into a discussion about an engagement, marriage, grandchildren, and safe sex—then finally somehow detour into planning an appointment for me with a gynecologist with both you and your mother present?"

I.

Had.

Nothing.

"If you can't laugh about it, you'll just cry. Believe me, I grew up in that household. It won't be that bad."

Avery jerked to attention, her green eyes lit up with hatred. "Did you just say it won't be *that* bad? Look, I agreed to help so you should just shut the hell up!"

"Um, well—"

"Have you ever, and I do mean EVER, had a man digging through your parts like he was searching for gold?"

"No," I choked out, then mumbled, "thank God."

I turned on the ignition, put the car in drive, and we took off.

She slugged me in the face with her purse. "IT HURTS!"

"THEN DON'T TENSE UP!"

"ARE YOU SERIOUS RIGHT NOW?" Damn it, she was beautiful when she was angry, chest heaving, lips pressed together like she was building up enough energy to use that dirty mouth to yell at me.

"No?" I scooted away from her. "Just, I don't know, do a yoga breathing exercise thing." I waved her off and reached into my pocket for my phone. I needed a distraction before my mouth accidentally hit hers in a vain attempt to repeat the kiss that shouldn't have even happened.

"I SHOULDN'T HAVE TO!"

"Stop yelling. You're completely overreacting."

Avery's response was to smack me with her purse again, this time in the chest. "Your mom said 'penis' at least ten times tonight. She encouraged me to lie in your bed with my legs in the air while your lazy-ass sperm swim upstream!"

"Lazy?" I shoved the phone in my pocket. "My sperm are ANYTHING but lazy, alright? Hell, you'd be LUCKY to have them floating down your river!"

"See!" She threw her hands in the air. "Floating! What? They don't even know how to swim? Hmm, reminds me of someone else. Tell me, how were those swimming lessons with the five-year-old class? How old were you, twelve?"

"Go to hell," I muttered. "And you're getting off point. Many a woman is thankful for my . . . juices."

Avery burst out laughing. "Your juices? Your perfectly golden and lazy-ass Lucas Thorn juices? Do you hear yourself?"

"Yeah"—I rolled my eyes—"and it's like I'm losing IQ points the longer I discuss this with you. Just plan to go to the appointment. I'll drop you guys off, you can spread for the dude, get your results. We'll all do lunch, and I'll make up a fake meeting we have to get back for—then in a few weeks, we'll convince my mom that we decided to break things off."

Avery tapped her fingernails against her luscious thigh. What I wouldn't do for one night, just one night, when I could run my tongue up and down that smooth piece of skin.

"I hate going to the doctor. Ugh. When she mentioned making the appointment, I didn't think I'd have to spread my legs for a total stranger." Avery exhaled roughly. "A few weeks is nothing. Besides, it's not like they live close to us. And we're adults, responsible adults."

"Who made out in the wine cellar," I just had to add.

"Sexual tension is just that, sexual tension. Besides, don't you have a few more girls to please this week?"

"Yeah." Guilt stabbed me in the chest because suddenly the only lips I wanted to kiss were hers. What the hell was wrong with me? "I do. At least they don't push me away."

She glanced down at her hands, then looked out the window and whispered, "Yeah, well, some girls aren't okay with sharing. Besides, you know that when I was little I stuffed animal crackers in my pockets during snack time, only to have them end up in the washer later. I didn't do it because I was hungry—I just didn't want other people to have what I had."

"Still possessive, hey, Avery Bug?"

She glanced back at me. "In every way that matters, yes. When a man loves me, he's going to get all of me, not twenty-four hours."

Lucky bastard.

Lucky freaking bastard.

I wanted to say something else.

I wanted so many things.

My heart twisted and slammed against my rib cage in defiance of the words I knew I needed to utter.

It begged me to think before speaking.

But I'd stopped listening to my heart a long time ago.

Back when it told me to pick Avery.

And dump the only girl I'd ever been with—her sister.

"Yeah, well, don't knock it until you try it." I smirked.

Avery stiffened. I pulled the car up to the curb of her building. "See you tomorrow, Thorn."

The car door slammed.

Blanketing me in darkness.

Leaving me to wonder if I was making another epic mistake with the one Black girl I swore I'd never hurt.

Chapter Twenty

Avery

I dreamed of strangling Lucas Thorn with my bare hands and woke up smiling, only to stop the minute I realized that he wasn't in fact dead—thanks to the text waiting for me on my cell:

Be ready in 40.

Why? I asked the universe that question over and over. First when I took a shower, again when I quickly got dressed and applied my makeup, and then when my unruly hair refused to do anything except shoot out in every direction, giving me a very hot Medusa look that I'm sure Lucas would comment on.

When I was finally dressed and ready to go, I had three minutes of freedom left.

Minutes before I was going to have to go to the gyno because of a stupid fake engagement I didn't even want in the first place. But his face at dinner. I knew that look. He had taken a huge deep breath and lowered his head like he was about ready to tell the truth and, in the process, disappoint his parents. And for some reason I decided to fall on my own sword, and jump into the depths of hell with him.

I stared at the door, willing time to stop so that the knock wouldn't happen. Hey, maybe I was in one of those alternate-universe movies, meaning the main character THINKS that everything is real but is actually hooked up to a giant human-hating computer.

I squeezed my eyes shut and mumbled, "I'm Neo, I'm Neo, I'm Neo."

A knock sounded at my door.

"Why can't I live in the damn Matrix?" I muttered, slumping all the way to the door and jerking it open.

"Did you say something?" Lucas asked, looking sexier than what should be allowed for the devil. His white shirt was crisp, ironed, and tucked into perfect-fitting pin-striped trousers that screamed class, money, man.

NO!

I shook my head. "I was just wishing on a falling star, asking it to fall right on your head." I grabbed the coffee from his hand and peeked behind his back. "Where's my pastry?"

He rolled his eyes. "It's in the car."

I scrunched my nose up and took a sip of coffee as I stepped out of the apartment. "Last night I killed you." I smiled triumphantly.

Lucas exhaled and shut the door behind me, placing his hand on my back as we walked down the dimly lit hall. "Wow, tell me more, please. I'm dying to know. Was it a gunshot wound to the head or something more graphic, like a machete to the balls?"

"HAH, don't give me ideas, Thorn." I chugged more coffee, allowing the heat of the bitter liquid to soothe my nerves.

The last time I'd been to the gyno was right in the middle of college. Not only was the checkup expensive, but it was also after I'd stupidly had sex with a relative stranger just to get the whole thing over with.

I was the only virgin left in my group of friends, and for some reason I thought that part of growing up was giving my virginity up in the most awkward experience possible.

Not only was it the most unromantic experience of my life.

But I later found out the guy had given another girl an STD. I swore I'd never have random sex again and went to get tested.

Thankfully, I was healthy.

But the trauma of the Pap smear remained.

Not that I would ever reveal that to Lucas. Who knows? I wouldn't put it past him to somehow use the info as ammo and turn the whole damn thing against me. That was the last thing I needed. Besides, he probably couldn't have cared less about my sexual (in)experience. He was a complete man whore.

"In you go." He opened the door to the back of the nice black Uber Escalade.

I slid across the plush leather seats, grabbed the paper bags of warm pastries, and inhaled them like a drug addict.

Lucas slid in behind me and slammed the door. "I figured the easiest way to put you at ease was to drug you with sugar."

"I take it back." I grabbed a sugary donut and stuffed half of it in my mouth. "I didn't enjoy killing you last night. I shed a tear, it was small." I held up two fingers that were almost touching. "Like this big. Hardly noticeable, kind of like your penis."

Lucas choked on his coffee.

"Well, maybe not as small as that"—I elbowed him—"but close. At any rate, thanks for the donut." I squeezed his leg, unable to keep my hands away from his stupid body.

"I got you a breakfast sandwich too. You know, protein."

I waved him off.

"Typical," he snorted.

"What?" I asked midbite. "What's typical?"

"You need to take care of yourself, go to bed early . . ." His voice was strained. "Make sure you do your annual checkups."

I rolled my eyes. "Yeah, because that's been so necessary this past year."

Damn it!

I waited.

Hoping he missed it.

But he was Lucas Thorn, so instead of missing my meaning, he leaned toward me and licked his stupidly attractive big lips. "Oh?"

I averted my eyes.

To the cleft in his chin.

Which made me think of our kiss.

I clenched my thighs together and then crossed my legs. Nope. Not happening, not getting anywhere near the lower region of my anatomy, not now, not ever.

My body was notorious for betraying me when it came to Lucas, and I wasn't going to lose control again.

Ugh, the sugar on the donut didn't taste as good as his tongue. The same tongue he thrust into other women's mouths.

Lust cooled. I turned to him and shrugged. "What?" Lucas's eyes pinned me.

"Admit it." He grinned. "There is no Carl."

"Fine, no Carl. Gee, you got me—doesn't change anything. I'm still a sexually active wildcat just waiting to pounce on my next prey." I tore a piece of donut and made a growling noise.

He swore violently and adjusted the collar of his shirt.

"What?" I smirked. "Something I said?"

"Nope, just imagining what that would be like, getting mounted by Avery Black."

It was my turn to choke.

The driver stopped in front of a large building a few blocks away from our downtown offices, closer to Pike Place Market, which made me want to go shopping for flowers and toss some fish around while sipping coffee.

I reached for my seatbelt; Lucas pressed a hand to my fingers and whispered in my ear, "Admit it, you're thinking about it too."

I exhaled and tried to even out my breathing. "I don't know what you're talking about."

"Liar." His chuckle was warm, seductive. "You're right—I bet you're crazy in bed, wild, violent. If there was a Carl, I'd have half a mind to be jealous."

"That would be the day." My voice was raspy and stupidly turned on.

Our eyes locked.

He leaned forward, just as the rear door opened beside me.

I jumped back and quickly wiped my mouth of any remnants of sugared donut, then numbly reached for my purse.

Walking was an issue.

You know, for obvious reasons. You needed legs to walk, and mine had turned to jelly. I couldn't even feel my legs, or my face, and it was all Lucas's fault.

Hating him was difficult.

Being attracted to him was inevitable.

Because many years ago—my life goal had been to find and marry someone just like Lucas Thorn.

Not the one I was helping lie to his entire family or the one who slept with a different woman almost every night, but the one who had held my hand when I watched scary movies.

Or the one who'd kissed me on the night he was found in bed with my look-alike sister after promising me things he had no right to promise.

I was a pawn in his game.

He'd just needed someone to save him from himself.

Great. History was repeating itself, because back then I had been willing to save him over a stupid crush and maybe because I thought he actually cared more about me than about my sister. And since I'd always been in Kayla's shadow—he made me feel special.

My morose thoughts really weren't helping things.

The morning went from bad to worse when Lucas's mom jumped up in the waiting room and shouted by way of greeting Lucas and me: "We're GOING TO HAVE A BABY!"

"Run!" I gripped Lucas's hand. "We can still make the elevator if we run." The elevator doors closed in our faces.

Lucas cursed. "We could always jump through the glass window and pray a garbage truck is driving by."

Patty barreled toward us, arms outstretched, tears running down her face.

"I'm in." I nodded earnestly.

Lucas let out a defeated sigh as his mom gripped him by the ears and pressed a kiss to each cheek. She then turned her attention to me and began crying even harder as we all headed back toward the doctor's office.

Why did she have to cry?

"I just knew it." She wiped under her eyes. "I'm so sorry, but you've just always been my favorite of you three sisters, and when poor Lucas confessed his true feelings for you—"

"Mom!" Lucas yelled.

My mouth dropped open.

"Oh"—Patty covered her mouth with her hands—"I thought she knew?"

"Knew that I adored this little slugger?" He, no joke, pulled me into his arms and noogied my head, then poked me in the chest.

I smacked him in the arm and shoved him away.

His mom blinked in confusion at our exchange, while Lucas turned bright red and pointed to the receptionist's counter. "Shouldn't Avery fill out her paperwork?"

His mom's eyes narrowed. "Yes, we'll just . . . Why don't we go get that and you can find a seat."

Lucas laughed. "Mom, I'm not staying. I came with Avery, but I'll go wait in the car."

He was already backing away.

"No." Patty shook her head sternly. "If you're going to be together forever, you go through thick and thin together, in sickness and in health!"

"But Avery's completely healthy!" he argued. "Look at her!"

I preened, couldn't help it.

"She has a history of anemia!"

I paused as sweat started to pool down my back. How would she know that? There was no way unless—oh no, oh no, no, no, no. I squeezed Lucas's hand, nearly cutting off the circulation. His eyes narrowed.

"Just how would you know that?" Lucas asked while Patty fidgeted with her purse and then cleared her throat. "Mom?" No doubt, he was ready to make a run for it. Again.

"I may have made a call." She smiled cheerfully. "But it was for the best."

Moms.

Whenever they did something wrong, they always justified it by saying, "It was for the best." As if their manipulation made it all okay because, *HEY, I'm looking out for your best interests.*

"What was 'for the best'?" I repeated, my entire body going numb this time. The sweat ran down my back and trickled even more—great, just great.

"The engagement party," she said, dodging the question. "I'll just go get a clipboard."

I gasped.

Lucas swore and looked ready to commit murder.

I quickly dug into my purse to find I had five missed calls from my mom. Five.

I didn't even want to look at the text messages.

"Not what I had in mind when I agreed to help last night." I smacked him in the chest with my purse and glared at him. "You need

157

to control her!" I pointed at his mom, who was already on her way back with the clipboard, practically skipping.

"Hey, you're the one who just HAD to say something to my sister. If anyone points fingers, they go to you," he said under his breath.

"Oh PLEASE!" I sneered. "Like it was my fault your best friend kidnapped mine and got everyone drunk!"

"Damn it, I should have left you on the street corner."

I jerked away as though he'd slapped me. "So that's what I get for helping you with all of your family drama? 'I should have left you on the street corner'?"

His mom was dangerously close to us.

Ugh, why did I keep doing that? Imagining he cared about me when he was probably checking his watch, counting down the hours until he could be with his next girl.

"Well"—I fought back tears—"we agreed to do this together, to help each other. Though God knows I must have been drunk when I said yes last night. Either we make a plan for how to get out of the party, or we end up pissing everyone off and hurting our families . . . again. Grandpa still hasn't forgotten what you did, and I can guarantee he still has nightmares from being a POW. The last thing you want is for him to turn all his attention toward you. He's a very violent man."

"Your grandfather makes bikes for children," Lucas said dryly, rocking back on his heels.

"He was a *sniper*."

"Fine." Lucas's shoulders hunched. "Let's just get this part over with, and we'll deal with everything else later."

I nodded, too tired to argue, then begrudgingly took the clipboard from his mom and started filling in my information.

Chapter Twenty-One

LUCAS

Don't panic.

Don't show fear.

My mom was sitting on one side of me with Avery on the other. I was in absolute hell and was going to have to change my shirt and get another brand of deodorant, since the one I had used clearly wasn't doing the job.

Then again, deodorants aren't made for situations that involve trying to right a wrong between two families in the worst possible circumstances. In my case that meant keeping my mom from finding out about my unique sex life while faking an engagement to the younger sister of the ex-fiancée I'd cheated on.

I think if it had been just that tangle, the deodorant would have been like, *Chill, Lucas, I've got this.*

But I was in a damn gynecologist's office; no male deodorant should have to put up with that shit.

With my mother.

With. My. Mother.

The receptionist called out Avery's name.

Avery directed a look of pure hatred at me before slowly standing and wiping her hands on her jeans.

The nurse eyed me up and down and smirked.

I tried to keep my groan in.

I knew that look. It was interest. Blatant interest.

But I was here with my girlfriend.

Fiancée.

Even with the fake fiancée, I didn't appreciate the nurse's leer.

I stood.

The hell?

I dated multiple women all the time!

Why would I have qualms now when my fiancée wasn't even real?

Avery glanced back at me, her face pale.

Slowly, numbly, I reached out and took her hand in mine, and for reasons I would probably overanalyze later—I kissed her fingertips and winked.

Ignoring the nurse completely.

And locking eyes with the only woman that mattered.

Only to have my mom ruin the moment by shoving her body between us and wrapping an arm around both my waist and Avery's. "This is so responsible of you guys."

"Yes, exactly what I was thinking," Avery said dryly. "How responsible of you, Lucas."

I glared at her over the top of my mom's head and mouthed a curse.

Avery carried on cheerfully until we entered the exam room and she spotted the table she had to sit on.

It had metal stirrups.

I coughed out a laugh. "I'll just be outside."

Mom grabbed me by the collar of my shirt. "Just where do you think you're going?"

I gave her a helpless look. "Mom, she needs privacy. I'll wait outside the door while the nurse and doctor . . . examine Avery."

"I completely agree." Mom nodded and crossed her arms. "So if you need me, I'll be reading that new book about the naughty duke on my Kindle. In the waiting room. You two have fun!"

She was gone before I could argue.

Leaving both Avery and me staring at the table in horror.

"We could pay him off."

"What was that?" I asked.

"And when I say 'we,' I mean *you*. You can pay off the doctor, tell him not to make me take off all my clothes and get on the death contraption."

"Avery, I—"

"They make me spread my legs, Lucas!" she wailed. "And this thing"—she made an alligator motion with her arms—"clamps together and gets shoved up into . . . Well . . ." Her cheeks turned pink. "You know where, and then it does THIS!" Her arms slowly opened. "WIDE!"

I was a sick man.

Because the image wasn't at all horrifying.

In fact, I had half a mind to ask if I could watch.

What the hell was wrong with me?

"Lucas!" she hissed. "Pay attention." She snapped her fingers in front of my face. "I'll be completely exposed!"

I tugged the collar of my shirt and nodded. "Avery, relax, it's going to be over with before you know it."

She hung her head and made a little whimper, then said, "Okay, well, I need to put on the gown of death, so you—you can go."

I sighed. "I'll turn around while you change, and at least wait until the doctor and his nurse get in here, okay?"

Avery's shoulders slumped. "I can't believe you got us into this predicament."

Sadly, I had to turn around, and I nearly passed out when I heard the sound of a zipper lowering. I clenched my hands. "How do you figure? You're the one who got drunk and then lied to Erin the next day, not me."

"You were right. You should have left me to die on the street corner, Lucas."

"Believe me, I would have, but you said you frowned upon prostitution, and I guarantee leaving you on a street corner would have been a very quick way to put you on the exact career path that working for me is keeping you from."

The sound of paper rustling had me too curious to resist peeking over my shoulder. Avery was already up on the exam table, her knees exposed and her small body completely swallowed up in an ugly pink hospital gown.

"Don't . . ." she said through clenched teeth, looking down at the pink fabric, ". . . laugh."

I shoved my hands in my pockets. "Wasn't even tempted to look beneath the paper sheet."

She rolled her eyes. "I'd like to think we're beyond the lying."

I bit down on my lip to keep from smiling.

"Fine." She looked heavenward. "You can laugh for three seconds, then you have to stop and tell me how sexy my legs look."

I laughed and then reached for her knee, which was warm, like the rest of her skin. My fingers bristled at the innocent touch, greedy for more. We locked eyes. "Your legs look sexy."

Her lips parted.

My fingers slid up her gown.

After a couple of soft knocks, the door opened before Avery could answer. "Avery Black?" One of the most attractive men I'd ever seen, damn it, walked in, clipboard in hand, plastic smile on his face. He had bleached-blond hair and dimples, and he was built like a tank. Oh, hell no.

His nurse followed and stood politely in the corner. I could feel the heat of her gaze on me, but my focus was entirely on Avery and her reaction to Dr. McDreamy.

"That's me!" Avery practically leaped off the table in an attempt to shake the doctor's hand.

The bastard grinned and touched her shoulder. If that wasn't a malpractice suit, I wasn't sure what was.

I moved quickly to intercept the hand that was already nearing hers. "Lucas Thorn."

He shook my hand, his eyebrows knitting together. "Oh, hi."

Damn it, he wasn't gay.

I was really banking on him being gay; at least then I could divert his attention away from Avery.

No chance in hell was he getting anywhere near the lower part of her body . . . Shit, was it hot in here?

"Do those windows open?" I pointed to a window and started rolling my sleeves up like I was going to be elbows deep between Avery's thighs, a mental picture that would land me in hell.

"No." The doctor laughed. "We're on the sixteenth floor, and people tend to jump."

"Hah-hah," I nodded. "What about pushing someone off? That happen often, Doctor?"

"Dr. Dupper." He grinned and turned to Avery. "But you can call me Dustin."

"Wow, *Dustin*"—I made sure to say his name loudly—"aren't you a bit young to be a doctor?"

His face hardened. "I'm thirty-three. I've been out of residency two and a half years. So, no. Would you like to see my degree from Yale School of Medicine?"

Of course he'd gone to Yale.

"No," I said through clenched teeth. Who would name their kid Dustin Dupper? "No, I'm sure you're more than qualified." It hurt like hell to keep a smile on my face while he eyed me up and down before he finally turned his attention back to Avery.

"Let's get started, shall we?"

Avery gulped. "Yeah." She peered around Dustin. "Lucas, you should wait outside."

"No!" I barked, then cleared my throat. "I mean, what kind of fiancé would I be if I bailed during the hard times, right, pumpkin face?"

"But, cupcake . . ." Now her teeth clenched, and she subjected me to a hard stare. "You said that—"

"I love you." The words tumbled out of my mouth before I could stop them, making every logical bone in my body panic while my heart continued to steadily beat against my chest. It was an odd feeling. My brain wanted me to run, but my heart was . . . content.

The feeling didn't last long.

Because the minute I released those three words, Avery hung her head, and every ounce of teasing left her body. Like I'd just zapped her of all the happy hormones she had floating around and told her I was going to kill her favorite pet.

"Avery?" Dustin asked. "Is everything okay?"

She nodded. "Yeah, let's just get this over with, okay?"

The doctor grinned, then eyed his clipboard. "Fantastic. Now, it says here that you're currently sexually active."

"The hell she is!" I yelled.

Both turned to me.

"Oh." I decided to backpedal before I made more of an ass out of myself. "Sorry—I mean, yes, with me, her fiancé."

"Do you mind?" Dustin barked out.

I held my hands up.

"Are you currently on any sort of birth control?"

Avery shook her head and whispered a no.

"Do you want to be?"

Wasn't that kind of personal?

"Yes," she answered thoughtfully. "I think it's time."

"Whoa, whoa, whoa." Was I sweating? "Avery Bug, maybe you're, I mean, *we're* rushing into this . . ."

"Safe sex?" The doctor gave me a confused look. "She's rushing into safe sex with her fiancé?"

I was shaking with the urge to strangle him. "No, you're right, ignore me."

Avery rolled her eyes at me while he checked something off his list.

There were about a million questions he went on to ask her, and I had to sit and listen to her answer every single one.

Chapter Twenty-Two

Avery

One of the most common questions when you're in a new group of people or introducing yourself at school—heck, it's the favorite question that gets asked at parties—is, "What's your most embarrassing moment?"

People confide in one another, laugh, create an emotional bond over their sad, unfortunate situations, and move on.

Before today, I would have said my most embarrassing moment was when I accidentally flashed the entire senior class at high school graduation because I'd tucked my miniskirt into my thong. Luckily, there was a nice wind that day, which clued me in when I was halfway up the stairs, ready to receive my diploma, that I had a cheek exposed.

It could have been worse.

That moment made a killing my freshman year at college. People laughed, guys hit on me and asked if I still had the skirt—so really it wasn't as bad as it could have been. Until today, I'd never truly understood the word "embarrassment," its definition, its meaning, and everything else attached to it.

Until Lucas Thorn.

Until his mother.

Until now.

"If you would just relax and lean back, this will be over with before you know it!" Dr. Dupper patted my leg with his latex glove. He then pulled a curtain around the examination table so that I was partially blocked from Lucas's view, for which I was grateful.

Shaking, I tried to go to my happy place, but I was miserable. Lucas had said the three words I'd dreamed of him saying to me when I still wasn't over my crush in high school—and he'd looked like he meant them.

I'd rather be rejected than given a taste of what it would feel like to be loved by him, only to realize two seconds later that it wasn't real.

I squeezed my eyes shut and waited for the inevitable, but Lucas peeked from around the curtain and whispered in my ear, "This will be funny tomorrow, I promise."

I opened one eye. "You aren't the one with your legs spread."

He looked down at my legs and smirked. He couldn't see anything, but it was still horrifying for me.

"I can at least appreciate the flexibility." He winked.

I smiled. "Really? That's what you're going to say?"

"Beautiful," Dr. Dupper commented.

I frowned and propped myself up on my elbows. "Excuse me?"

He peered up at us in confusion. "Oh, I just appreciate it when a woman takes care of her health." He winked.

Lucas cursed on the other side of the curtain. "More doing, less talking, Doc."

The doctor snapped back at him, "Please don't tell me how to do my job."

"Lucas . . ." I shook my head slowly even though he couldn't see me. "Just leave it."

"He called your parts 'beautiful'!" Lucas hissed as if he was actually angry that a doctor was doing his job.

I burst out laughing. "So?"

"So!" He swore violently and then gripped the edge of the curtain like he was getting ready to tear it down. "Just, that's not . . . professional."

"Okay, big guy." I patted the part of his arm that was visible and then let out a little whimper.

"What?" He poked his face around the curtain, his eyes locking on mine. "What's wrong? What did the bastard do?"

"You know I can hear both of you, right?" Dr. Dupper asked in a detached voice. "And, Avery, I need you to stop clenching or it's going to hurt a lot worse."

"THEN STOP DOING IT!" Lucas yelled.

The doctor ignored him and shoved the metal thingy further in. I clutched the paper sheet and started to sweat.

By this point the curtain was long gone and Lucas was at my side, gripping my hand like I was getting ready to pop out a kid.

"What do I do?" Lucas looked like he was ready to pass out.

"You could have just told the truth to begin with instead of making me go through with dinner last night," I said through gritted teeth.

"And miss this amazing team-building opportunity?" he joked. "Never."

"You're a jackass and should burn in hell."

"Thanks, sweetie." He patted my head. I swatted his hand away and swore.

"Almost there," the doctor said for what felt like the fifth time.

"He's said that at least twice, right?" My eyes were watering. "Never again. I'm never going to the doctor again."

Finally, Dr. Dupper, the doctor of death, pulled the metal thingy away and stood. "You can sit up now."

I jerked the paper sheet over my lap.

I almost burst into tears with relief, until he locked eyes with me and said, "Is there something you'd like to discuss with me, Avery?"

I frowned and then shivered. "Um, no, I don't think so."

Lucas's hand on my arm tightened.

Dr. Dupper looked between the two of us. "Your hymen is still intact."

I looked up at Lucas and grinned, suddenly feeling quite pleased with the whole situation when I answered, "Well, he's really small."

Dr. Dupper burst out laughing.

And suddenly? The whole trip to the gyno?

Worth it.

Chapter Twenty-Three

AVERY

After the gyno adventure, we decided to skip having lunch together and sent Lucas's mom on her way. I told her I was traumatized, and Lucas looked traumatized, so it worked. I whistled the entire afternoon at work—not because I'd had such a stellar start to my day but because I had every intention of going back to a certain doctor and getting a date.

That was, once I flushed Lucas Thorn down the toilet with all the penile enlargement pamphlets Dr. Dupper had given him. Hey, there was a thought. Instead of flowers at his burial, I'd litter the casket with those. Perfect. And he said I was evil for making fun of his small penis!

At least I can still be thoughtful!

"Lunch." Lucas rapped his knuckles on my desk. "What do you want? Hot dog? Hamburger?"

"Gee." I pretended to think about it. "How big is this hot dog?" I held two fingers an inch apart. "Would you say it's this big? Or"—I moved them two inches apart—"this big?"

He glowered. "I'm never living this down, am I?"

"It was one of my favorite life moments," I answered sweetly. "Ever."

"That makes one of us. The bastard gave me pamphlets for a penile enlargement. He looked genuinely concerned, Avery. Think of what that does to a man! He thinks I can't please you!"

I laughed. "And why does that bother you? You'll never please me. Think of it that way."

"But I could," he pointed out. "And put your fingers down. It's embarrassing how little you know about hot dogs—mine especially."

My eyebrows shot up. "Oh?"

"Careful." He leaned over the desk and whispered, "Your innocence is showing."

"Is not." Mature, Avery. Well done.

"You're blushing."

"It's hot in here." I made a fan motion in front of my face to deflect his attention.

He eyed me up and down. "Yup, I see what you mean, very hot. Hot enough to give you a nice flush down your neck—hey, where's that sweater from?"

I ignored him and pretended that I was checking my email so he'd leave. It didn't help that my fingers shook a bit over the computer keyboard. "I'd like a hamburger. I think I've had enough hot dog talk for the day."

"Done." He nodded and started to walk away but then backtracked and scratched his head, like he was nervous. "When Chelsea gets here, can you show her to my office?"

My hands froze over the keyboard. I could only nod and mutter out a "Yup."

"Thanks."

Fortunately, my embarrassment at the doctor's office was trumped by Lucas's, so he hadn't even touched on the subject of me being technically a virgin. I can only imagine how that conversation would go, especially since by some miracle of God the only guy I'd had sex with hadn't really done his job.

Needing to busy myself, I reviewed the calendar for the next few weeks. We had app training four times a week in addition to two more school visits this week before I could be done with work, which meant basically every day of my life—both business and personal—was with Lucas.

I exhaled and tried to get myself to think of anything but Lucas.

And the way he had held my hand.

And said he loved me.

And kissed me.

The pencil I was holding snapped in half. My phone lit up the minute the pencil tip nearly impaled my thigh.

Kayla.

Ah!

"Hi!" I answered on the first ring, my voice breathy and high. "What's up?"

"You," she sniffled. "You."

"Me?" I started to have that dizzy feeling you get when you know that you're in trouble and something bad is about to happen. I knew that the moms would talk. I just assumed they wouldn't break the news to Kayla, of all people, that quickly. "Me, what?"

"Y-you and Lucas are g-getting married?" she shrieked. Loudly.

Oh no.

I wished I could blame Austin and Thatch and the stupid wine at his house, but this was all me.

All me and my stupid need to save Lucas from his parents' wrath and possibly mend my own parents' hearts in the process.

I quickly tried to think of a way I could lie my way out of it.

"Kayla, calm down."

"CALM DOWN?"

"I mean, what I mean is, you don't know all the details, and—"

"He cheated on me!" she wailed. "With our SISTER!"

Hah! Wondered what she'd do if she knew he always cheated on everyone. Would that make her feel better or worse? Decisions, decisions.

"Kayla." I wondered if the day could get any gnarlier. "Look, I can explain—why don't we meet for dinner tonight?"

Not only did I have absolutely no money, but now I'd have to sit across from my amazing sister and make her believe that I was in love with her ex-fiancé and that he'd turned over a new leaf—though none of it was actually true.

Liar. My heart thudded.

I had adored him once. Past tense. And even then it was a high school crush.

This. This is why they always tell you during all those health-class talks to never have sex. Men only complicated things. One minute you're a happy single female living in downtown Seattle, the next, you're lying to your family and planning a fake engagement while behind their back you're hoping to date the doctor who saw your parts! Ugh, ever since seeing Satan again I was going insane.

"Avery?" She sniffled. "Are you still there?"

"Yeah." Unfortunately. "Tonight, dinner, it'll be great."

"Okay."

Thank God Kayla was reasonable. Sort of. She was the nice daughter, the one who never did anything wrong and looked weird in red lipstick. She was the girl next door.

Perfect.

"Seven?" At least she wasn't yelling anymore. Or crying.

"Great." Shaking, I hung up and looked up to see a gorgeous redhead who could have been someone in my family. She grinned down at me and announced, "I'm Chelsea." Her shoulders bounced up and down as if she had so much energy it was impossible for her to be still. "You know, Lucas Thorn's Wednesday."

I glared. "Of course you are." Did everyone have to full-name him? It just reminded me of everything I wanted to forget.

She didn't seem to mind that I was pissed.

In fact, I was 99 percent sure that if I peered around the desk, I'd see a rainbow shooting out of her ass while little unicorns danced next to her in a circle singing "Kumbaya."

"You can just wait in his office," I said in a flat tone.

Her perfect straight teeth nearly sparkled as she scampered on her feet and marched into his office without me needing to point the way.

She'd been there before.

In his office.

How many times, I wondered, had he bent her over that desk. I leaned back in my chair and watched as she comfortably sat on the leather couch and pulled out her cell.

She moved out of view, so I leaned back farther.

"Something interesting, I hope?" Lucas's voice made my feet jerk up, causing my chair to fall backward.

Make that two embarrassing situations in one day.

I was on a serious roll when it came to Lucas Thorn.

Ah, now I was doing it too. Full-naming him.

Feet in the air, I let out an "oomph" before managing to get on my hands and knees and then look up at the most perfect male specimen God had ever cursed.

"Thorn." I cursed his name. As per usual. And grabbed his outstretched hand as he helped me to my wobbly feet.

With a smirk, he thrust a paper bag against my chest and leaned in. "I got you a milk shake too."

"Brings all the boys to the yard," I joked, riffing on the song.

"Funny because word on the street is that your yard's been closed . . ."

I gulped. "Chelsea's nice."

His smile faded, and he took a step back. "Yeah, yeah, she is."

"She's in your office. On your couch. Texting Barney."

"Huh?"

"She's superpeppy and kind of loud."

"You would be too if I was about to rip your clothes from your body."

My mouth dropped open.

So did his.

And then he ran a hand down his neck. "Sorry, that was uncalled for."

"Nooooo," I teased. "I'm just going to sit here and eat and not watch you cheat on your Monday, Tuesday, Thursday, Friday, and Saturday, alright?"

"Right." He didn't move.

I ignored him and started pulling the food from the bag.

I knew Lucas well enough to be aware that he wanted to say something else, but I couldn't handle any more conversation.

When Chelsea left an hour later, her hair didn't look mussed, and her skirt was on straight. I'd expected it to be backward or at least ripped.

I couldn't help it—my eyes greedily searched for any part of her that looked like Lucas had marked it. But I got nothing.

I was still staring when the elevator doors closed.

"Curious?" Lucas asked from behind me.

Straightening my shoulders, I refused to look at him and pretended to check my email. "Let me guess. You kiss her, she moans, she screams out your name, you both get your rocks off in less than a half hour—because, let's be honest, you seem to like efficiency—and you send her on her way with a nice slap on the ass."

His dark chuckle infuriated me.

Rage was good.

Anger kept me safe.

It solidified the wall between us.

He walked away.

At least I thought it was safe—thought that he'd left.

But the devil reappeared and dropped something onto my desk.

It was a gold envelope.

I peeked down at it, then shoved it to the side of the table with my pen. "What's that?"

His muscled forearms pressed against the desk, and he shrugged his massive shoulders. "Open it."

I just loved surprises, which Lucas of course knew.

So I tore into the envelope like it was my birthday and nearly cried when I saw what he'd given me.

"I know money is tight, and as far as apologies go, this is the only way I can think of to make sure you eat tonight—and maybe then you'll offer me a little bit of forgiveness for the gynecologist episode."

I smiled up at him. "This is my favorite restaurant."

"I'm aware."

"They have steak."

"Other foods too, but yes." He chuckled. "Leave early, go eat, order whatever you want."

"This gift certificate is for three hundred dollars."

"Yup."

"Lucas, that's enough food for like four really good meals."

"Yup."

"You're feeding me!" I yelled.

He looked around and then down at me, his eyes twinkling. "You had a man with surprisingly large hands stick God knows what between your legs—it's the least I can do."

Tears welled in my eyes. He was being so nice. And it was confusing. And I both hated and loved him for it.

I don't think I realized how stressed I was over the whole fake engagement scenario and the prospect of meeting up with Kayla until that moment. "Thank you."

Before I could stop myself, I stood and reached across the desk, then kissed him on the cheek.

His skin was scruffy, deliciously warm.

He swallowed slowly, his eyes locking with mine in a hazy blur of desire. "Have fun."

"Why don't you come with me? I mean, later this week or . . ."

He backed away, his smile gone. "I have to meet with Chelsea tonight, and the rest of my week is booked."

"Oh." Rejection sucked. I was in deep. Maybe I'd always been that way with Lucas, maybe I just never realized how deep until now. Regardless, the realization stung, and my pride was taking a whopping hit as he backed away farther, cursed, and then went to his office, slamming the door behind him.

One step forward. A moment when he showed me he was actually a decent human worth saving. Worth loving.

Ten giant steps back.

Chapter Twenty-Four

Avery

I figured I may as well use the gift card Lucas gave me for dinner that night—it wasn't like I had any extra money to spare, and I still had a little less than a week before I'd receive my first paycheck.

And my options for three meals a day were slowly turning into cold cereal or oatmeal or whatever was in the funky-smelling box in the back of the fridge.

Just how long could I keep Chinese takeout before eating it would kill me?

I braced myself and stopped in front of Lowell's. It was a Seattle staple and boasted everything from oysters to steak, salmon, clams . . . Well, you get the point—it had meat and fish, and that's all that really mattered.

Plus the prices weren't totally ridiculous, so I could probably stretch the gift card—unless my sister decided to order two bottles of expensive wine and drink away her sorrows.

I pressed my hands down along my short black cocktail dress and checked my red lipstick using the camera on my phone.

Stalling.

I was stalling.

But Kayla was . . . Kayla. I loved her—she was an amazing teacher and an even more amazing sister. Growing up, I'd wanted to be just like her and even tried out for cheerleading because of her. After finding out I lacked the necessary coordination, I played sports instead, favoring headbands and basketball shorts over miniskirts and makeup.

I was the black sheep. The tomboy. Now that I was older I'd ditched the basketball shorts and giant T-shirts. But every time I saw Kayla or Brooke, I felt like that teenager again, the awkward girl with braces and no fashion sense who just wished she was as pretty and smart as they were. Even though I knew I wasn't stupid, my sisters always had a way of making me feel that way when I was younger.

Kayla had never really done anything wrong, although she used to tease me a lot about my insecurities—often in front of Lucas. I pretended it didn't bother me when she giggled and asked me if I even knew what lipstick was. But her words stung.

And now I had to face her like I'd somehow won this giant prize and lie about everything. I had to pretend Lucas was the greatest— and the real sucky part? He was. I saw greatness in him still, in the small moments he tried to hide from me. But he covered it with anger—and with cheating and unnecessary meanness that threatened to choke me.

I would be defending him to the one woman who I could never measure up to.

And I had to sell it all like he loved me.

When I never stood a chance. Never would.

Shoot. I still didn't know what I was going to say.

I chewed my lower lip and quickly dialed Lucas's number, thankful that he'd actually added it to my contacts.

"Miss me already?" he crooned.

I rolled my eyes and absolutely hated that my lips curved into a happy smile while my heart did that little leap and thud against my chest. "How do I explain us?"

"Huh?"

"I may be having dinner with Kayla."

Absolute silence. And then he said, "Did you just say you're having dinner with Kayla?"

"Yes." I closed my eyes and willed my headache away. "Because your mom has a huge mouth, no offense, and doesn't understand the concept of secrecy, she mentioned something to my mom, remember? If my voice mails from my irate mother are any indication, it took your mother less than twenty-four hours to try to mend the bond between our families and plan our engagement party. You know, the one we lied about not being able to make because we're taking that trip to South America to save the children?"

"I don't recall having this conversation at all."

"Exactly!" I jabbed my finger in the air. "That's twice I've saved your reputation—you can thank me later. Actually, thank me in the form of giving me an amazing review for my internship. This is above and beyond, Thorn!"

"We're going to South America?"

"No, not really. You know what? I don't have time for this. Just tell me what I'll need to say to turn Kayla's frown upside down. I've always been awkward with her when it comes to relationships, especially with you."

He sighed. "She's *your* sister. Don't you have like magic sister-speak?"

I paused. "No, idiot, we don't! We're not exactly close. Stop asking stupid questions and just tell me what to say!"

He sighed again. "Okay, um."

"Wow, Lucas, don't talk so fast—I can't keep up!"

"Stop being such a smart-ass." I could practically hear his eyes rolling. "Okay, how about"—he sounded nervous—"how about this . . ."

"I'm waiting."

"You're also annoying, and yet here I am, talking to you."

"Thorn!'

"I've always had a thing for you." His voice was confident, smooth. "I ignored my feelings because I'd never dated anyone but Kayla, and once you and I reconnected at work, things just sort of happened. We fought it for—"

"—a day," I finished, wishing it were true and hating myself more than I cared to admit for being that weak over a man who said the same nice things to every girl he slept with during a one-week period.

"Right," he fessed up. "After all, you can't control these things, or plan for them. Some things just happen."

"Yeah." Why were my eyes welling with tears? WHY? "They do."

He coughed. "Is that good enough, Avery Bug?"

I clenched my eyes shut and opened them to see Kayla standing in front of me. "Gotta go," I said into the phone.

"Hey where are you anyway—"

I hung up and pasted a smile on my face as Kayla and I hugged awkwardly.

"Who was that?" she asked, her gaze zeroing in on the phone still clenched in my hand.

"Plumber," I announced. "Getting those pipes cleaned, and you know how I feel about tools."

Her face cracked into a smile. "You wouldn't know what to do with a wrench if it hit you in the face and came with voice-automated instructions."

I held my hands in the air. "It's not my job to wield man tools."

"So"—she shrugged and gestured at the restaurant—"this looks nice."

"It's awesome." When I looped my arm through hers, she stiffened, once again reminding me that I wasn't her favorite sister. I wasn't the one who had anything in common with her. I was the outcast, little

Avery Bug, with her sports and her braces. Pulling away would have made things more awkward, so I held my chin high as we walked into Lowell's together.

The hostess seated us at a nice table for four in the back corner, which was dark enough to cover any sort of bloodstains, in case Kayla decided to turn her steak knife on me.

She ordered a glass of wine, and I got the same thing, not because I wanted it, but so Kayla wouldn't have to drink alone.

She stared down at the table.

Kayla's reddish-blonde hair was pulled into a low, tight bun. She wore minimal makeup, and her black slacks and black blouse made her appear more sophisticated than I could ever hope to look. Even on a teacher's salary, she was dressed like some millionaire's wife out having drinks after spending all day on her veranda getting fed grapes.

"So"—she sipped her wine and stared at her fork—"you and Lucas."

Here we go.

Just say what Lucas said and explain the story, make it sound real. Except. It wasn't real. None of it.

I opened my mouth just as someone approached our table.

"We're not ready yet," I barked out without even looking up.

Whoever it was scurried away.

Kayla finally made eye contact. It killed me that her eyes were filled with tears, that I was lying to her to protect Lucas and bring our families together again—and that the mess was partially my fault. Lucas and I were in it together, but for some reason I didn't want her to think the worst of him. Memories of my time with Lucas for all of those years hit me square in the face.

It was getting harder and harder to ignore the truth of what had happened between Lucas and me.

That night, years before.

I just had no idea why it was okay for me to hate him—but nobody else.

Kayla sighed, and her lower lip wobbled. "He's a good guy," she said. "I think—I mean, he panicked. I get why. We'd been together since junior high, and he was drunk that night. I don't forgive him, but . . . Brooke even admitted that nothing happened. He stumbled into her room by accident, you know?"

I fought back a snort. "Yeah, he's . . . great." At stumbling into EVERY room.

Hell, one might even say he had a revolving door to his own room!

"We would have never worked out." She clutched the stem of her wineglass too tightly, and I was afraid she was going to either shatter the glass or spill the wine. "I know that now. Besides, we hadn't had sex in forever."

"Um, Kayla—"

"I mean, that's not normal, right?" Tears spilled onto her cheeks. "Six months! We hadn't slept together in six months. And look, I'm not blaming you, but all he wanted to do was hang out with you. You always had a soccer game, or work that he drove you to, or whatever. The whole situation isn't even a big deal anymore, but in the end you guys were like best friends. I was too busy with grad school to really notice."

I felt like I was going to puke.

Because if Kayla's memory of the no-sex timing served.

He stopped having sex with her.

The very first night we almost kissed.

But that could mean anything.

Plus between starting his new job and wedding planning, he'd probably been exhausted.

And I'd been downright terrified over all the feelings I had for him and the looks we gave each other when we hung out.

I downed the rest of my wine and nodded. "You guys were both just really busy, going in different directions."

"I need you to be honest with me, Avery." Kayla leaned forward. "Did you sleep with Lucas when we were together?"

"WHAT?" I yelled. "No, Kayla, believe me, I would NEVER have done that to you."

"So you guys never kissed or anything?"

I opened my mouth to deny it—but I hesitated. Because we had kissed, the night that changed everything. But he was drunk.

"No," I lied. Hating myself for it. Hating him all over again for breaking up my family. And to what aim? When, in the end, he simply moved on to having six or seven girls at a time and left us behind—left *me* behind.

"Don't lie to me, Avery Bug." Tears spilled onto Kayla's cheeks again.

I was just about to confess everything when, out of the corner of my eye, I saw Lucas enter the restaurant.

Kayla started to turn just as Chelsea sat down with him. Oh holy hot dog, no, no, just . . .

"OH NO!" I yelled, purposely spilling my wine all over the table.

Hopefully, the racket was loud enough to gain his attention.

And it was.

But the minute Kayla looked where I was looking, it was too late.

He was at dinner with another girl.

I was at dinner with his ex.

Oh dear.

To his credit, Lucas smiled, waved, and got up. He said something to Chelsea that I'm sure meant he'd make up for it later—in the bedroom—for having to abandon her unexpectedly and sauntered over to us while she gathered her things and left.

Damn the man. He didn't have a right to look so good in a suit jacket.

Kayla started shaking.

I wasn't sure who I felt worse for: her, Chelsea, or Satan, as he made his way toward us, his jaw twitching like he was clenching his teeth.

"Hey, um, hey there . . . baby." I choked and threw my arms around his neck.

He wheezed, coughed, then did what Lucas Thorn always does when he's cornered by a female—he kissed me.

Chapter Twenty-Five

Lucas

It was hard to feel disappointed about losing yet another one of my girls when my lips were in the process of plundering Avery's mouth—with the aid of my tongue. Ten more minutes, and I was going to be tossing her over my shoulder.

Because that's what a grown man did in fancy restaurants—screw a girl he wasn't even on a date with, against the very table where his ex-fiancée is seated.

Perfect plan.

"Chelsea works here, thus the gift card I got for you," I whispered against Avery's ear. Since I was in that general vicinity I decided a slow nibble wouldn't hurt. She let out a little squeak, tightening her arms around my neck.

It felt too real.

All of it.

And I wanted that, the realness, the feel of her body against mine, her smooth curves filling my hands, her fingers stretched across my neck—and then slowly, sadly, she pulled away and hung her head. "I missed you."

"Surprise!" I said, trying to wing it. "I figured you would come here, so I had Chelsea get me a table far enough away from the drama so I could at least intervene if need be."

"How heroic." Avery blinked and then nodded toward Kayla.

I didn't want to look at Kayla.

I didn't want to talk to her.

I didn't want to be put in a position where I had to explain myself to the very woman who I'd left at the altar—because I was in love with her little sister.

Shit.

Admitting the situation in my head was almost as bad as finally saying it out loud. I wrapped my arm around Avery and faced Kayla.

Tears streamed down her face.

I was the cause of them.

And I hated myself for it. Even if Kayla had doubts too, there was no justification for what I did to her—not that she forced me to do something as horrible as I did.

There was no justification for what I did to Kayla.

Everyone had expected us to get married. But we'd been fighting, and deep down she must have known that we'd been growing apart. That we'd stayed together out of familiarity and habit.

Even though I knew it wasn't the time to say it, she had to know, in her gut, that we would have never worked.

"Kayla, you look really good." I held out my hand. She hesitated and then sat up a little taller, taking the compliment and pressing her hand firmer against mine. I'd always hated how she shook hands. She'd always been a bit vain, needing attention and adulation to feel good about herself. I hoped that my greeting would set her at ease—and though she did look good, she didn't compare to Avery.

The breadbasket arrived.

Avery ripped into it like a hungry lion, while Kayla tore small pieces and put them on her plate, only to plop one in her mouth, chew a billion times, and finally swallow.

God, it was like seeing her for the first time—and suddenly I wondered how we'd stayed together as long as we did. So many things had started to pull us apart before we even got engaged. I'd always despised Kayla's eating habits, especially after all the fights we got into about her not eating. Back then she thought the perfect body was about being skinny, and it was apparent she hadn't changed much in that regard. I'd never noticed how thin her face was, or how clothes hung so loosely on her body. Most women would probably envy her wispy frame, but it made my fingers itch to run up and down Avery's legs, then hold her tight.

"So this is . . . so nice," Avery choked out, taking a huge sip of wine between her giant bites of bread. "Should we order?"

"YES!" I said a little too loudly.

"Look, guys"—Kayla's shoulders slumped—"I appreciate the show, but honestly this is awkward and it's not going to get better. I haven't had an appetite all day, so why don't you two just enjoy dinner tonight." She stood. "Avery, I love you. I'll talk to you later."

Her eyes locked on mine. "Lucas."

And she was gone.

I exhaled in relief while Avery pointed at the breadbasket, her mouth filled with bread, and said, "Are you going to eat that?"

"By all means, have all five pieces. It's not communal or anything," I joked as the waiter dropped off two menus.

"That was . . ." I glanced back at the door. "How is she?"

Avery made a noise. "How would you be if you dated someone for most of your life and thought it meant forever, only to find him in someone else's bed and then, plot twist." She was really tearing into that bread. "Now that she's finally over it, her goofy little sister suddenly steps in and decides she wants a piece."

I reached for a roll, but my hand was slapped away.

"No," Avery growled.

With a sigh, I leaned forward and said in a low voice, "Don't you think I know how bad it hurt? How awful it was the next day when I woke up with the hangover from hell? I never meant to hurt her. I wouldn't—look, regardless of how things were between us, the last thing she deserved was that."

A hunk of bread fell from Avery's lips. "You really mean that, don't you?"

"Of course I do." I rolled my eyes. "I'm not a complete monster— I'd think you would know me better than that." I tried to keep the hurt out of my voice, but it was impossible.

Our gazes locked.

The air was tense with all the words left unsaid.

Four years' worth of them.

I looked away, suddenly grateful for Kayla's exit.

Because it gave me time with the only girl I actually wanted to be having dinner with on a Wednesday.

Avery.

Shit. I was already in so deep, wasn't I?

I couldn't see beyond the hole I was digging for myself. The kiss had unlocked every damn thing, and the more I pushed her away, the more I hurt her. She was probably ready to strangle me half the time whenever I brought up my girls, and yet she held her head high and met me with a fierceness I found so damn irresistible and admirable that I couldn't help but crave her more.

A waiter approached.

"Steak." I winked at Avery. "Just bring us two giant steaks, mashed potatoes, the house salad, and—"

"Corn!" Avery added, shoving another piece of bread in her mouth.

"You heard the lady." I chuckled and handed him the menus.

"Would you like something to drink, sir?" he asked.

"No, I'm good." For some reason, I wanted a clear head, and after that kiss, I was already half-drunk on Avery's mouth, the same mouth she was still stuffing bread into.

I raised my eyebrows.

"I'm a nervous eater," she said defensively. "Thanks for coming by and making Kayla believe it's real, but you can run along and hang out with Chelsea, who I'm sure is pissed."

And as I often did around Avery, I felt like an ass. "Actually, she thought it was going to be a group orgy. I let her down slowly though, told her you weren't into anything sexual and still wore a training bra."

"How sweet of you." Avery kicked my foot under the table.

I winced. "That was uncalled for."

"You insulted my boobs—I'll have you know they're very sensitive."

I bit out a curse and reached for my water. She was young, inexperienced, and probably didn't intend for her words to affect me, and yet I was nursing fast-moving arousal under the table.

"That came out wrong." Her cheeks blushed bright pink.

"Funny, I'd say it came out just right." I leaned in. "Let's discuss this further."

"Aw, sorry, can't. I'm not your normal Wednesday, so no matter how this night ends, whether I'm at my place or yours—my private parts are on lockdown."

"You really need to stop drawing my attention to your breasts. Might give me the wrong idea."

She gulped, her eyes locking on my mouth. "Yeah, well, when I'm stressed I blurt out things that make no sense. You're free to ignore me the rest of the night. Say, where are we with that whole leaving and forgetting about this idea?"

"Staying." I wrapped my arm around her. "Right here."

She slumped forward. "But . . ."

"That didn't seem to go well." I changed the subject and reached for the last piece of bread.

She shrugged. "It sucked actually. At least I didn't have to defend your lifestyle and why you were sitting with another girl." She scowled as a blush heated her cheeks. "I didn't want her to look at you that way, I just . . . I mean, I hate you—you get that, right?"

"Do you?" My heart thudded slowly in my chest, waiting for her answer. "Do you really hate me so much?"

She blinked and looked down at her hands. "I want to."

"You want to hate me, but you don't."

She nodded.

"So that must mean you kind of like me?"

"What is this, middle school?"

"I wouldn't know, that was a long time ago for me, but for you—hey, wasn't that like five years—"

She smacked me in the chest. I grabbed her hand and held her sizzling fingertips against my neck until they began slowly inching up to cup my cheek. "Tell me one thing, and I want the truth, Thorn."

I sighed, body buzzing with awareness. "Okay."

She licked her pink lips, and her hand continued to move back and forth against my jaw, driving me insane with the need to kiss her. "Why did you guys stop having sex?"

My head told me to lie.

My heart told me that was all I'd been doing for the past four years.

"Because I kissed you, and I knew in that moment that if I could kiss a seventeen-year-old girl—if I looked forward to stupid things like picking you up at work or you coming to me when your boyfriend dumped you—then I was already screwed. In my mind, I was cheating. I was a cheater then, Avery. I'm a cheater now. At least now I admit it. When I was with Kayla . . . all I wanted. Was. You."

Avery kissed me.

I swallowed her moan as I tangled my hands in her hair and gripped her head, deepening the kiss by sucking on her tongue while she tried to crawl into my lap.

"We'll"—I broke off the kiss, then went in for another—"get it to go?"

She nodded and kissed me again, and when Avery pulled back, her green eyes sparkled. I knew in that moment, the connection had never just been a crush.

I hadn't kissed her four years ago because it was wrong and felt good.

Or forbidden.

Illegal.

Or even stupid.

It's because what we had between us was real. The most real thing I'd ever experienced with anyone.

Only now?

I had nothing holding me back, except for the guilty feeling in the back of my head that told me—even if she gave me her heart, I'd never be able to give her mine. Not when so many other women currently had a piece of it.

Chapter Twenty-Six

AVERY

I used to make fun of this kind of girl.

The one who threw caution to the wind and made a poor life choice and then cried into a box of Lucky Charms when the guy ended up being a total asshole.

And even though I knew the ending long before it happened, I couldn't help but make the same stupid choice.

Kiss him again.

And again.

And again.

Until my lips were swollen from the friction of his, until my greedy hands were burned by the scruff on his cheeks.

I craved more of him.

And sadly, pathetically, I always had. And probably always would.

That's the thing about crushes—if you're lucky, they go away and you find someone so incredible that the whole crush is laughable, a distant memory you think about or maybe dream about once every three years after having too much sangria.

But the crush I'd had on Lucas?

It had always been more.

It went from being a crush, to hero worship, to him being my best friend—and the minute we locked eyes that fateful day on his couch?

I knew it could be more.

If my sister—my adorable, amazing older sister—hadn't been standing in the way. With a ring on her finger.

Did that make me just as bad as Lucas?

Just as guilty?

Did that mean I was a cheater too?

No! A voice screamed in my head, or maybe it was just my heart yelling as loud as it could. My sister had lost Lucas. Ignored Lucas. She hadn't been thankful for what was right in front of her—and their relationship ended.

This was different.

I was an adult.

So was he.

We didn't need permission to actually follow through with what everyone else already assumed was happening.

Right?

My head hurt just thinking about it. His mouth met mine again and again, and the scent of his body hung in the air as I clutched the front of his shirt and tried not to be "that" girl in the back of the cab who straddles the dude before they even make it to his apartment.

By the time we made it into his building's elevator, both of us were breathing heavily, and the guilt at what I was doing had somehow transformed into this white-hot need to strip every inch of his clothing from his hot man-candy body and see if I could make him tremble beneath my touch—the way I did beneath his.

Five steps to his door.

Still. No talking.

It opened.

The lock clicked shut.

Darkness enveloped the entire apartment—the only light was the moon as it glowed across the Sound and stretched through the floor-to-ceiling bay windows.

And still no talking.

It wasn't an uncomfortable silence, which should have been my first clue that this wasn't a one-night stand or a test to see if we were compatible.

This was Lucas and me following through with something we both had wanted a long time ago—something that we were never allowed to have because of factors that felt beyond our control. And something that involved feelings neither of us had ever admitted to out loud.

Until now.

My heart kept trying to remind me that there were other women, that he'd cheated on my sister, that this too was cheating—that I wasn't different because tomorrow he'd be with someone else.

But stupidly, like I said, I was becoming the girl—the girl who did bad things, the girl who was convinced that she was different, that she was the game changer.

My mind reacted to that possibility in a completely logical way by reminding me of his calendar—of who he'd been on a date with just before he kissed me.

Warm hands cupped my shoulders and then slowly made their way down to my wrists. "You're so soft."

I leaned my head back against his chest. "What's happening?"

"I stopped asking that the minute you kissed me back. Figured it would be better for my sanity."

"So you admit this is insane, right?"

"Right."

Protect your heart, protect your heart! Don't be that girl, don't be that girl! My brain screamed, and my heart thudded wildly. I turned in his arms. "I'll be your Wednesday, but only for this week, only for tonight.

And then this is over with, whatever this is, whatever itch that needs scratching or desire that needs to be fulfilled. Once I walk out that door, we go back to hating each other and under no circumstances do we ever discuss it. Ever."

Say no. Please say no.

Give me more than one day.

Be different.

Let this be the game changer.

Instead, Lucas's expression turned cold as he whispered the word. "Okay."

I wasn't different.

I was going to be just like the others, desperate for him, thrown aside when the sun rose the next morning.

One night.

It was all I needed anyway, right? It's not as if he was going to really commit to me, marry me, offer to impregnate me and father all our children.

"Are you sure about this, Avery?" He cupped my face with his rough hands. "You still have a choice. You can turn that cute ass around and march out that door—hell, you can even slam it on the way out. I'll even let you keep the steak."

"Are you offering me an out?"

He nodded.

"Do you offer that to every girl?"

Another nod.

"Do they ever take it?"

"Sometimes."

"What do you want me to do?"

He paused. "You know, nobody has ever asked me that before."

Probably because nobody cared about what else he had to offer besides what was dangling between his legs.

"I'm asking. Right now." I wrapped my arms around his neck. "What does Thorn want?"

"You didn't full-name me."

"It seems to make you even more arrogant, God forbid."

His grin made me weak, so weak that I had to hold on to him for strength. Funny how things come full circle. How he'd always been my rock.

Dependable.

Loving.

And now?

He held all the power. Lucas Thorn . . . could destroy me.

"Stay." He brushed a soft kiss across my lower lip. "I want you to stay."

Chapter Twenty-Seven

Lucas

She asked me what I wanted—and meant it. But she'd also taken my heart and beat it against the door, stomped on it for good measure, then shoved it back into my chest with a smile on her face.

She wasn't like my other women.

Not at all.

But I didn't want her to be, and it pissed me off that she was categorizing herself the exact same way—like she was planning sex, like she was just another freaking day of the week.

All I had to do was look in the mirror to know whose fault that was.

And all I had to do was tell her no—in order to fix it.

But I'd always been selfish—once a cheater, always a cheater, right? Only this time, this time it really did feel wrong.

This felt like cheating.

I wasn't cheating her.

I was cheating *us*.

And when the idea of cheating suddenly transformed into something plural, like an "us"—that's when you were in the wrong, that's when you fought like hell. So I decided to give her this night, I decided to do the wrong thing—in hopes of doing the first right thing I'd ever done.

I'd hold her in my arms.

I'd kiss her lips, draw out each moan and scream, and if she tried to leave me, I'd simply chain her to my bed and provide enough food and water for her to survive until she agreed to be with me for longer than a twenty-four-hour period.

Okay, so it wasn't a solid plan.

But it was all I had.

And because of my lifestyle I knew if I told her she was different, she'd want to believe me but wouldn't be able to—and seeing the doubt in her eyes would hurt me as badly as her asking for one day had when what I wanted to give her was a week, a year, a lifetime.

Something bad was happening to me.

Either I had a tumor in my chest.

Or my heart was . . . beating.

Hell, I knew it had been there all along—it just needed a conniving little snot to weasel her way inside and clang around a bit with a hammer. It needed Avery.

"Come on"—I kissed her nose—"I have something to show you."

Avery rolled her eyes. "Does that work on the other girls too?"

"I rarely have to say that, usually they just strip me at the door and—"

Avery covered my mouth with her hand and shook her head. "Not helping your case."

I moved her hand and kissed her palm, and her breath hitched when my lips touched her skin. "I was kidding."

"Too soon," she said with a breathy sigh.

I led her by the hand down the hall and into my bedroom. "Go ahead, ask me."

Avery gazed at the large bed and then the window and then back at me. "Who's your decorator?"

"Avery Bug, come on—ask me."

"How many women?" she blurted. "How many women have been in that bed?" It killed me that she had to squeeze her eyes shut as if she was expecting the number to be such a blow that she couldn't look at me when I confessed it.

"One." I kissed her forehead. "Though last time she was in it, she was really cranky, drunk, made fun of my pancakes, and threatened my life."

"She sounds awesome. Can I have her number?" Avery grinned up at me.

"She's alright I guess."

"I bet she has amazing boobs and knows how to moonwalk, and can eat an entire block of cheese within a ten-hour period."

"One *whole* block?" I repeated.

"With wine," she added with a smile and then looked back at the bed. "Any reason why no other girl has been in here?"

"Easy." I shrugged. "This is the only part of me that's for me."

Avery reached for my hand, then squeezed it. "I think this is the part where I say I'm honored that you're sharing your eight-hundred-thread-count sheets with me, but I can't quite manage to choke out a thank-you before sex."

"I'll expect one after." I chuckled. "Or you could just tell me to go to hell and run out the door."

There it was again.

The push.

We did banter well—I made her think I didn't care, and she treated me like a disease—and yet when we connected, we felt it. Words can lie, and the words said between Avery and me? Absolutely necessary to avoid the truth of our touch.

A touch can't lie.

A touch may as well be a confession—and in that confession, you have no choice but to acknowledge the truth.

"I think you better kiss me right now." Avery stood on her tiptoes and brushed her lips across my chin. "Before I say more stupid things or just bail on you altogether."

"We're doing this." I wasn't sure if I should be excited, elated, or disappointed that she wasn't telling me to go to hell when, according to her, I'd be seeing another girl in less than twenty-four hours.

"It's not cheating if you know." She repeated those same damn words I'd told her less than a week ago. And I only had myself to blame. Funny, when I said them I'd meant them. Truly believed that if you were that transparent, then it really wasn't a bad thing. Everyone wins.

Until now.

I'd never been on the receiving end, and it hurt.

It cut deep.

Because if she left my bed to warm someone else's, I'd end up in prison.

Another kiss to my chin and then my lips. I knew I should push her away—we needed to have the dreaded talk, we needed to . . . I let out a moan as her hands fumbled with the buttons of my shirt.

"What are you doing?" I asked, gently grasping her wrists.

"Taking your clothes off, Thorn. Why? You got a problem with that?"

"Are you going to mount me if I do?" I teased.

Her scowl deepened while her face flushed bright red. "I guess I brought that on myself."

"Yes." Still holding her wrists, I backed her up against the bed until she had no choice but to fall backward onto the pillows. I straddled her and pinned her arms above her head. "Now, why don't you let me kiss you first? It's only polite before you start pulling my clothes off."

She nodded and swallowed as I lowered my head to hers. We were a breath apart.

Chapter Twenty-Eight

AVERY

Bad idea.

    Bad idea.

    Good.

    Oh my hell.

    Was that his tongue?

    So.

    Knees buckling, I held on to his firm body to keep myself from collapsing against him.

    Good.

    I shivered as the aching tension between us intensified past anything I had ever experienced.

    Why hadn't I jumped into his bed before? This was a splendid idea. His lips trailed up and down my neck, causing me to shiver, and then his fingers moved to my dress and tugged it down my shoulders. My flesh was too sensitive for words, and that was just from kissing.

    Something about the way his lips caressed my body—something about the way he held me—signaled what we were about to do was a way bigger deal than anything he had with his other girls.

    Was this how he treated all of them?

With awestruck worship?

Because it could get addictive—his touch wasn't like anything I'd ever experienced. You know it's bad when the way someone touches you alters the way you feel about yourself. No longer was I the young, inexperienced brat he'd grown up with.

In Lucas Thorn's arms, I, Avery Black, was a woman.

"You're shivering." His lips nibbled mine before he took a step backward and pulled his shirt off over his head.

I sucked in a breath. "Can you do that again? Maybe slower next time?"

His lips spread into a wide, arrogant smile. "That depends. Will you gasp louder next time?"

"Ladies don't gasp, and if they do, a true gentleman wouldn't point it out." My lips were moving, but my eyes were locked on his insane chest.

"Good thing," he said as he took a step toward me, "I'm not a gentleman."

"Good thing," I repeated, my voice sounding airy, nervous as he very slowly snaked his right arm around the back of my neck and tugged me forward against his solid wall of muscle and heat.

With a moan, I pressed an openmouthed kiss to his chest. "I may just hang out here for a bit."

I could feel his chuckle against my mouth—I hated how good the vibrations felt. I hated how they made my heart pick up speed, and how warmth spread from my head all the way down to my toes when his grip on my body tightened possessively. I hated all of it.

Not.

"You know this has to be the slowest seduction ever," he grumbled. "I've been waiting years to see you naked, and you nearly pass out when I take off my shirt."

"Years?" My ears perked up. I waited for details while his hands ran down my back, his fingers locating the zipper to my dress and pulling it.

"Years," he repeated. "Years."

"You've said that twice—no, three times." Cold air hit my back as Lucas slid my dress all the way down.

Lucas stepped back and cursed. "Oh, Avery, the things I'm going to do to you."

I gulped.

His eyes seemed to darken as if a switch had been flipped. I was in his territory, where he ruled—and I had no idea how to proceed.

The last time I had sex hadn't been so great.

It was rushed.

It was a blur.

It was messy.

Awkward.

Embarrassing.

I left with one sock.

"Tell me if I hurt you," he warned, his voice on edge like he was about to pounce or something—and then, with a wicked grin, he charged me, gripped me by the hips, and flung me farther up on the bed.

Like he was a freaking superhuman.

I'd love to say being manhandled was horrible. *Lucas Thorn, boo, you suck in bed—well, may as well make my grocery list while he does what guys do.*

Nope.

False.

I bounced once.

"Don't move."

I licked my lips and watched in utter fascination as black slacks fell to the floor.

He made black boxer briefs look too sexy. But of course he did.

And then he tilted his head and ran one hand up my right leg, pulling my thong down with his fingers before tossing it on the floor. I hadn't worn a bra with my dress, so now I was naked.

What happened to fast?

Like, *Oh look—let's take off our clothes, have sex, and get the awkward staring at each other part over with?*

He didn't do fast.

His hand slid up my right leg again, and then the man hooked my leg up on his shoulder and flashed me a cocky grin. "You're gorgeous."

I would have argued, but I had no voice.

We locked eyes.

And I almost passed out when he lowered his head. I opened my mouth, assuming he was going to kiss me.

"Thorn!" I yelled. "Totally not necess—" Words. I lost them completely as he pressed his lips at my center and swirled his tongue. Warmth pooled where he was kissing, and my entire body went red-hot and then cold again, only to get hotter and hotter as he worked magic that mere mortals with penises should never possess! I accidentally smacked his head and used the opportunity to grab a fistful of his hair. At the moment holding on for dear life and trying not to lose my mind while he devoured every inch of me like I was his own brand of chocolate seemed like a good choice.

His head popped up. "You were saying?"

"Nothing." I sighed, aching for more of what he'd just been doing. "Absolutely nothing. I'm silent. Mute." I released his hair and sucked in a breath as his eyes locked on mine.

"Well, we don't want that either." He disappeared again.

My muscles flexed, contracted. He added fingers to his tongue until I felt so thoroughly worked over, I was certain I would explode. Fire raced through my veins and gathered where he was sucking and licking and thrusting with his fingers. The room dimmed, and I realized I'd forgotten to breathe. When I gulped in air, my arms and legs went numb and tingly. Is that what Lucas Thorn did? He gave women strokes in the bedroom?

I released his head a second time as a white-hot sensation rushed over my lady bits, slamming into me in rapid succession. I let out a scream. "THORN!"

He said my name against my skin, sent a vibration through me, giving the impression that I had the most beautiful name in the world. He murmured it once more, and little aftershocks rocked me.

I became lost in my own desire again.

I was happy to stay there forever.

Or until he got tired.

Amazingly, the man's mouth was good for something. "Thorn!"

I needed him to stop.

Or keep going.

Or just give me a two-second time-out before I lost my mind. Just when I felt like I couldn't take any more of his moves, he jerked away from me and said gruffly, "I can't take it anymore."

"Oh thank God!" I reached for his head the minute he reached for mine, our mouths fused together in a frenzy of tongue sucking and near teeth knocking. I tasted what had to be me on his lips, and it only made me want him more. In the hazy distance I recalled this was Thorn. Lucas Thorn. Someone who'd broken my sister's heart, someone who cheated, someone who was bad, but was still so, so, so good . . .

There was something oddly arousing about the sound of our kissing, of our bodies hitting the sheets, crumpling them.

Lucas groaned as I jerked his briefs violently down his legs and kicked them off the rest of the way.

"What? No more patience?" he teased between searing kisses.

"No." I kissed him harder, my hands digging into his muscular back as our bodies rubbed against one another. Fierce, aching need between my thighs drove my hips upward, pressing against his thigh.

I could kiss him all night long.

And not get tired of it.

But I suddenly wanted more.

His cheek rubbed against my face as he cupped my breast. "I didn't even spend any time—"

"Not now!" I smacked his hand away, my body dying for the release his mouth had earlier promised.

"Sorry!" He gripped my ass and pulled me to my knees. "I got distracted."

"No more!" I shoved his chest.

He let out a rough exhale and then chuckled. "Angry makeup sex, and we haven't even been fighting . . . incredible."

"If you want to tie me up, just say it. Otherwise, get on with it." I winked and then wrapped my arms around his neck; my legs followed as I straddled him on the bed. Desperation burst through me. My already sensitive nipples hardened as they brushed against his chest, and chills spread outward, raising goose bumps all over my body.

"If I knew it would make you stay I probably would," he admitted. The smile fell from his face briefly before he let out a moan and touched his forehead against mine, then pushed his erection against my thigh. "I need to be inside you, I need to feel you."

I nodded as searing waves of anticipated pleasure throbbed at my core.

"Avery—" He groaned again as I ground against his hips, easing some of the craving between my legs.

"Yes?"

"Just"—his breath hitched—"just tell me if it hurts."

I silenced him with my mouth, hoping to end that certain conversation about my past sexual experience. Then I shocked myself by guiding him exactly where I needed him to be, not that a man like *him* needed help.

I just wanted to be in control of it.

Because that would end up protecting me, right?

Protection! Oh God!

"THORN!" I wriggled away from his hard length even as my body protested the move with a surge of pulsing desire. "Condom," I gasped, feeling like a complete tease.

"Shit." He stared at me in horror. "Avery, I completely forgot."

Part of me deflated just a little, but I didn't ask if that happened often. I did notice he was shaking when I pulled away so he could walk over to the nightstand.

I was ready to die.

I wanted him that badly.

"Could you walk any slower?" I demanded, my body twitching with anticipation.

He burst out laughing. "I figured it was better this way." Seriously, an ant carrying a picnic basket could have walked faster. His eyes lit up with amusement. "You know, to make you so desperate for me that it consumes you the way it's consuming me—the way it's consumed me ever since you walked that tight ass into my office."

I gasped, more turned on than I'd ever been in my entire life, damn him.

"So, yeah, I'll walk slower." He pulled a foil packet out of the nightstand and walked toward me. The foil crinkled as he tore it open. "I'll go as slow as I can because a woman like Avery Black should be savored."

I gulped.

I knew he shouldn't say things like that to me.

Tenderness made me want what wasn't mine.

He made me want more than Wednesday.

My eyes filled with tears, and I looked away and forced my emotions out of the situation, which just meant later I was going to end up crying into a box of chocolates while I dipped a serving spoon into a carton of rocky road.

He leaned over the bed and kissed me, and then very slowly pushed me back against the mattress. His hands grabbed mine as he pressed openmouthed kisses to my neck, his tongue making trails down my jaw, until he nudged my knees wider apart and I felt him press into me, stretching me, filling me.

It felt familiar.

It felt right.

Like coming home.

Chapter Twenty-Nine

LUCAS

It felt wrong.

Because of how right it felt.

With other women, I was easily able to objectify the situation—to go to that place in my head where, in each instance, I truly convinced myself we were in a mutually beneficial relationship that meant I pleased her, she pleased me, and eventually we both moved on.

I was a jackass.

And the minute I felt Avery's tight body surrounding mine—I knew.

This would end badly.

Sex would change us.

I would break her heart.

Logically, that meant I needed to stop.

I tried pulling back, but the vixen hooked her feet behind me, trapping me in the most perfect hell I'd ever experienced, where the heat from her tight walls nearly suffocated me—brought me sweet death and then constricted, releasing me, only to tighten again. And from the look on her face, she was doing it on purpose. Tightening and releasing, tightening and releasing, building a rhythm I became driven to match. Looser . . . press forward, tighter . . . pull back. In and out. I was past that point of no return, past rational thinking and into straight-up pleasure.

So I stayed.

I tried to control it.

But the thing about sex—when it's with someone you have feelings for, you can't hold back.

She moaned.

We locked eyes.

I thrust harder.

She groaned louder.

Her lips parted.

I captured her mouth, my body slamming into hers in a punishing thrust as I gripped her hips and kissed her, bruised her mouth in an effort to make sure she never forgot it was me, it was us—together.

"Thorn—"

I pulled back and clenched my teeth in an effort to make the moment last longer—you'd think with all the sex I'd had, it would have been a simple matter of control.

But that's another thing—when you're with the right woman, you can't help it.

One last thrust, and she clawed at my back and screamed my name so loud that I was pretty sure the neighbors were going to complain.

Release exploded through me with Avery Black's name on my lips. I lowered my head and fused my mouth to hers, swallowing her cries as she contracted around me.

My heart would never be the same.

Because when we both pulled away from one another, I could have sworn I saw her grab the still beating vessel from my chest and hold it in the palm of her hands.

Without her—I felt empty.

Or maybe I'd always been that way.

The moment was crushed when she burst into tears.

I was still inside her.

And she was crying.

"Did I hurt you?" I tried to sound gentle rather than horrified that I might have harmed her physically.

Her answer was to shake her head and cry harder. Tears streamed down her cheeks to her swollen lips—and damn, I knew she was crying, but could she have looked any more beautiful?

"Avery, you gotta help me out. I don't know how to fix it if you don't tell me what's wrong." I wiped her tears away with both of my thumbs and waited.

She sniffled. "I kind of wish you were a jackass right now. Quick, do you think you can go back to being really insulting?"

"I'm still inside you. We just had sex," I said slowly. Incredible, brain-numbing, heart-stopping, wanna-do-it-again-soon sex. "And you want me to . . . insult you?"

She nodded quickly and then pounded a fist against the mattress. "Damn it, Thorn!" Her eyes widened. "Insult me!"

"You're, um"—I coughed—"short?"

Avery flicked my nipple.

"Hey!" I swatted her hand away. "What the hell kind of postcoital ritual is this?"

With a grin, she shrugged. "I just needed a reminder."

"A reminder," I repeated. "Of how to inflict pain on me?"

"No." Her expression sobered. "That I'm not different."

"This is a fun game, Avery Bug, really, talking in circles and then hitting me every time I do exactly as you say . . ."

"Never mind." She waved me away. "Also, you're really heavy."

"It's called muscle." I rolled my eyes as I pulled away from her and dropped back against the feather pillows. I thrust my hands behind my head to keep myself from grabbing her again and asking for another round.

Asking.

Since when had I ever asked?

"Thorn?"

"Hmm?"

Avery scooted toward me until her face was in the crook of my arm, her hand pressed against my chest. "Will you do me a favor?"

"Depends. Will you tell me why you cried?"

"I'm a girl."

"Woman," I corrected. "And what's this favor you speak of?"

"Can we have steak in bed?"

"As opposed to the table?" I smiled, unable to help it. "Oh, I see what this is—you like all your meat in bed."

A pillow pummeled my face, once, twice.

Laughing, I grabbed it and let it fly against her face.

She cursed. "THORN!"

"Ah, there it is. You know how many times you screamed my name during—"

The pillow cut me off, and then I found myself getting strangled by a curvy vixen who, not five minutes ago, had been sobbing in my arms.

I liked her this way better.

"Are you trying to beat me up?" I burst out laughing. "And stop squirming if you don't want to end up tied to this bed, Avery."

Her eyes lit up.

I groaned.

"What?" She lifted a shoulder and gave me a coy look. "I bet you tie good knots."

"Hmm, maybe after we eat the steak?" I was about ready to beg for her body, when she hopped out of bed and grabbed my shirt from the floor.

"I agree to these terms."

I quickly disposed of the condom and wrapper, then pulled on my briefs, only to see her staring at me, jaw nearly hitting the floor.

"Avery?" I snapped my fingers in front of her. "Steak?"

Her eyes never left my cock. "I could just eat you." And then slowly, her gaze lifted to my face and she winked. "But steak first."

"Tease." My body strained toward her.

She shrugged and skipped out of the room, leaving me too aroused and confused for my own damn good.

Chapter Thirty

AVERY

Be normal. No sweat. I could totally be normal after having the best mind-blowing sex of my life. Admittedly, that wasn't saying much, given my lone previous disaster in the sack, but that was already ancient history, and my body was still overheating at the memory of his hands, my hips, or his mouth.

That.

Mouth.

I took a deep breath and braced my body against the kitchen sink. All I needed was air, just a bit of air, and I'd be totally fine.

Air and steak.

In that order.

The microwave dinged.

But when I turned around to bolt toward the food, Lucas was already there, pulling out the plate, serving it up for both of us—nearly naked.

His body glistened—seriously, it glowed with a mixture of sweat and awesomeness.

How did I get myself in this situation?

Oh, right, it all started with wine.

Most poor life choices start and end with alcohol.

But tonight?

I was completely sober.

And I had still jumped into bed with the devil. What was worse? I enjoyed it.

"Avery"—Lucas didn't look up from the steak—"you've been staring at me for a good four minutes, and it's starting to freak me out, even if it is a bit flattering. You keep eying the knife too, so could you move that sweet ass over here and eat before I use the plate as a cock shield?"

Rolling my eyes, I moseyed over to him in what I thought was a sexy, confident stroll.

Fake it 'til you make it.

Don't cry.

I was torn between wanting more of him and making up some lame excuse about being sick so I could make a run for it.

One session in his arms was incredible.

But two? Two would be like poison.

Suicide.

Another round would kill me.

I was sure of it.

I'd be down for the count.

Lucas patted the barstool next to him. I climbed up onto it and inhaled the aroma of steak, closing my eyes as the scent of pepper and spices filled my nostrils.

A fork was placed in my hand. I opened my eyes. "You're giving me weapons?"

"Just be careful where you point the sharp points, Avery Bug." He winked.

I grinned and stabbed a piece of meat, then shoved it into my mouth. The steak, even though it was reheated, was amazing.

"So . . ." Lucas ate a bite.

I ate a bite.

It felt normal.

Push it away, Avery, he doesn't want normal.

He wants a different girl every night. The steak almost got stuck in my throat—I had to chug water to wash it down.

"So . . ." I licked my lips.

Lucas's eyes darted to one corner of my mouth. He leaned forward and wiped it with his fingers. "You always were a messy eater."

"I embrace food the way most people embrace life—with extreme purpose and vigor."

His sexy mouth twitched, and then he was full on smiling. "I like that."

"Well, I like food." I shrugged.

His hands moved down my arms, then back up, then down. The tension was so thick it was hard to breathe.

"Fuck it." He slammed his mouth against mine and lifted me by the ass off the chair and placed me on the counter. I bit back a hiss as my skin came into contact with cold granite.

Lucas ripped open the shirt.

A button flew past my ear and made a pinging noise as it landed.

It was five seconds.

Before I felt him inside me again.

Before he was yelling my name—before I was maiming his back with my fingernails and begging for more.

When I almost slid off the counter because I was trying to get a better angle, he lifted me in the air and walked us over to the couch, then bent me over it, only to apologize for being so rough.

I was too busy kissing him to care.

Too busy tasting him and hating myself for letting it happen again.

When I'd promised myself it would only be once.

When I'd promised myself that I wouldn't be one of those girls.

It was over too quick.

Sweat dripped from his head onto my chest; both of us out of breath, we stared at one another—the gap of silence was deafening.

I waited for it.

"Sorry," I whispered. "For the scratches."

"Believe me when I say"—his voice was hoarse—"I didn't feel a damn thing."

"Oh?" I teased.

"You know what I mean." His tone turned serious, and then he paled and pulled away from me. "Avery, we need to talk about this—"

"Nope." I shook my head way too many times. "No talking, remember? We agreed not to talk about it."

"But—"

"You know what? I think I should go. It's late and"—I yawned—"you have a big day tomorrow because it's Thursday . . ."

"Avery—"

"And Thursday's—"

"I have a feeling my Thursday isn't going to work out anymore." He crossed his arms.

"Sad for you." My fake laugh needed work. "But anyways, I'm just going to—"

Lucas swept me up into his arms and carried me to the bedroom. I banged his back the entire way with my fists.

"Put me down!"

"There." He tossed me onto the bed and crossed his arms. "You're staying the night."

"Lucas." Why was he being so nice! I needed the jackass more than air right now. "It's fine; just treat me like you treat them."

His nostrils flared as he joined me on the bed, flipped me over onto my stomach, and slapped my ass. Hard. "If you ever compare yourself to another girl again, I'm going to leave a mark."

"Thorn!" I yelled. "I'm not a child!"

He laughed. "Oh, I know."

"Hell, if you weren't such an arrogant ass, I'd maybe actually admit that you were superhot right now, all dominant and such."

"Well, my life purpose has been met—you called me hot."

"You know you're hot, that's the problem."

"Or the solution? It's all in how you see things, Avery Bug."

I rolled my eyes and willed the smile away from my face. The last thing that man needed was encouragement. "If I stay, I need to shower."

He rolled off the bed and held out his hand. "Follow me."

Chapter Thirty-One

Lucas

"Hey." Avery sniffled—her eyes were watery, her smile nonexistent. "Mom just wanted to know if you needed anything before the rehearsal dinner tonight."

"Avery Bug." I opened the screen door and leaned against it. "What happened?"

"I hate men. Except you, Grandpa, and my dad. Well, I guess I like your dad too, and my dog is amazing—at least he doesn't run around humping random girl dogs like that bastard son of a . . ." She burst into tears. "I'm sorry. Ugh, it's the day before your wedding and—" She wiped her eyes and forced a smile. "See? Totally fine. So do you need anything? I can go to Starbucks for you. Run some errands. Do you have your tux?"

I frowned. "Avery?"

She blinked up at me.

"Did your mom really send you?"

"I believe her words were 'Leave the house before you upset your sister again,'" Avery said in a wobbly voice.

I snorted. Unbelievable. I loved her mom—hell, I loved their entire family. But Kayla had a tendency to make everything about her, especially *lately, and with the wedding so close she'd turned into a bitch. Especially to Avery.*

Damn it. I was literally five minutes away from calling the entire marriage off. But people were already here for the wedding, and what was I supposed to do? Tell Kayla that it just didn't feel right? That I didn't feel the same way I used to?

That I felt more connected to Avery than to her?

That whenever Avery smiled at me, it made my day?

That when Kayla told me she didn't have time for me, a giant weight lifted from my shoulders and my first instinct was to call Avery?

Yeah, I was sure all that would go over like a car wreck.

With a sigh, I opened the screen door and Avery came barreling into my arms, all snot and tears.

My heart sank when she started crying harder. "It's not even that I was in love with him—but he cheated on me with Desiree! Austin saw them making out last night at Taco Bell."

I smirked. Oh, to be in high school again. "Avery, do you really want a guy that makes out with some girl at Taco Bell, of all places?"

She pulled back and grinned up at me. "You know how I feel about food, Thorn. But Taco Bell?" She scrunched up her nose. "Where's the decorum? The class? As in 'No, you may not kiss my mouth while you eat that taco!'"

"That's a girl." I burst out laughing and pulled her in for a hug again. "I promise that one of these days you're going to find someone that sees your true worth, and he's not going to cheat on you." My entire body tensed. Because it would never be me.

"Swear?"

"Swear." I kissed the top of her head, itching to bring my lips lower. Her beautiful green eyes blinked up at me. She was so trusting, so unaware of the battle that raged within me.

Wanting to do the right thing.

When the wrong thing looked so damn good.
Time stood still in that moment.
Again.
Because I was touching her, and my body wanted more.
She clung to my shirt.
Just seventeen. She wouldn't be eighteen for a few more days.
"Let's hang out for a bit," I encouraged—well aware that I was adding kindling to the already growing flame. And when she skipped ahead of me into my parents' house, I saw her as more than a passing flirtation.
I saw her as my future.
The day before I was supposed to say "I do"—to her sister.

◆ ◆ ◆

"Thorn!" Avery slapped me across the cheek. "Swear to the steak gods that if you snore one more time, I'm suffocating you with your boxers!"

My vision was blurry from sleep—and my breathing out of control from the dream I'd had. "Huh?"

"You. Dead. Steak gods. Boxers," Avery grumbled, tucking her body next to mine. "And for the record, I'm only cuddling because you're a coldblooded psychopath who clearly doesn't believe in heat!"

I glanced at the clock. "Why? Why are you yelling at me at three in the morning? Is this what living with you is like? Waking up with screaming? About hell? Threatening talk about killer food?"

"Huh? Killer food?"

"Death," I said in a gravelly voice. "Steak?"

"Go to sleep, Thorn."

"I *was* asleep," I grumbled. "Until a little hellion woke me up."

She yawned. "Stop complaining. Now go back to being my human blanket."

I fell asleep with Avery in my arms.

And a smile on my face.

It was a first because—though Avery didn't know it—I never slept with girls.

I had sex with them.

I never slept with them.

I never held them and allowed myself to imagine anything past the twenty-four hours we spent together.

It was a first since Kayla.

But with Kayla it hadn't felt this way.

Not at all.

I was . . . happy.

◆ ◆ ◆

My alarm went off too early. I begged for time to go in reverse.

I rubbed my face and wiped the grit from my eyes, then glanced at a sleeping Avery. Her mouth was open, and she had one leg spread across my legs, the other touching the other side of the bed. Apparently, she slept like she ate—with abandon.

"Avery Bug," I whispered, "time to get up."

"Sleep." She shook her head.

"I wish," I confessed. "But we have to work."

At the mention of work, she bolted out of bed and nearly fell backward against my window. She righted herself with the curtains, only to have them break and fall against the floor while she still clung to the fabric.

"Oops," she whispered groggily. "Sorry, I don't wake up well."

"Obviously." I pointed at my poor abused curtains.

She dropped the fabric, stepped over the rod, and nodded repeatedly at me. "Well, I guess it's Thursday."

"It is." I tried not to grin. Why was she nodding so much?

"And"—she held out her hand—"I will now bid you farewell."

I smirked. "Tell me how much you hate yourself for saying 'bid' and 'farewell' in the same sentence."

"So, so much." Her cheeks reddened. "Now shake on it."

"What exactly are we shaking on?"

"No discussing last night, ever."

I stood toe to toe with her, chest to chest. "I think I'll pass, but thanks for the offer."

"YOU PROMISED!"

"You're the one who has a problem with it. Not me."

"But—"

"I'm thinking I may redecorate my office with pictures of your ass. Hey, I know, a screen saver of you in nothing but my shirt—"

"You are seriously the devil!" She clenched her fists and with jerky movements tried to put on her dress. "I can't believe I thought this would be kept between us."

"It will be," I said smoothly.

She paused. "Then what—"

"I'm just making the point that the minute you walk out this door, there will be another time when we will discuss this—and, Avery?"

"What?" She gritted her teeth.

"You will be in my bed again before this week's over."

"Don't hold your breath."

I shrugged.

"You're a menacing man whore! I refuse to sleep with you after you've stuck your . . ." She screwed up her face and pointed at my dick. "Business all over town."

"I'm hurt." I really was, but I wasn't going to let her see it. "And why do you care? Didn't you say only one day?" I had her there.

"Exactly." She nodded. "One day."

My phone buzzed in my pocket.

"Well . . ." I grinned as I read the short message. "Look at that. The universe is even on my side. I don't have a Thursday anymore." Nothing like being dumped via text.

"But . . ."—her eyes narrowed—"are you tricking me?"

"You know what sounds fantastic?" I ignored her anger. "A hamburger, say, tonight?"

"YOU HORRIBLE HUMAN BEING!" she shouted. "How dare you lure me into your bed with beef!"

"And extra cheese. I'm thinking . . ." I tapped my chin, trying to think of her favorite. "Swiss?"

Her mouth dropped open.

"Extra fries."

She glanced down. "Does this meal include fry sauce?"

"Do I look like I'm insane? Of course it includes sauce."

She cleared her throat, put her hands on her hips, then smoothed down her dress, only to then put her hands on her hips again. "Pick me up at seven."

It was cute as hell how she tried to stomp by me, stopped, backed up, and then very innocently stood up on her tiptoes and kissed me on the cheek. "Thanks for the steak."

I felt the buzz from that kiss hours later when I was in my office, and later that afternoon when I was staring at my phone and the five missed calls from my mother—the buzzing finally stopped.

Mom: PROBLEM.

Chapter Thirty-Two

AVERY

"I slept with the devil," I whispered as I cupped my hand over Austin's ear and prayed she wouldn't repeat what I'd just said in the packed Starbucks.

"Huh?" Her eyes narrowed as she looked back and forth between me and her ever-present iPhone, which was lighting up with a new message every few minutes.

I rolled my eyes. "Answer your stupid boyfriend, and then I need all of your focus!"

"One sec." She held up her hand and started furiously texting, then smiled like an insane person down at the screen. She was like five seconds away from kissing a mobile device. "He's so sweet."

"Uh-huh." I took a sip of my drip coffee, irritated that my best friend couldn't spare five seconds of her time to help me through my first pre-midlife crisis—because that's what this was. I'd made a poor life choice, twice, and had somehow found myself on the road to hell because he'd convinced me to say yes again!

I chugged.

And then Austin's hand was on mine. She pulled the cup from my mouth, and coffee dribbled down my chin.

"Oh, honey, I didn't know it was that bad—and drip is meant to be sipped." She handed me a napkin. "So what happened?"

"I don't know!" I wailed. "I mean, I know what happened. I can't stop thinking about what happened, and then I went ahead and did it again because that always makes things better, more sex!"

I shouted the last part, earning the glare of another patron. I lifted my coffee in salute and was promptly ignored.

Austin was quiet for a second and then leaned forward. "Can you please repeat that . . . ?"

"AUSTIN!"

"You said 'sex.'"

"Yes." I nodded slowly. "When a man and woman decide they find each other attractive and all the hormones start firing and juices release and your ability to make logical choices flies out the window because you see a naked chest—but, Austin . . . that man's chest."

"Back up, who's the man?"

"The devil. Did we not just establish this?"

Her eyes widened. "Holy shit, you slept with Lucas Thorn?"

A barista walked over to us and handed Austin her pastry, then locked eyes with me. "You know Lucas Thorn?"

"I, uh . . ." I lifted my coffee into the air to buy some time. "He's my boss?"

She blinked. "You slept with your boss?"

"I'm sorry, who are you?" I asked sweetly.

"I used to be Thursday." She held out her hand.

I had no choice but to shake it.

"And you are?" She was being nice. But meeting someone who he used to sleep with only hours after leaving his bed? Not the best way to start a morning. Just another painful reminder that I was in over my head.

"I'm nobody," I finally answered. "No day attached to my name or anything. I mean, not that that's bad—I mean, good for you, woman power, *rawr*."

Austin kicked me under the table.

The barista started laughing. "If it makes you feel better, I only lasted a week before I told him I couldn't take it." She smiled. "Do yourself a favor, do him a favor—don't let him label you with a meaningless day. If he tries, he's not the one for you."

"Thanks." My voice came out scratchy and emotional. By the time she left the table I was dabbing my eyes with a brown crinkled napkin, and Austin was staring at me like I'd grown five heads.

"You slept with him," she said. Again. As if I wasn't painfully aware of what had taken place last night.

"Yes."

"And now you have a weird chest fantasy."

I grinned. "You have no idea."

"And I never will, because I'm not asking for those types of details, but . . ." She leaned forward. "Are you seeing him again? I don't want to be that bitchy friend that warns you not to go there—"

"Then don't."

"But . . ." She patted my hand, the one that was holding the napkin. "Thatch says the guy doesn't commit—ever. And need I mention that your entire family is going to shit a brick? What about Kayla? Do you even realize the ramifications?"

I slouched. "Well, I mean, long story short . . . Because you and Thatch hooked up, Lucas had to take me home and make sure I didn't get kidnapped on the street corner, then one thing led to another and his sister saw me at his place."

Austin's eyes widened. "Tell me this story has a happy ending." She raised both hands and crossed her fingers in front of her face.

"It did last night," I said under my breath and then inhaled loudly. "I felt bad that his sister was going to assume the worst about him, okay? Our families have never been the same ever since the fallout."

"Right," Austin said slowly. "The fallout from when he was found in bed with your sister!" She shouted that last part.

I covered her mouth with my hand to shush her. "Look, I haven't forgotten what happened. It's just for now. I mean, it's just temporary. All the parents start talking again, everyone's happy, crisis averted."

Yeah, I so wished it would be that easy.

Austin slowly shook her head. "Except you slept with him. Lying to protect him, however misguided, is one thing—but having sex with him? Especially when you KNOW how he is?"

"What if this is the new me?" I asked, giving a nonchalant shrug. "What if I want to cut my hair, dye it pink, get a nose ring, and become the girl who only wants no-strings sex?"

My best friend knew me too well, knew my defensiveness was just my insecurity screaming at the top of its lungs and pounding its chest.

"Then you wouldn't be you, Avery." She handed me her pastry. Only a true friend would have noticed I'd been looking at the paper bag like I had tractor-beam eyes and could will it to float toward me. "And the last thing you need to do is change just because a man looks good naked."

"So. *Good*," I whimpered.

Austin raised her hands in the air. "Look, I know you've always sort of had a thing for Lucas—I mean, what girl in our high school didn't? What teacher, for that matter?"

I nodded in agreement.

"But"—Austin sighed and lowered her voice—"I think it's a bad idea. Noble that you want to help bring your families back together, but you just crossed a pretty big line, and now he's going to just want his cake and eat it too."

I swallowed back the emotion building up in my throat. Hating that she could be right. Hating that I was thinking of the same possibility. "Or"—I lifted my chin—"this changes everything."

After a few moments of silence, she finally heaved a long drawn-out sigh and changed the subject. "Look, I have to get to class and I'm meeting Thatch later." Her eyes got all dreamy, the bitch. "He's clearing the rest of his afternoon so we can go to a matinee."

"Aw, Thatch is just so sweet," I said sarcastically, lashing out at her because she was making me feel even more nervous about what had transpired between Lucas and me. "You know he's a complete player, right? As in, he isn't the devil, but he's his half brother?"

Austin's dreamy expression remained. "You don't know him like I do. He's not like that anymore."

Look at us. A pair of idiots.

"If you say so."

"Well, I do." She stood. "You're just trashing Thatch because your new sex partner can't keep it in his pants."

I gaped at her. "Low blow, Austin. I don't want to fight." My throat got tight. "I just wanted my best friend, the person who knows me best, to tell me what to do."

"Not how this works, honey." Austin shoved her sunglasses on her face. "You want me to tell you it's okay, and I can't. Look, I've known Lucas just as long as you have. He's not the same guy he was when we were in high school. He's changed, Avery. The Lucas Thorn you crushed on isn't the one you just slept with. He's like a tiger that's lived in captivity, only to be set loose in the jungle. Do you think he's going to actually volunteer to go back in the cage? Trust me. No matter how sexy the lion tamer is—he won't stay. He'll stray."

"Wait, I thought he was a tiger?"

She waved me off. "They're both cats, and the point remains—why would any sane guy choose to settle down when he doesn't have to? He's getting the milk and the cow for free."

"So now I'm fat?"

"I'm leaving. Enjoy the pastry."

"Enjoy your date," I grumbled, feeling worse than before, if that was even possible.

As luck would have it.

My day was about to get even better.
My text alert lit up.

Thorn: Mayday! Mayday! RED ALERT!

I rolled my eyes and texted him back.

Me: Stop overreacting and use your words.

Thorn: The mothers.

Really, that's the only thing a person ever has to say to inflict horror
and absolute terror.
Because if I read that text correctly—it was plural.
As in, our mothers. Which meant only one thing. They'd gone
beyond a casual phone call and were now planning world domination.
Mine.
His.
Oh dear God.
I texted back slowly.

Me: Apocalypse.

Thorn: We may have to fake our own deaths.

Me: I know people.

Thorn: Meet at office in 5.

Chapter Thirty-Three

LUCAS

"You know, all this pacing isn't helping—in fact, it's making me more nervous. Just. Stop. Walking."

I ignored Avery's plea and kept going back and forth, back and forth in my office. My phone conversation with my mom had gone something like this:

"Oh, hi, Mom—how's Dad?"

"The party's back on!" she squealed. "Bill, stop that! I said *stop*. Your father! You know how he gets on Thursdays—between you and me, I think it's because it's so close to Saturday, and *S* stands for—"

"MOM!" My ears were bleeding. "What do you mean the party's back on?" A cold sweat broke out across my forehead.

"The problem I texted about?" She sighed. "Well, I don't want to get too personal, but Avery's mother is having a rough time with Brooke being back home, and, well, she needed some cheering up, so . . ."

Just thinking about that bitch Brooke had me ready to ram my fist into a wall. She had always been conniving and manipulative, and I blamed her partly for what happened, even though it was still my mistake.

Between her and Kayla I felt like my head was going to explode.

"Stop that!" Mom giggled like she was swatting something—most likely my father. "Anyways, we talked last week and it was . . . tense, you know? But I saw her on my morning walk this morning. We got to talking again, and it felt so good! Just like old times."

My heart sank.

"I've missed her," Mom sniffled. "We hugged, and of course the topic of conversation floated over to you and Avery—and I may have hinted that I'd be more than happy to throw a party to celebrate. Not just you two getting together but our families as well."

Oh hell.

She sighed loudly. "I know you said you guys don't want to do one and that you are planning a long engagement, but honestly—I don't know why you wouldn't want this! It's a way of righting a wrong, and, well, the minute I told Tess we would host, she burst into tears!"

"From happiness?"

"Well, she sure as heck isn't sad!" There was a strange rustling sound. "Bill, stop that! Your son's on the phone."

"Hi, Dad."

"Son, you'd understand if you saw what this woman is wearing right now."

"Please don't tell me what she's—"

"Nothing but an apron, son, nothing but an apron."

"The chicken one?" I winced. "With the giant—"

"Cock on the back." Dad chuckled. "Oh, son, it's a glorious day! I think I see the moon!"

"Oh, hush, you!" Mom giggled. "Now, the party's this Saturday—no backing out. Think of all the people you're going to make happy! And the best part! EVERYONE is going to be here, even Avery's grandfather!"

I felt my entire body go numb, and then hot. "Is he?" How the hell did they all put this together so fast?

"Sure, sure, and Kayla too, but Tess said Kayla is really excited for you guys. Isn't that sweet of her? She actually said, and I'm quoting Tess, 'They make a lovely couple!'"

"Did she now?" Yeah, I highly doubted those were her exact words, and I was even more convinced that whatever nice thing she might have said, it was with more sarcasm than Tess could possibly comprehend. She didn't know Kayla the way I did, or Brooke for that matter.

Both had mean streaks that Avery didn't possess.

I hung up the phone and texted Avery, asking her to meet me in my office in five minutes.

◆ ◆ ◆

"Do you think she was serious about the party?" Avery asked, chewing the shit out of a green Starbucks straw as she drummed her fingers against the chair. "We could get in a car accident."

"So we're back to that?" I groaned. "Back to the whole faking our own deaths scenario."

Avery stopped chewing the straw. "Kayla, Brooke, Mom, Dad, Grandpa with his guns, and your family of fun, all in one house. Yeah, Thorn, I'm back to death instead. Is that a problem?"

"Hell no," I growled.

I was having the damnedest time concentrating, what with the way Avery was sitting, her black pencil skirt hiked up around her thighs. She wasn't wearing nylons, just really high nude-colored shoes that reminded me of what her pink skin looked like beneath the clothes.

Her crop top revealed a sliver of her stomach.

And her eyes were outlined with some sort of dark liner that made them pop, and made me want to throw caution to the wind and attack her with my mouth.

"Thorn." She snapped her fingers. "Eyes up here, Casanova."

I blinked, unaware I was even staring at her breasts until she said something, and then it was impossible not to stare.

With a sigh, she tossed the straw onto the chair next to her and sauntered over to me, her hips swaying slowly enough to put me in a trance.

"What are we going to do?" She breathed out a shaky sigh.

It was instinct. I pulled her into my arms and rubbed her back. "We go to the mattresses."

"Oooh." She shivered in my arms, and I loved it. "So we war?"

I nodded. "What other choice do we have?"

Her body went rigid against mine. "We could tell them the truth."

"Oh great, I'll go first." I smirked. "Hi, guys, we aren't really engaged, nor should you be expecting a grandchild anytime soon. You see, it was a little white lie that got a bit out of hand. But here's a bonus—we did see each other naked last night, twice, and damn, watching your daughter orgasm has to be one of the sexiest things I've ever seen. Oh, hey, Grandpa, it's been a few years!"

"You've made your point." Avery's face was as red as a tomato. "Is it true?"

"Is what true?"

She broke eye contact and crossed her arms, putting space between us. "Was it the sexiest thing you've ever seen?" Finally, she gazed directly at me.

I jerked her against me and captured her mouth in a heated kiss, my hands finding her ass and giving it a tight squeeze before my lips grazed her ear. "Sexiest thing I've ever had the pleasure of seeing."

"Oh." She blushed an even deeper shade of red.

"But," I said, sighing, "I may need to do more research in the field. The first session was so fleeting that the results could be skewed."

"Is that your nerdy way of asking if you can see my boobs again?" She grinned.

"That depends. Does nerdy Lucas work better than dominant Lucas?"

"I'll let you know." She grabbed me by the shoulders and swayed.

"It's okay to kiss me," I whispered, touching her chin with my fingertips.

Emotion flickered across her face. What had just happened? A second ago she was laughing, and now she looked ready to burst into tears.

"No, it's not." She swallowed and pulled away. "Because that was a one-time thing. It's Thursday, after all."

"Avery?"

"Hmm?" She looked so insecure, hugging her body, refusing to let me in. I hated that I didn't know why, although I assumed I was probably the cause. But I didn't know how to fix it.

"Let's get back to work and we'll discuss this later tonight."

She nodded and quickly walked out of the office, but not before snatching her chewed straw from the chair, glancing back over her shoulder, and giving me one last heated stare.

The minute my door clicked shut, I breathed out a curse and adjusted myself. I'd been ready to close the blinds and do just about every wicked thing to her my mind could conjure up.

With a groan, I walked around my desk and sat down in my leather chair, rubbing my temples with my fingers.

How the hell was I supposed to face her family?

As if the universe needed to remind me of my many sins, my calendar popped up with a reminder to find a new Thursday—and to make reservations for Nadia and me for Friday.

I heard a few raised voices.

And then Avery saying, "I said he's busy, don't—"

I heard a knock at my door as it jerked open. "Come in?"

Nadia grinned at me. Speak of the she-devil.

Well, at least Avery no longer looked sad. Nope, she looked ready to stab me with the nearest sharp object.

"I have missed you, Lucas Thorn," Nadia purred. Her red lipstick was like a magnet; it drew a person in to the shape of her mouth and then caused you to look lower as her breasts jiggled in the barely there black dress she was wearing.

Frustrated, I stood. "Nadia, this is a surprise."

She crossed her arms. "A good surprise, I hope."

"It's Thursday," I said pointedly. "Not Friday."

Her lips formed a pout, then she uncrossed her arms and swayed closer to me. "I was lonely."

"You know that's not how this works, Nadia."

She kicked the door shut behind her and arched a brow. "When have you ever said no to me, Lucas Thorn?"

It was on the tip of my tongue to say "Now." Instead, I sighed and pointed to the chair. "You've brought up a good point. Sit. We need to talk."

Chapter Thirty-Four

AVERY

The minute the door clicked shut, my entire body shook with rage. The bastard son of a bitch was going to have an accidental death if he touched her mere minutes after kissing me!

I was hurt.

And embarrassed.

The mixture of both was almost too much to bear, and my stomach roiled and tensed.

Ten minutes later, and the witch was still in his office.

I went and grabbed a bottle of water from the hospitality room and slowly walked back to my desk, praying I'd find Lucas's door open and the gorgeous woman gone.

When everything looked exactly the same, I checked both calendars, his whore one and his work one. Neither said anything about a meeting with Nadia, plus it was Thursday! Did the woman not know her place? Her designated day?

Then again, even if I had a day, I'd want more time.

Maybe that's what this was about, a friendly negotiation during which she would beg for more time.

Not that *that* was an acceptable explanation, since it still meant they'd be seeing each other.

I groaned and pressed my forehead against the keyboard of my computer, praying for the phone to ring so I had an excuse to interrupt their meeting.

An hour later the door finally opened. Thank God, I'd been minutes away from pulling the fire alarm.

Nadia's eyes locked on mine. At least I had the good sense to roll my chair far away from the door as she glared at me and then turned around and planted a horrible, nasty, openmouthed kiss on Lucas's lips.

He didn't grab her.

But he also didn't push her away.

"Good-bye, Lucas Thorn." She arched a brow at me and wiped her mouth with the back of her hand. Maybe it made me a bad person—but I may have prayed that the elevator would break and send her and her giant boobs careening headfirst into the lobby. I smiled at the thought.

"Sorry." Lucas sounded exhausted.

My heart wasn't prepared to see lipstick on his mouth. I'd seen the kiss, but the lipstick? The remnant of what they shared? My brain didn't know how to process what just happened, even though it wanted to. Because if I could justify it, then everything would be okay. We could move forward, carry on, skip into the sunset, and have a picnic.

But he was wearing her lipstick.

And she'd been in his office for over an hour.

And he looked guilty.

I knew that look.

It used to haunt me.

The last time I saw that look he was stumbling out of bed with the wrong Black sister.

Thank God the phone rang. I knocked over the receiver in an attempt to grab it, then fumbled with it against my ear and said, "Lucas Thorn's office. How can I help you?"

"Hi, this is Molly. Can I please speak to Lucas Thorn?"

And the hits just keep on coming.

I clenched my teeth. "Just one minute."

I slammed the receiver onto the desk twice before sweetly calling over my shoulder. "It's your Monday."

"I'll call her back." Lucas wiped the lipstick from his mouth with the back of his hand.

I held out the phone to him, but he shook his head.

With a sigh, I hung up without an explanation.

"Avery!" he yelled. "What the hell? You can't just hang up on people!"

"Just did," I fired back. "Now, is there anything else I can help you with, Mr. Thorn, or can I get back to work?"

"Don't"—he shook his head—"nothing happened."

"Whatever you say. I just work here."

"Avery Bug—"

"Not now. I can't do this here. Remember, I *need* this internship."

Lucas swore, turned on his heel, and slammed his office door. I flinched when the blinds were aggressively pulled up so I could see directly into his office.

But I wasn't sure if what I saw should make me feel better or worse.

One of his office chairs appeared to have been knocked over, and papers were strewn everywhere.

It would be a nightmare to clean up.

I smiled and decided to enjoy imagining Lucas Thorn on his hands and knees, cleaning up the consequences of his sin.

◆ ◆ ◆

I ignored him all day.

And learned one thing.

Lucas Thorn was not easy to ignore. Not easy at all. I never realized how much of a presence he had, until I was trying *not* to notice.

He smelled nice too. He wore only enough cologne to give you a little bit of a tease, which of course made you want to lean in more and take another good sniff.

Oh good, so now I was daydreaming about sniffing him. That was not healthy for my sanity, not at all.

I think the worst part of the day, so far, was that it was just lunchtime. I couldn't escape—I was at my desk, after all—and the bastard ordered Thai food, then proceeded to eat it in the lobby.

Directly across from me.

As slowly as humanly possible.

While licking his lips with that . . . tongue.

"You hungry?" he asked.

"Nope." My stomach growled in protest. The heart might want what it wants, but the stomach? It wanted Thai food, and it was completely willing to tell the heart to shut the hell up so it could get fed.

"You sure?" The man just wouldn't leave it alone!

"I've got a protein bar." My stomach growled in irritation. *Chill, stomach. I'm not exactly thrilled about the chewy concoction I found in my desk either.*

"Because I ordered extra."

Stand your ground, Avery! You will not fall to his charms again because of food.

"Hey, you like peanut sauce, don't you?"

I jerked to attention, and my eyes widened, mouth watering. "Nope."

"Oh, because I'm just going to throw it out, so—"

"No!" I wailed and charged toward him, ready to save the peanut sauce and sacrifice my body if necessary.

I tripped over my own feet, stumbled against the chair, and barely grabbed the peanut sauce from his hands before he dropped it into the trash can.

"Someone should hold out a piece of bacon and time your sprints," he joked.

I glowered down at his perfect face and stupid chest and sexy smile—and I prayed for all his teeth to fall out, except for one. Because then I could call him Toothclops—like a Cyclops of teeth!

Clearly, my blood sugar was dipping.

"Avery"—his eyes pleaded with me—"sit."

"I'll stand."

"Fine." He handed me a carton of pad Thai and a fork.

"Fine," I repeated like a six-year-old.

He sighed.

We ate in silence.

I stood, moaned, made a few whimpering noises, and nearly licked the box. Lucas sat and watched me.

Normally, I would care about having food on my face.

But today wasn't normal.

Nope, today was the day that a Friday came in on a Thursday and reminded me why sleeping with Lucas Thorn was a bad life choice.

"Nothing happened."

"Not my business."

"I broke it off with her."

This, this intrigued me. "I'm sure you'll find a replacement soon enough, you always do."

"Funny, since I've met you, I've done nothing but lose girls."

"I'm not interviewing potential whores for you, Thorn. I don't give a rat's ass that you kiss like a god. I will not be sucked in"—I fidgeted with my hands—"again."

"Not even for a hamburger?"

"STOP BRIBING ME WITH FOOD!"

"STOP ACCUSING ME OF CHEATING!"

We were chest to chest. How did that happen? Again?

He grabbed my hand and tugged me into his office, slamming the door behind us and causing the blinds to slam against the windows—all before his mouth was on mine.

He tasted like peanut sauce.

So I licked.

Because that's what starving women do when they're placed in a situation like that!

Low blood sugar.

Bad choices.

Thai food.

And Lucas Thorn.

Nobody had a right to taste that good after having lunch—it wasn't fair. I ran my hands over his cheeks, and currents of desire washed over me as his mesmerizing eyes searched mine. He sighed. "I didn't kiss her."

"She kissed you?" I hated how weak my voice sounded. "You know it doesn't matter."

"It matters." He gave my body a little shake. "Believe me, it matters."

Sighing, I tried to pull away, but he locked his arms around me, and I was powerless. "Today may be Thursday, but tomorrow's Friday."

"And I'm never seeing Nadia again."

I tried to calm my racing pulse.

"And you don't have a Saturday anymore either. Should we hold auditions at the homeless shelter?"

He slapped me on the ass. Hard. "Why do you have to be so difficult?"

"Me? Difficult? Why all you have to do is feed me, and I'm calm, cool, and collected—while also being sexy and downright aloof when I want to be."

His eyes raked me over before he silenced me with another kiss and released me. "This isn't over."

"This?" I hid my shaking hands behind my back. "Thorn, there isn't anything to be over. Remember—one day?"

"I owe you a burger tonight."

"It's just a meal, breaking bread—not sex, Thorn. Get your mind out of the gutter."

"If you wouldn't wear such a tight skirt, my brain wouldn't be functioning at such a dirty level, Avery Bug."

I hated that his comment had me smiling all the way to my desk, until I looked at his calendar again.

He was bored.

He wanted sex.

I was available.

And convenient.

Nothing more.

Chapter Thirty-Five

LUCAS

"Right. There." I moaned and then broke out in a cold sweat. "Wait, just a little to the left. No, right! Left!"

"Did you FAIL when you were taught direction in first grade?" Avery asked. "Just tell me where it is."

"You were just there. Damn it!"

"Right or left!"

"RIGHT!" I pointed to the nightstand, not that she could see.

Avery made a triumphant noise, clearly forgetting she was under the table and giving me the show of a lifetime. She bumped her head while attempting to jump to her feet, no doubt to celebrate her ability to locate the penny she'd dropped.

"Ouch." Avery rubbed her head and then thrust the penny against my chest. "Heads we go with the death scenario, or tails we power through, man up, and make them think that we are together for real. We eat the food, we talk to the people, we wave, we kiss for pictures, and"—her eyes widened—"Uh-oh. I don't have a ring."

"We haven't even flipped the coin yet." My hands moved to her hips in a vain attempt to pull her against my body.

"Stop that"—she swatted my hands—"I'm off-limits, remember?"

"I keep forgetting."

"How convenient for your penis."

"This is a bad idea."

"Thank you!" She threw her hands in the air. "Finally, you get it. Sex? Always a bad idea."

I reached for her again, only to be shoved back.

"Not the sex, the sex is always a solid plan—I mean, going home for the so-called engagement party."

Hurt clouded her eyes. "Which is why we decided to flip the coin."

"No, *you* decided to flip the coin after I fed you a hamburger and you declared that the beef inspired you."

She shrugged. "Foodspiration. I called it foodspiration, Thorn."

Groaning, I positioned the coin on my palm. "Fine. Are you ready?"

"I've never really thought about planning my own death—so, no, I'm not ready, Thorn. But what other choice do we have? You said my mom cried! She cried and hugged your mom! They're finally back together! Peace has been restored. If we fess up now, we're completely screwed, and you know it. Suddenly, we're back at square one, and they'll think you somehow brainwashed me to go through with this plan and"—she was starting to hyperventilate—"Kayla, will hate you all over again. And it's not fair, not when—"

I swallowed and looked away.

Not when it always takes two.

The truth loomed over both of us.

"Clearly, sticking to the plan has caused a domino effect," I said.

She shook her head.

"But going to the engagement party and continuing on with this plan . . . Well, the last time we said yes to one of the mothers, you were spread-eagled on the doctor's table and—"

"I was there, Thorn, don't need a recap." She covered my mouth with her hand. Her skin smelled like coconut. "Stop looking at me like you want to eat me."

"I do want to eat you."

"Lucas . . ."

"Oh, so it's Lucas now?"

"Flip the damn coin."

I held my breath and tossed it in the air. Once it hit the ground, Avery and I stood over it and simultaneously let out a sigh of relief.

"Tails!" we said in unison. I reached out and grabbed her hand, rubbing her skin softly.

When she looked into my eyes, tears were already filling hers. "We've come this far. They can't know the truth."

"The truth." What was the truth anyway? That I was falling for her? That I didn't know what the hell I was doing? That I was a cheating bastard who fell for her long ago even though I'd asked her sister to marry me?

Avery squeezed my hand. "Here's our story: I was your intern, one thing led to another . . ." She chewed on a fingernail. "Love at first sight. I sharpened your pencils, saved the day by fixing the copy machine—we shared a laugh in the break room, hah-hah." She was bordering on delirious. "And then we kissed. End of story. No, I'm not pregnant. Yes, we'll eventually get married. No, I don't have a ring because it's too conventional. Done."

"Wow, you've thought of everything."

"I have." She exhaled, looking pleased with herself. "I really have."

"You barely started your new job, Avery Bug."

"Curses."

"So unless we were dating in secret, that part of the story isn't going to work. It's going to seem like we're moving too fast. It may have worked when we told my parents, but they've been too busy thinking about grandkids to actually process the whole time line."

"We need another story." Her expression softened, and she went all doe-eyed. "Come on, Thorn, you cheat on women all the time—you're good at dealing with estrogen. How do we do this, make it believable, keep everyone happy, and the families on friendly footing? Because I refuse to let you ruin our families again."

"Me? I ruined your family? And Brooke? What did she do? Nothing?"

Avery gasped. "You tried to seduce her!"

"What?" I hissed. "What did you just say?"

"You. Seduced. Her. In. Her. Bedroom. MINUTES after kissing me."

"I was drunk—I stumbled into the wrong room, saw red hair, and thought . . ." Shit. I'd gone too far. Shit. Shit. Take it back, take it back.

"Thought *what*?"

"So, a story?" I pasted a fake smile on my face. "I say we go with—"

"Thought. What?" Her fingers gripped my T-shirt and twisted.

With a groan, I broke eye contact and looked down at the ground. "I thought it was you. In my muddled drunken brain, I thought it was you, not Brooke—so, yeah, she wasn't the sister I'd planned on seducing."

There. I'd said it.

Let her hate me.

"You thought you were crawling into my bed?"

"I figured if I could just talk to you and see how you really felt— then I'd be brave enough to call everything off, or if that failed, at least I'd be drunk enough to pull the plug on the wedding."

The silence stretched out long past uncomfortable, making the tension between us nearly unbearable.

"You felt that way because you were drunk."

"No, Avery Bug, not because I was drunk."

She waited.

I exhaled through my clenched teeth and finally admitted the truth. "One day you were my friend, and then you became something completely different. Because I wanted you. Because I've always wanted you. Because even when it was wrong—and you were only seventeen years old—I wanted you."

"And now?"

I kissed her.

She didn't kiss me back.

Not at first.

And then slowly, her hands snaked around my neck, her lips parted—and I was completely awakened to what it would feel like to belong to Avery Black.

"Stay," I heard myself begging between each heated kiss. "Stay."

"You're a bad habit, Thorn." Her chest heaved, and her green eyes glistened. "An addiction I can't kick—each kiss gets me drunker than the first, until I lose all sense of right and wrong."

"This is right," I urged, already backing her up against the wall and parting her lips with my tongue. Her body melted under my touch. I was pretty sure I could taste her forever and still be ravenous for her mouth.

Her hand slid down my chest, pushing me away, putting maybe two inches of space between us. "What about your Monday?"

"Screw Monday." I slid my hands under her shirt and slowly inched it off her body. "I'm talking about today. Do you think you can handle that?"

She nodded.

"Thank God, because plan B involved duct tape, rope, my bed, and an infrared sensor."

"Classy." Avery's questioning gaze had me ready to bolt already, but if she needed more, I needed to be willing to give it. "One question."

I waited.

"Are you even capable of commitment?"

I wasn't sure how to answer.

"Thorn?"

"Honestly? I don't know. The last time I tried I fell for someone else. A girl with bright green eyes and strawberry-blonde hair who smelled like grape gum and called me by my last name. She made me feel alive. I think she's the only one capable of giving a cheater a reason to change his ways. That's all I can give you, the truth."

She brushed a kiss across my lips. "It's enough."

Chapter Thirty-Six

AVERY

I yawned behind my hand. My eyes watered a bit, and my vision was starting to double and then triple. "Two months ago. Starbucks. You stood in line and yelled obscenities at the poor old lady getting trained. I, being the hero in this scenario, stepped in, punched you in the face—we both ended up in jail and then started dating."

Lucas gave me a thumbs-down, and his abs glistened beneath the soft glow of the bedside lamp. "Is there a reason that every story you come up with involves you being the hero, while I end up maimed, in prison, or almost murdered?"

I giggled. "I think my favorite one was when you got jumped, and I saved your life with my kung fu."

His menacing grin did funny things to my stomach. "Admit it. The closest you've been to kung fu is the movie *Kung Fu Panda*, which you probably watched because you're convinced the panda is your spirit animal since it's always eating."

My mouth dropped open.

"Next!" Lucas pressed down on the red beeper I'd stolen out of one of his board games and yawned. "And please let me keep all of my teeth this time."

"Flaws make people human!"

"Avery Bug, in one of the stories you were wearing a crown . . . Now, something realistic, please."

"Okay, okay." I moved onto my knees and started crawling across the king-size mattress toward him.

His smile fell, replaced by a heated look that had me ready to jump all over him—again—and get distracted—again—and fail to come up with a believable story for our families—again.

"How about . . ." I licked my lips and grinned. "I've got it. The perfect story."

"Oh?" He started kissing my neck. I shivered. "Are you going to share this perfect story or just keep it on lockdown and then surprise the shit out of me? Careful how you answer—I'm already old, remember? Surprises age people, Avery Bug."

"You're a male dancer, like Carl. On the weekends you shake your ass to make more cash—and then you donate said cash to the children because you, Lucas Thorn"—I imitated his voice the way every female imitated his voice—"are a giver."

He glared at me.

"Or"—I held up one hand—"we tell them a partial truth."

"I'm listening."

"Great, could you perchance not kiss me while listening though because it makes me stumble over my words, and I hate feeding your ego. Tonight, I saw you preening at yourself in the mirror, so stop that."

He laughed against my neck.

And I briefly wondered if I would survive the day Lucas Thorn walked out of my life.

Again.

Chapter Thirty-Seven

LUCAS

Work had been hell, probably because I spent most of my workday trying not to stare at Avery and imagine her naked.

Time passed too fast, meaning I blinked and it was Saturday, the day of the party. We'd stayed up most of the two nights before. I couldn't keep my hands off her, and I had this urgency to keep marking her—making her mine before we faced everyone.

Which in turn caused us to run late since she'd stayed over at my apartment again and said she had to go home and change into something presentable. I took a few deep breaths while parked out in front of Avery's building and drummed my fingers against the console while soft music floated through the car.

I adjusted my tie a dozen times.

And nearly choked myself to death at least six of those times.

"Sorry." The passenger door opened, and in a flurry of mouthwatering perfume, Avery hopped into the car. "I couldn't find my heels, and then I realized my shoes didn't match and—"

I wasn't aware I was swearing out loud, until she stopped talking and my mouth kept moving.

"Are you okay?" Her expression was one of concern.

"You look incredible." I breathed out a tense sigh. "That dress." I shook my head, mouth completely dry. "It's really . . . tight."

Her eyes narrowed. "Tight as in, maybe stop bonding so much with your panda spirit animal, or tight as in, wow, it fits you like a glove—carry on and here's a donut for your trouble?"

"The latter." I leaned across the console and captured her lips in mine. Relief washed through me when she threaded her hands through my hair and whispered my name. "I missed you."

"I was literally gone for eight minutes, maybe nine."

"The day you get ready in eight minutes, I'll run for president."

"Vote Thorn!" She nuzzled my neck and then sucked on my earlobe. "But seriously, we need to go. We're already late and I'm sweating."

"You and me both," I grumbled, putting the car into drive and inching into downtown traffic. "Though it's more of a cold sweat."

"That sounds lovely, Thorn. Tell me more about this 'cold sweat.'"

I studied her lithe body out of the corner of my eye and tried to remind myself of all the reasons we were actually going through with this.

"I have an idea." I pulled the car onto the freeway and turned down the music. "What if, instead of telling everybody a story, we just tell them it's none of their damn business?"

Avery's eyes twinkled, and her lips spread into a beautiful smile. "Thorn, I think that's the smartest thing you've ever said."

"I'm not sure that's a compliment."

"Since I'm never going to make it a habit to compliment you, I'd just take what I can get if I were you. Beggars can't be choosers."

I glowered and then barked out a laugh. "Fine."

She reached for my hand.

And the entire thing felt normal.

If normal was taking one giant step backward into a past I'd rather forget—and facing every single person I'd hurt by not admitting my feelings earlier for the girl sitting next to me.

Like when they originally started happening.

Which was long before the day of the rehearsal dinner.

Or in a vain attempt to jump into her bed because I was so damn miserable with my choice to marry her sister.

Unfortunately, the car ride didn't take long, which meant that we were in front of my childhood home sooner rather than later.

I turned off the ignition.

Avery let go of my hand.

"It's one traumatic night with our families," she said, more to herself than me. "And then we carry on with our lives and try not to figure out whatever this is between us, alright?"

"Oh, so we're not trying to figure this out?" I was surprised she wasn't overanalyzing every little thing or asking to see my phone, or imploding over the fact that never once had I said we were exclusive.

"Nope." Her hands trembled in her lap. "If I think past today, I get freaked out, not because I'm afraid of commitment."

"Because you're afraid of me," I finished for her.

She didn't deny it—how could she, when it was the truth? However ugly honesty may have been, at least we both knew where we stood.

Her lack of a denial hung in the air. It was the perfect moment for me to tell her how I felt—that what was happening between us was real—but I wasn't confident enough in my ability not to cheat.

And that's what sucked.

Which made me a horrible human being.

Because I wasn't sure if there was something broken inside me that made sure I stayed far away from any sort of relationship for fear I would hurt someone—even if that someone were myself.

"Thorn?" Her eyes were filled with a sadness that I alone was responsible for. "Let's just focus on today."

"Today," I repeated, lifting her hand to my lips and kissing her smooth coconut-infused skin. "I can do that."

"Now"—she puffed out a breath—"let's go face the firing squad."

"Wouldn't surprise me one bit if your grandfather brought his guns over to our house just so he could clean them in front of me."

"Rest assured, he's gone completely blind in his left eye. I highly doubt he'd be able to hit a moving target."

"Great, Avery, I'll just practice my zigzag."

Her laughter wasn't at all comforting as we joined hands and approached my childhood home.

It felt weird walking into my house with Avery by my side as more than a friend. I wondered if I should seem more excited about our fake engagement.

Hell, we'd made a mess of things, and now I had the worst partner in crime that history had ever seen. The girl couldn't lie to save her life, and at least 80 percent of the time she picked a fight with me just because she couldn't help herself. Now we had to spend the entire night pretending to be a couple in love and lying to the people who knew us best. Right, what could possibly go wrong?

Try everything.

"LUCAS!" Mom screamed my name like she hadn't seen me just a few days ago and held open her arms while my dad lifted his beer in acknowledgment and continued talking to Avery's grandpa, Lewis.

"Mom." I kissed her soft cheek and pulled back while she examined Avery from head to toe and then burst into giant, wailing sobs. "Mom."

Avery gave me a panicked look.

"Just let her cry it out." I sighed and looked up at the ceiling. "Huh, is that light new?"

"Just installed it last night." Dad wrapped an arm around Mom and handed her a paper towel.

"Sorry, kids." She blew her nose. "I just—it's happening, this is really happening." She leaned in and whispered, "It's just like old times, and we're so excited."

"Us too!" Avery said in a strangled voice. I shot her a pleading look while she quickly hugged my mom and then linked arms with her, abandoning me to my father and a very angry-looking Grandpa Lewis.

"Lewis." I nodded toward him and then held out my hand.

He stared down at it and grimaced. "We killed traitors back in Nam."

Interesting, please tell me more about how you killed people for less than what I did four years ago. "And we're all so thankful for your service."

He grunted, then pointed at his good eye and back at me. "Don't think I won't be watching you like a hawk."

Thank God he was half-blind.

"I've got my eye on you, son." He let out something that sounded a hell of a lot like a growl, then left me and Dad in blissful silence.

"Is he wearing a pink shirt?" I asked once the man was out of earshot.

"Can't tell pink from blue, poor bastard." Dad sighed. "Besides, bright colors are easier to see; last week Tess lost him in the grocery store and only located him because he was wearing yellow and telling anyone who would listen about Agent Orange."

"How . . . nice for him." This. This was why I rarely came home. Everyone in both our families was certifiable.

Which is also why it was so sad when they stopped spending time together.

One thing was for sure—our families belonged together. Both dads slightly crazy, the moms loud, and the one living grandparent who talked about the good ol' days when everything cost a nickel.

Gas? A nickel.

Shoes? A nickel.

Meat? A nickel.

According to Lewis, everything was a nickel.

Which also meant that, to him, everything in this day and age was too damn expensive.

257

I sighed and weaved through the halls toward the loud chatter in the kitchen and braced myself for the impact of seeing the rest of the Black family for the first time in four years.

I noticed Tess first. She was wearing a short black dress with white pearls and had a white apron with a dog on it wrapped around her petite body. Her reading glasses were perched on the top of her head, and she had a glass of white wine in her hand.

"Lucas Thorn." One penciled eyebrow arched, then the other; her red lips pressed together, and then she was walking toward me. The kitchen fell silent.

"I'm so happy to see you." Her smile was tense. That made sense. The last time I'd seen her she was sobbing her eyes out and holding Kayla after Brooke confessed I'd kissed her. And that was before I'd called off the wedding.

I hugged her as tightly as I could, hoping to at least convey in that hug that I was sorry, so damn sorry.

She relaxed in my arms and kissed me on the cheek. "I can't say I'm surprised—I know how close you and Avery were." No accusation tinted her voice, but I couldn't be sure if she was being honest and kind or passive-aggressive. "I wasn't surprised at all to hear the good news."

Please let the good news be the marriage and not some other random made-up story that I had to lie about.

Avery saved me by snaking an arm around my waist and shrugging. "Thanks, Mom. We're really excited we were able to reconnect."

"Yeah." A familiar voice echoed through the kitchen. "And we're all dying to know how *that* happened." Brooke threw back her glass of wine and zeroed in on Avery and me with an intensity that had me wanting to both strangle her and run in the opposite direction. Her hair was dyed a fake red that made her face look harsh, and her dark eye makeup didn't help, nor did the slutty white dress that showed enough boob and ass to make her look like a prostitute.

"I think"—Avery glanced up at me—"that's a secret we'd like to keep between us."

I could have kissed her for that save.

So I did.

Hard.

She gasped against my mouth as I mauled her in my parents' kitchen and shoved all the doubt anyone may have had about us out the window. Take that, nasty witch.

When we broke apart, Avery's chest was heaving. God, I wanted to devour her right next to the cheese plate.

Her cheeks bloomed with a pretty pink before she laid her head against my chest and laughed. "Sorry, got a bit carried away."

Tess sighed happily, then poured more wine. "This really is wonderful—we've always wanted Lucas to be a part of our family, and now he will be."

"Yay," Brooke said sarcastically from her spot near the bar.

I was about to tell her to shut the hell up when Kayla appeared from around the corner, wearing a dress that was even more scandalous than her sister's. Red, with a plunging neckline, plus high heels and dark makeup to complete the look.

What the hell was wrong with Avery's sisters?

"Wow, this is so familiar." Brooke tapped her chin. "But wait, we just need to switch out the sister." She sighed. "Maybe next time I'll get my shot. God knows our kiss was briefer than the one you guys just shared."

Avery lunged toward her as gasps ricocheted around the room. God, Brooke was such a bitch.

I held her back even as her nails dug into my arm, most likely deflecting her anger toward me to keep from ripping her sister's head off.

"Brooke," Avery's father said, shaking his head. "That's enough out of you."

"What did I do?" she asked innocently. "I'm just kidding."

"The hell you are." I curled my lip.

Brooke's eyes widened. I'd had to put up with her shit all through high school when she bullied both Avery and Kayla.

"Apologize," I demanded, crossing my arms.

The kitchen was silent again.

Avery groaned.

"Now."

With a sigh and a fake smile, Brooke winked at her sister and said, "I was just kidding, Avery Bug. You're so lucky to have Lucas Thorn in your bed. Just make sure he stumbles into the right one—we don't want a repeat of last time."

She sauntered off, leaving me burning with rage and a heavy, heavy dose of guilt. Because she was right. I did go into the wrong bedroom, and I did pursue the sister of my fiancée. It was my mistake. And now I was paying for it all over again—and so was Avery. Which just made me all the more enraged because I wanted to protect her.

I wanted to love her.

And Avery's eyes filled with tears.

"Come here." I tugged her into my arms. "Don't listen to her, okay?" I knew we had an audience, but my only goal was to make sure Avery didn't take what her sister had said to heart, because Brooke had no idea just how her comments had hit home.

Because I was a cheater.

I knew it.

Avery knew it.

And she was looking at me like she knew it—like she knew I was one choice away from ruining whatever we had, even though that was the last thing I wanted.

"Let's go for a walk." I gripped her hand, grabbed two full glasses of wine, and shoved past Brooke and Kayla, who were already conspiring in the corner—at least that's what it looked like, though Kayla was wiping tears from her cheeks.

Hell. I was in absolute hell.

"Happy engagement," Avery muttered. "You know, if this was real, I'd be pissed."

I froze. "The engagement? Or us?"

"The engagement." She stopped walking. "I know you're real—I sleep with you."

I sighed and kissed her head.

"Once all the family members from both sides are here, we'll make our apologies and leave," Avery said in a steady voice. "Austin and Thatch are already planning on giving us an out."

I'd forgotten they were coming.

At least I'd have one person other than the moms and Avery who didn't want to kill me, right?

Chapter Thirty-Eight

AVERY

"Hey"—Lucas kissed my temple—"you alive?"

"Well, for now, but if looks could kill . . ." I set down my wine-glass and turned around so I wouldn't have to watch Brooke's angry scowl.

Lucas gripped my hand. "She's just unhappy, Avery. And when people are unhappy they like to make everyone around them unhappy too."

I turned and examined my sister with new eyes. "Has she always been this horrible though? Or is this new?"

"Polite Lucas would say this is completely new—she must have had a hard life. Poor Brooke, I feel sorry for her. Let's go pat her on the head."

"Eh, I'm tired of polite Lucas already."

"God, so am I," his voice rumbled in my ear as he tugged me into his arms. "Okay, so asshole Lucas Thorn—the one you've grown quite attached to—would just say out of complete honesty that your sister has always been cruel. In high school she picked on anyone she thought was beneath her and walked around like the world owed her something. Brooke has always had a superior attitude and is clearly dealing with some serious emotional issues since she's been forced to move back home with your parents. Besides"—he cupped my cheek—"you're prettier, and the red in your hair is real. This battle between you guys? You're not going to win it, because she will always find a reason to justify her nastiness toward you, only to apologize and try to gain your love and then stomp all over it again."

I gazed at him in wide-eyed amazement. "You really didn't seduce her."

His eyes lowered to my mouth. "Believe me when I say, your mouth, your body, you, Avery Black, were the only thing I was craving that night."

"Other than water," I added with a smirk.

He barked out a laugh. "Yes, other than water."

"This could work," I blurted. "I know we aren't supposed to talk about other days but—"

He silenced me with his mouth and then whispered across my lips. "This is working."

"Present tense."

He nodded.

I grabbed his hand and led him down the hall, fully aware that Brooke's eyes followed us like a laser beam the entire way.

Once we reached his old bedroom, I opened the door, pushed him inside, turned the lock, and waited.

"Something on your mind, Avery Bug?" His eyes burned with passion.

I leaped into his arms, not really giving him a chance to say anything since the minute he balanced us, our mouths were already meeting, caressing one another in a fiery explosion of desire.

"How do I get this damn thing off?" He cursed against my neck as his hands blindly reached for the zipper to my dress.

Laughing as he continued to fumble, I finally smacked his cheek lightly and said, "Allow me."

Lucas Thorn. Damn it. I was full-naming him in my head because I had no choice but to accept the full name of the man who had captured my heart, who was so perfect for me that it made my head hurt.

He crooked his finger, signaling me to turn around.

His hands grazed my back, his fingers running down the zipper—and then he slowly inched up my tight dress past my thighs and whispered, "I improvised."

"I see that," I hissed as cold air hit the back of my legs, and then his hands moved to my hips as he slowly brought my body back against his.

Shivering, I leaned my head back and tilted my chin up, accepting his hungry kiss as his hands moved down the front of my dress. It was almost more erotic than being naked, his hands roaming across the sleek fabric as it pressed against my skin.

My body ached for him in a way that terrified me—because it wasn't just this physical attraction. It was so much more, more than I could have possibly imagined, with a man I used to hate—a man who, for all intents and purposes, deserved that hate.

"Promise me," I whispered as his hands slid past my ribs and cupped my breasts. I let out a moan as he massaged and teased, the evidence of his arousal pressed against my back. I wanted him. With serious desperation. But I needed the words.

"Anything."

"I get all of the days." I said it in a rush.

His hands dropped.

Rejection slammed into me.

And then those same hands flipped me around, bracing my body while I hung my head in shame. I had done the unthinkable.

I'd gone and fallen in love with Lucas Thorn.

Stupid.

Idiot.

"Look at me," he whispered.

I shook my head no.

"Avery Bug." He trailed a finger down my jaw. "I've wanted you for years. Do you really think I'd toss all of this between us aside, for a Molly Monday or a Flight Attendant Tuesday?"

"Yes." I sighed. "No." My shoulders slumped. "Maybe."

"You don't trust me yet," he acknowledged. "And since I owe you honesty—I don't completely trust myself either. Do us both a favor."

His eyes were so clear, the prominent cleft in his chin made his mouth so much more tempting. Why couldn't it be easy?

Just sex?

"What's this favor?"

He pressed his hand to my chest. "Keep this—until you know, without a doubt, it's safe in my hands."

I frowned and looked down; his hand was placed over my heart. Understanding dawned. "What if it's not all mine anymore?"

Silence.

"Lucas—"

His lips met mine softly and then more aggressively as he lifted me into his arms, our bodies grinding together.

I reached for the button of his pants, my hands greedily tearing at whatever I could find to get there faster.

"Damn it, Avery." He kissed me harder. "What have you done to me?"

His pants were free. I glanced up at him and saw such a raw intensity I almost backed away and ran out of the room.

The real Lucas Thorn was staring at me, not the cheater, not the one who told me he couldn't be trusted. The real thing.

And he was mine.

I reached out, grazing his abdomen with my knuckles. His sharp intake of breath quickened my heart. I gripped his thick erection and moved my hand slowly up and down, squeezing gently.

He cursed and bit down on my bottom lip, then lifted me onto the dresser. A feral gleam lit his eyes as he parted my legs and our bodies joined, and he claimed me with one abrupt thrust, stealing my breath.

He kissed away my whimper.

He covered my mouth when I screamed out his name. The tension built, hard and fast, as he pumped and I bucked. The room filled with a musky scent that made me even hotter.

The hot pressure at my center became unbearable just as he stiffened and drove himself into me in a ragged rhythm. He swallowed my helpless cries with a deep kiss. And as we both floated on the devastation of our release, I knew it was too late.

He had me.

He'd always owned me.

I just didn't know it until now.

Chapter Thirty-Nine

LUCAS

I loved her.

I still didn't trust myself not to hurt her—but I loved her. The last thing in this world I wanted was to make Avery Black cry, again, because of me.

When she was done biting the hell out of my shoulder, she jerked back, her eyes filled with horror. "How loud were we?"

"Quiet," I lied. "Like church mice." I coughed.

Her eyes narrowed. "I think it's best we leave the nice polite church mice out of this scenario, Thorn."

I flashed her a smile and helped her off the dresser, then made sure my shirt was tucked in again while she shimmied her dress back down her thighs.

It was no use.

Our clothes looked fine.

But our faces told a completely different story. She was biting her lip and trying not to smile; her cheeks were flushed, and her mouth was red.

Her hair looked like I'd used it as a harness and held on for dear life while I screwed her.

"You look fine," I said quickly. "And nobody heard." I was pretty sure that even the neighbors at the end of the street had heard. "Just act normal." Which would be hard, considering it was Avery we were talking about.

"If you weren't so pretty to look at, I'd punch you for all of those lies." She pointed at me, then jabbed me in the chest. "I'm just going to hold my head high and get another glass of wine."

"Solid plan."

She smacked me on the chest before opening the door and then slamming it again.

"Avery?"

"The moms." She breathed out the words like a curse.

"What do you mean 'the moms'?"

"They're there."

A knock sounded.

Avery backed up.

I rolled my eyes. "What are they going to do, ground you?"

When I opened the door, I grinned wide and tried to think of a good greeting for Avery's mother other than "Lovely day" or "You look just like your daughter!" Because neither was going to earn me any points since I'd just had my way with her daughter on my childhood dresser.

"Lucas Thorn!" Mom stomped her foot. "We have guests!"

"We were just, um"—Avery piped in—"looking for . . ." And silence. Good, Avery, great lie.

"I know exactly what you were looking for, young lady!" Tess pressed her hands on her temples. "I can't believe you two! You"—she thrust a finger at me—"keep it in your pants. Do you even realize how high we had to raise the volume on the music to keep people from asking questions! Your father started dropping metal pans . . . on purpose."

My lips twitched.

Mom smacked me in the arm. "This isn't funny."

"No, ma'am." Avery nodded sternly. "And I apologize that I allowed him to lure me into his sex lair."

Tess rolled her eyes heavenward, and I elbowed Avery in the side.

"You poor, poor girl," Mom said, dripping with sarcasm. "That must have been why you screamed his name. You were angry, terrified, I imagine."

"He's very . . . intimidating."

"All Thorn men are that way . . . in the bedroom."

I groaned and waved my hands in the air. "This conversation just took a really unfortunate turn. We'll go make sure the guests are happy and eat cake, and forget this ever happened."

"I highly doubt poor Rocko will forget." Mom sighed. "Poor dog was in the corner howling and then tried to hump your father's leg!"

"Rocko always humps things."

"That doesn't change the fact that you caused it."

I caused a dog to hump my father? Yeah, I needed a drink. "Avery"—I grabbed her hand—"let's leave the moms to their scheming."

A smile tugged at my lips—it felt good to see them together again, even if they had the worst timing in the world.

We sidestepped our mothers and quickly headed to the kitchen. The music was so loud it was almost painful.

Avery grabbed two glasses of wine and handed one to me, then stole mine back and started sipping from both.

"Avery Bug, they're the same."

Her face paled.

I frowned and then felt a tap-tap-tap on my shoulder. There are times in a man's life when he can sense something is wrong with the universe, and in that strange moment, as the hair on my arms stood on end and as the room fell relatively silent, I knew that turning around would change everything—but it didn't stop me from doing it.

From turning.

And coming face to face with Molly.

My Monday.

On the arm of Brooke Black.

Chapter Forty

AVERY

I froze.

It was an unfortunate time for my body to become that of a traitorous whore, but there it was. I froze while Brooke eyed me up and down with smug amusement and then grinned, which hurt worse than she could ever imagine or possibly know, because she was my sister! Why would she be happy to hurt me? After that night four years ago, I'd believed Brooke's lie that Lucas had seduced her and practically begged her for sex.

Was it Lucas who had broken my family?

Maybe what I thought was petty jealousy among sisters was actually something deeper and more hateful. Maybe it was easier to put the blame at Lucas's feet than to take responsibility for the state of our relationship.

I was just as guilty. Because the minute I saw the evidence, I cut Lucas from my life, when a true friend, a friend who really loved someone, would have asked why or at least listened to what he had to say.

He'd begged me to let him explain, and I'd yelled at him that I never wanted to see him again.

Because, yes, he'd cheated on my sister.

But he'd also cheated on me—that's how I felt in my heart.

"Lucas Thorn." Molly spoke his name with reverence and a bit of a hussy-sounding sigh. "I hear congratulations are in order."

Oh no.

"Thank you." He reached blindly for my hand, but I held a wineglass in each, so I chugged one and set the other on the table, then secured my hand in his and squeezed.

Molly tilted her head at me. "Now, that's strange."

"What's strange?" I asked in what I hoped sounded like a semibored voice, although inside I felt terror—terror that all our friends and family would discover the truth.

That he wasn't who they thought he was.

And yet, he was.

I mean, he could be.

I was confusing myself.

He wasn't a cheater anymore. I knew that in my heart. A man wouldn't look at a woman the way he looked at me—and keep seven girls on the side.

Would he?

"I haven't seen you in a little over a week."

I did the math and deflated a bit. That meant he'd slept with her just a few days before I'd started working for him and started our little flirtation.

My hand went stiff in his.

"Are you sure about that?" Lucas looked pissed. "I could have sworn it's been a lot longer, not that it matters since clearly I've moved on."

"Yes"—her eyebrows shot up—"clearly." She nodded toward me. "I'll see you guys around. And Lucas, you know how to get ahold of me when you get bored. Which you will. Because, let's face it, you need a little variety in your life from time to time—it's how people like us work."

"Please leave." His teeth snapped together.

Molly shrugged and walked off with Brooke in tow.

I thought the worst was over, but then Brooke leaned over and whispered in my ear, "Too bad you only get one day, huh, Sis?"

I hung my head, ready to defend him and ready to defend myself too, but I knew it would be in vain.

And as people laughed and celebrated around me, I suddenly felt lost, like a girl who was playing a part that was never mine to play.

I eyed Kayla in the corner. She wore her hurt like armor.

She stared at me as though I was an interloper.

Oh God.

She stared at me like I was the cheater.

I sucked in a breath as memories of my past with Lucas assaulted me, all our stolen moments together, our almost kisses that led to the kiss the night before the wedding. I was just like him.

I'd done nothing to push him away, because I loved him.

And I used that love to justify my actions, even though they were wrong.

And now? Now it was too late.

Lucas Thorn didn't break my family.

Brooke didn't break my family.

My actions.

My obsession.

My love for a man who was never mine to begin with broke my family, and in turn—I glanced up at him—it broke Lucas Thorn.

And made him a cheater.

Chapter Forty-One

Lucas

"Avery"—I tugged her hand—"are you okay?"

She was immobile, her face pale, her eyes wide like she'd just witnessed something shocking, which I knew couldn't be true. She'd known about Molly all along, and in the end, if the truth got out, I couldn't care less.

I loved Avery.

Therefore my focus shifted from myself to her—to protecting her, to making sure she was okay, even if revealing myself caused my parents pain.

This lie was a reflection on me—my flaws, my character—not her. Seeing Molly had the opposite effect that it should have.

I felt pity.

And anger at myself.

For ever thinking that once I had Avery I would cheat on her or turn my back on her. Seeing Molly had solidified the knowledge that I wouldn't; it made my phone burn in my pocket.

The phone that had my "other" calendar.

God, I was such a complete asshole.

"Y-yes." Avery nodded jerkily. "I just need some air."

"I'll come with you—"

"Alone." She released my hand. "Just for a minute."

I reached for her again, my fingers brushing her warm skin, but she shook her head.

The last thing I wanted was to embarrass her in front of her family, so I let her go and hoped I wasn't making a giant mistake as I watched her slowly put one foot in front of the other and walk away from me.

"Dude." Thatch's voice shook me out of my weird funk concerning Avery. "You never told me how hot Kayla is!"

I glanced back at Kayla, who looked more hot mess than hot, and shrugged. "Yeah, well, she's had work done."

His eyes lit up. "Serious?"

"No, you asshole, and stop looking so excited every time I tell you that I know a girl who likes plastic surgery."

"It's my job."

"Shame you aren't better at it."

"What crawled up your ass and died?" He pushed my shoulder. "You're at your engagement party to a hot-as-hell chick who actually likes having sex with you."

"Hilarious."

"And even better, you've got like five more on the side."

I froze. "What did you say?"

"Or is it six? I can never keep track." He popped a cracker in his mouth and crunched down. "Not that it matters, since you have them in your trusty calendar."

"Thatch."

"What?"

"Shut the hell up."

He wrapped an arm around my body. "Why are you pissed about this? You've got the girl you want to commit to and a few others who are obsessed with the great Lucas Thorn—I really don't see a problem."

"It's cheating."

"Not cheating if they know about it, and your girl knows." He shrugged again as if we were having a completely sane and logical conversation.

My words kept crashing back to bite me in the ass.

I groaned. "Thatch, I'm not going to keep seeing other girls."

His eyes narrowed. "But . . . why?"

"Because"—I gritted my teeth, then shouted—"I. LOVE. HER."

Maybe I shouted it a bit too loud.

Because all talking around me ceased, and then some ladies to my right emitted a few happy sighs.

Kayla looked guiltily down at her feet and then tried to grab Brooke. Fire lit up Brooke's eyes as she stomped toward me, hands on her hips. "I need to talk to you."

"So talk."

"In private."

"Been there, done that," I sneered. "I think I'll pass."

"Thatch can come." She nodded at him, her eyes raking him over in a way that made me want to strangle her.

"Fine."

The three of us walked down the hall to one of the guest bedrooms. I was turning to close the door when Kayla walked in.

I wondered whether I was being set up. But Thatch was there. And Thatch had my back.

I backed away slowly and glared at Brooke. "Make it quick."

"We know what you're doing."

"And what exactly is that?" I crossed my arms.

"Using our baby sister to hide from your parents—what a complete jackass you are! Once a cheater, always a cheater!"

I winced, but Thatch just shrugged and mumbled, "Not too far from the mark."

"Pick a side, Thatch." I glowered at him.

"Hi, I'm Kayla." She stepped forward, and Thatch reached for her hand.

What the hell?

I wanted to strangle him. He was dating Austin. He had come with Austin, who deserved better than a guy who couldn't be loyal to her. Damn it, I was going soft.

They freaking rode to the party in the same car.

What a douche!

"We'll, uh . . ." Thatch was abandoning me for Kayla. Unbelievable. Though in the furthest shameful corner of my brain, I realized I'd been that guy—even just a day ago I still identified with that guy. "We'll be letting you guys have that talk."

Kayla squeezed Thatch's hand and winked.

He stared at her hand as a flurry of emotions—from defeat, to anger—seemed to cross his face. Hanging his head, he then took her hand and left with her, like he had no choice.

What the hell was that?

The minute they were gone, Brooke moved closer, her chest heaving. "Admit it, you're using her."

"I'm not using her," I said in a tired voice. "I love her, not you, not Kayla. I love Avery."

"She's a child!" Brooke burst out laughing. "You forget you stumbled into my bedroom, *my* bed!" She thrust her chin up in the air.

"I THOUGHT YOU WERE AVERY!" I shouted.

Brooke stumbled backward. "What did you say?"

I pinched the bridge of my nose. "I thought you were Avery."

"But—"

"Brooke, I say this as a friend—get your shit together. Nobody likes this type of drama, and you're way too old to be stirring things up."

She hung her head as a tear streamed down her cheek. "I know. You're r-right."

Damn it, why did I always have to make women cry?

"Don't cry."

She collapsed against my chest in a sob.

I patted her back but refused to hug her.

Because I didn't trust her.

Which proved to be accurate when she glanced up at me through fake lashes and gripped my face, then pressed her mouth to mine.

"Oh!" Molly's voice jerked us apart. "Sorry, wrong room, right, Avery?"

Avery's eyes zeroed in on the both of us.

I was aware how bad it looked.

How guilty I looked.

Brooke slapped me across the face. "How dare you kiss me? Avery, I'm so sorry, it just—"

Avery stomped up to her sister, drew back a fist, and before I could stop her knocked Brooke on her ass. Then she reached for her sister's hair and pulled.

Chapter Forty-Two

AVERY

I didn't want to believe that my older sister was capable of that kind of evil, but from the look in her eyes after I punched her in the face—I should have.

Her glare was venomous, eyes watering, as she poked me in the chest with her finger and spit out, "You're no different from the rest of them."

"Don't make me punch you again, Brooke. There are some things even our friend Thatch can't fix."

"You really are a stupid child, aren't you?" she snorted. "Look at him!" All eyes went to Lucas, who was staring at me with his jaw firmly clenched, muscles flexing in his cheeks like he was trying not to say something—or maybe just trying not to help me beat the crap out of my own sister.

I sighed in Brooke's direction. "All I see is the man I love."

She burst out laughing. "Oh?"

I nodded, suddenly feeling exposed, vulnerable, like I'd just stripped myself bare in front of the only person capable of hurting me—even when the track record pointed to all signs of doom.

"He can't help it, Avery." Brooke sighed. "Once a cheater, always a cheater. You think you're different. You're just like every other woman who's tried to trap Lucas Thorn."

"Well, you should know, Brooke. Get out of this room before I push you out the window," I hissed.

She raised her hands in the air. "You trust him, and yet he still hasn't canceled any of his appointments for next week. Ask Molly—they're still on for Monday." Her attention went to Lucas. "It's his MO. A dinner, a movie, they laugh and go back to her place for wild, crazy sex. He never kisses her mouth, and he promises to call but only does the day before they're going to meet again. Lucas Thorn is a cheater, and you've just been duped."

My heart sank.

Because Lucas had convinced me otherwise.

Because he'd told me to focus on today. Because I'd agreed to focus on a day at a time.

And blindly ignored the simple fact that he'd never promised commitment, never said we were exclusive.

I'd been given a few days with him.

So had the rest of them.

Brooke walked out, and tears slid down my cheeks.

◆ ◆ ◆

Lucas's arms wrapped around my body. "Are you okay?"

I shook my head no.

He bit out a curse and kissed the top of my head. Why did being in his arms have to feel so right? It felt like forever. And yet, even when Brooke had unleashed her tirade . . .

He'd said nothing.

"Tell me the truth, Thorn," I whispered. "Have you canceled all of your weekly dates?"

He stopped rubbing my back.

"Lucas Thorn." I whispered his name like the rest of them, with psychotic desire. And it hit me.

They full-named him.

Because that's what you did for those who are unreachable.

You put them on a pedestal because it's the only way to handle the inevitable.

If he was "Lucas Thorn," then it made sense that eventually he'd tire of me.

If he was just "Lucas," or just "Thorn," he was a person, reachable.

"Avery, I haven't talked to them yet, but I will, I swear."

I closed my eyes against the angry tears. "You haven't talked to them . . . yet?"

"Avery"—he sighed—"look at me."

I pulled back, afraid of what I'd see reflected in his eyes. But they were clear as day. There was no confusion or guilt, which was what I'd come to expect from Lucas: he had always been solid, incapable of feeling anything for one single person.

"I want you. Only you."

"Okay." My thoughts jumbled together. "And the thought of being with me and only me—no more Mondays or Fridays—that doesn't terrify you?"

He. Said. Nothing.

"I think I have my answer"—I nodded—"I'll just . . . Can you tell my parents I got sick? I'll catch a ride with Austin so that you don't have to drive me back."

"The hell!" Lucas gripped my shoulders, his fingers dug into my skin. "Would you rather I lie? Of course I'm terrified. I've never done this before! You can't judge our future by my past!"

"But that's the thing about pasts . . . As long as they stay in the past, you can move on. But you, Lucas Thorn, have not moved on.

You're stuck in between your past and our future—and that's not fair. To either of us."

"I love you!" His grip tightened. "Avery, I love you."

My heart cracked. Could he tell how hard this was for me? To be in his arms? To walk away when all I wanted to do was crash my mouth against his and beg him to say he loved me over and over again?

But when you love something . . .

You let it go . . .

"Prove it." I nodded.

He released me and turned on his heel, jerky movements that weren't normal for a man who did everything with a predatory smoothness that was most of the time absolutely terrifying.

"This is bullshit." He ran his hands through his hair. "All of it. I can't believe you'd listen to Brooke." He paced back and forth. "Avery, I don't know *how* to prove it! If I knew how, I would do it. Just tell me—I can't lose you." His eyes filled with tears.

"That's my point!" I choked back a sob. "You're hurting me without even knowing it. Your moral compass is so skewed that you don't even realize how you're hurting me!"

"HOW the hell am I the one hurting YOU?"

Speaking of hurting, my head was starting to throb. After a moment, I held out my hand. "Give me your phone."

His eyes narrowed. "Why?"

"Thorn . . ."

With a curse, he pulled out his cell and tossed it in the air. I caught it with both hands and pressed the home button to light up the screen.

Fifteen new messages.

All from different girls.

"This"—I pointed at the screen—"this hurts."

"Avery, I haven't even responded."

"I want you to choose me not because I'm pressuring you to, because I know you'll resent me for that. I want you to throw this life away because you want to. And right now you don't. You think you do, but it's a comfort, having someone on the side, just in case. I can't wait at home, knowing that one day you're going to smell like another woman's perfume. I want all of you, not a day, not five days—I want forever."

I chucked his phone at his head and walked out of the room.

And right into World War III in the living room to witness a screaming Austin holding Brooke in an impressive headlock. Grandpa Lewis was clapping his hands like they were doing some sort of country jig, and my mom was trying to pry Brooke and Austin apart while Thatch stood nearby, looking guilty and extremely sad, which made no sense at all.

I stomped over to him, shoved his ripped chest, and shouted, "What the hell did you do?"

"Nothing, I—"

Austin released Brooke. "NOTHING?"

He had the good sense to backpedal. "Austin, we aren't exclusive—we talked about this. We—"

In tears, she slapped him so hard across the cheek that my own face stung.

Thatch cursed and grabbed his cheek. "What the hell!" he roared. "Austin, we discussed this!"

"ONE WEEK AGO!" she yelled. "And I said I wanted more and you said okay!"

"How the hell does that translate into exclusive?" He dropped his hand. "Because when you said you wanted more, I took more time off so I could be with you—and you seemed happy." He reached for her. "Aren't you happy?"

"Yes." She wiped her tears. "I'm so thrilled. Just jumping for joy that I discovered that witch with her tongue down your throat!"

Brooke flushed bright red.

How the hell had she moved that fast with Thatch? Did she always set up men? And where was Kayla?

I seriously wanted to strangle my sister with my bare hands, and probably would have had Lucas not appeared just then in the living room.

I couldn't face him.

Not now.

And probably not tomorrow.

I breezed past him and whispered, "I'm quitting the internship."

Chapter Forty-Three

LUCAS

Things calmed down once Avery and Austin left, but it took a few bottles of wine for everyone to forget that I was mysteriously without Avery, the girl I had walked in with.

The one I was supposedly marrying.

I made excuses for her.

I lied to everyone about this mysterious illness that also made it look like she'd been crying.

I did what I did best: I Lucas Thorned everyone. And I hated that everyone believed me, that I was so damn good at lying and making people want my lies to be true that I wasn't even nervous about it. I could literally justify any lie.

And make myself and everyone around me believe it was the truth.

It was the first time in my life I believed what Avery had always said. I was the devil himself.

And I was too proud to go after the one girl who could give me salvation, save me from myself, from the depths of hell.

I grimaced and tipped back a bottle of beer.

Thatch had pursued Austin, but I knew it was already too late. He'd screwed up.

I knew he would—but I wanted things to be different for them, because Austin deserved a happy ending.

Even if she wasn't exactly my favorite person.

"She's not sick, is she?" Kayla's voice interrupted my morose thoughts. I set the beer bottle down and started to stand. "Wait, sit."

With a curse, I plopped back down on the chair and looked out at the giant oak tree that Avery had fallen out of when she was a kid. At least it was quiet outside—until now. "I really don't want to talk, Kayla, not now, not like this."

"She hides her sadness well." Kayla took the seat next to me. "I helped Brooke—I was supposed to distract Thatch and get him to leave the room."

"What?" I hissed as betrayal washed over me. "Why the hell would you help Brooke? You know she's insane. She's always been jealous of you and, apparently, now Avery."

"She's hurting." Kayla sighed. "And since I was hurting . . . We're all capable of making bad choices. My bad choice was made when I came home after seeing you and Avery together and cried myself to sleep." I winced. "Brooke came into my room and told me about your, um, calendar. Apparently, she and Molly work out at the same gym, and one thing led to another—then suddenly Brooke made the connection."

"Son of a bitch." I clenched my fists.

"I was so angry at you, angry at Avery for lying, and then Brooke planted the thought in my head that you didn't really love Avery—and maybe you still loved me, I just needed a chance to prove it." She let out a bitter laugh. "And look how that turned out? I look like a hooker, Brooke naturally betrayed my trust and wanted you for herself—and wonder of all wonders, you really do love Avery."

"That dress really is horrible, Kayla. I say that as a friend. You should burn it. You almost flashed Grandpa Lewis twice."

Her chuckle was low, familiar. Years ago I lived for it. Funny how we were able to sit together like we were friends again.

But the mess with Avery?

I cursed again.

"You love her."

"I do."

"You know, Lucas, I wish I could hate you."

"If I had a penny for every time I had a woman tell me that"—I stared down at my shoes—"I'd be a very rich man."

"That's a compliment, you know, the fact that you can roll through life like a complete asshole, yet women still want to like you."

"I should make a profession out of it." I sank down into my chair. My heart was so damn annoying—it hurt like hell. How could an organ hurt? It did. And it sucked.

"Start at the beginning," Kayla whispered.

"She works"—I caught myself—"she *worked* for me."

"Not that beginning."

My self-confidence cracked as I looked at the oak tree and let old memories take over. "It was her hair."

"Her hair?" Kayla repeated.

"I loved her hair. When she got back from summer camp, she had just turned seventeen, and it had been a few months since I'd seen her. I was just getting ready to start my first real job, you'd already left for grad school, and she knocked on my door, begging me for waffle mix."

Kayla laughed. "Sounds like her."

"Yeah, well, she offered me a kidney in exchange for Bisquick." I chuckled. "Naturally, I made her up her price and said I wanted to partake of this glorious food she was about to make. She grumbled about how greedy I was, and marched right into the kitchen like she owned it and started baking." Her legs had been so long, her shorts so ridiculously short, her tank top falling off her bronzed shoulders. "She started dancing slowly to the music that had just popped up on the TV, then looked over her shoulder and said, 'I could get used to this, Thorn.'"

I sighed. "What she meant and how I took it were two very different things. The sun was shining directly on her pretty strawberry-blonde hair, and the only thought that consumed me was 'God, I would give more than a kidney just to freeze this moment in time—and keep her forever.'"

Tears filled Kayla's eyes. "But we were engaged."

"Yes." My voice was hollow. "So I ignored it, thinking it was just cold feet, right? A passing fascination with a girl who'd suddenly grown up. And then one night, I almost kissed her. It freaked me out. I'd only ever been with you. I mean, we'd been together since the eighth grade. So then I told myself I was attracted to her because I was being a guy."

"And it got worse?" Kayla asked.

"So, so much worse," I groaned, remembering all the moments I almost took Avery in my arms and imagined kissing her. "The night of the rehearsal dinner was my breaking point. I realized I couldn't go through with it. I couldn't marry you and have such strong feelings for your sister. I was a coward. I should have said something, but I kept thinking it would pass, and when I saw her in her rehearsal dress . . ." I cursed and balled my hands into fists. "I started drinking because that always leads to good decisions, and then when I saw her later that night, I was already on my way to being completely drunk. She helped me back to the house, and I kissed her—kissed her so damn hard it probably terrified her. But she, she kissed me back, and for a few seconds in time I had the girl I'd always wanted, until she shoved me away. She looked at me as if I'd betrayed her. Her eyes said it all—*I want you, but not this way.*"

I hated the memory of that night.

The mistakes.

"I meant to sneak into Avery's room to talk about it, to apologize. Stupidly, I didn't think I would get caught, but I was loud, drunk—and of course Brooke being Brooke just encouraged me, and by the time I realized she wasn't Avery, it was too late."

Kayla and I sat in silence for a while. The breeze gently picked up the scent of rain in the air.

"And now you're pushing her away again," she finally said.

"The hell?" I blinked. "I'm sorry, did you miss the part of the story where I basically emotionally cheated on my fiancée for over a year? If I cheated on you—"

"You didn't love me." Kayla chewed her bottom lip. "Not like that. I can't remember a time you ever looked at me the way you look at Avery, with this raw devotion that makes the rest of the world fade away."

My heart felt heavy.

"You need to go after her."

"I figure she needs time before I start banging down her door."

Kayla rolled her eyes. "Men are so stupid."

"Says the girl dressed like a prostitute."

Kayla glared at me and then burst out laughing. "Lucas, she doesn't need time—she needs you to chase her, she needs you to be the man she fell for, the confident Lucas Thorn. Don't shy away from a girl who's half your size. Grow a pair and chase her. Isn't that what guys like anyway, the chasing?"

"I think I prefer the catching," I admitted.

Kayla stood and held out her hand. "Friends?"

I pressed my palm to hers. "Friends."

We shook, and something clicked into place. All my football games she'd cheered at, all the moments we'd shared—we had been together because we were friends, because it was always like that. I had loved Kayla, but as a friend.

I loved Avery . . .

The way a man is supposed to love a woman, with such blind madness that nothing made sense when she wasn't in my world.

"Tell my parents—"

"Yeah, yeah." Kayla waved me off. "I think they're still trying to make sure Austin doesn't come back and kill Brooke. But if the drama lessens, I'll be sure to tell them you went after your girl."

"Thanks, Kayla."

Tears filled her eyes as she nodded. "Go get her."

Chapter Forty-Four

Avery

I was too sad to be angry.

I really wished I were angry so I could go all Carrie Underwood on his ass, but his stupid car was still at his parents', and I was pretty sure if I slit his tires the hollow ache in my chest wouldn't ease. If anything, with my luck, I'd mess that up and somehow get arrested, only to be bailed out by the devil himself.

Austin was a mess. "Do you want to talk about it?" I asked, completely aware of my own heartbeat as I tried to steer the conversation toward her and not me.

"He was supposed to be different!" she wailed, slamming her hands against the steering wheel, then swerving into the other lane before righting the car. "He promised!"

I didn't know what to say. Or how to make her heartache better.

Because we were in the same boat, just on different sides. I was struggling with wanting to trust Lucas with my heart. And Austin was trying not to think of all the ways she could poison Thatch for being unable to keep his wandering eye on lockdown.

"Here." She tossed me her phone. "I can't take it anymore. Can you just turn it off?"

"Are you sure?" I studied her closely, seeking assurance that she was serious.

"Positive." Her lower lip quivered. "You know what sucks?"

With the slide of my finger, I turned the phone off. "What?"

"He asked me to be exclusive. He asked me! I told him I wasn't ready to get into anything serious because I still had school, and then he goes and buys me roses and takes me out to dinner and asks if we can take the next step. I have a key to his apartment! And now? Now he's kissing complete strangers? Putting his dick wherever he pleases? Is it some sort of sick game with these two or what?"

"I wish I knew," I whispered. "Believe me, I do."

That was the end of our meaningful conversation.

Both of us were too upset to say anything more until the car was about a mile from my apartment, and even then we basically took turns crying and cursing men to hell the entire last mile of the ride. When she dropped me off, we hugged, then did what best friends do: told each other never to date again and promised to eat ice cream the next day until we got sick.

She didn't have any of her things with her, and she had a huge test to study for—which left me alone with my peeping Tom neighbor and the same sly spider who still hadn't found the will to die.

Ah, a pet.

That's nice.

"Hi, spider." I opened up my laptop and breezed through a few TV shows. My fridge was empty. I had no ice cream. No wine. Water. I had water. I would get paid soon, but it would be my only paycheck since I'd just quit.

Stupid Avery.

I needed money!

And I quit over a man.

Not just any man.

I sniffled, then shouted, "DAMN YOU, LUCAS THORN! Curses on your perfect hair, and that stupid cleft in your chin. I hope it turns into a giant wart and grows a single tough hair that refuses to be plucked!"

The spider crawled back into its hole.

I had scared my pet.

A loud banging sounded at my door.

Cringing, I waited for it to stop, but it didn't.

Finally, I pulled open the door.

My landlord did not look pleased. "You've been warned, Avery."

"Warned?" I frowned. "Warned about what?"

"Rent."

"I paid rent."

"You paid *last* month's rent. This month's rent was due three weeks ago."

Impossible. I did the math. No, no, no, that couldn't be right.

"And I have someone willing to move in immediately, so . . ." He rocked back on his heels. "You have one day to get packed."

Great. I had one day to pack up my laptop and spider. No problem. I'd just go find a box to set up on the street corner and pray it didn't rain.

Tears filled my eyes.

"No." He shook his head. "No tears, Avery. This is business. I've put notices on your door for weeks. This ends now."

He walked off.

I glanced at my door.

To be fair, the notices were underneath another notice that the building was going to be under construction, and it's not like I'd actually been staying at my own apartment for the past few days.

I'd been with the devil at his.

My stomach grumbled. I should have eaten at the party.

I slumped to the ground, the door still open, and cried.

Footsteps neared. I didn't look up. Take your fill, creepy Mr. Thompson! This is the last you'll see of Avery Bla—

"Avery." Lucas breathed my name. "Avery Bug, what happened? Are you hurt?"

"Only everywhere," I mumbled through my tear-soaked fingers. "But you know that's to be expected when the man you love is an asshole and you just got evicted."

"You what?" He stood and stepped over me.

"Evicted, you know, meaning you're homeless, and—hey!" I clenched my fists. "What are you doing?"

He didn't answer. Instead, he rummaged through my only closet, grabbed two bags, and started pulling all my clothes, with hangers, onto the bed.

"Thorn!"

He didn't respond. He breezed into my kitchen, opened every single cupboard, frowned, and then asked over his shoulder, "Anything in the fridge?"

My stomach grumbled again.

"Guess that's my answer."

"You can't be here. I don't want to see you . . ." I was three seconds away from launching myself onto his buff body and beating his back with my fists until he left.

And then he stopped. He didn't smile; he just stopped, in the middle of the room, and stared me down.

It was uncomfortable.

I started to fidget.

"Any furniture other than this futon?"

Embarrassment washed over me. "No, I haven't had time to—"

"Good." He walked back into my bedroom and used my bedspread to hold all the clothes. He then stripped the sheets, threw both pillows at me, and said, "Let's go—I'll come back for the furniture later."

"I'm not going with you." I held my ground.

Lucas sighed. "It's me or the box near Pike and First, but I've heard that's currently occupied by a homeless guy and his cart. Your choice though."

I truly thought about it. A box would be nice; nobody would bother me except for the occasional homeless friend or possible rat.

"Avery Bug . . ." Lucas's eyes pleaded with me. "Let me take care of you."

I puffed out my chest. "This means nothing."

"Fine."

"It's temporary."

"Whatever you say."

"And I'm not sleeping in your bed."

"Did I ask you to?"

Well, that stung. "N-no."

"You can have the spare room."

"Right." Tears filled my eyes. So I'd just stay in his room of torture while he entertained Molly in two days. Great. I think I preferred homelessness.

I begrudgingly followed him down to his car.

We rode in silence all the way to his apartment building. And by the time we settled all my stuff into the guest bedroom, the tension was so thick I was actually sick to my stomach—either that or my stomach was eating itself out of desperation.

At least Lucas left me alone while I put my clothes away in the closet.

A half hour later he knocked on the door and motioned for me to follow him, still no words. So this was fun. Not stressful at all.

I was about five seconds away from having a mental breakdown, and I've heard those aren't pretty.

The kitchen smelled like Thai food.

Mouth watering, I floated over to the breakfast bar and burst into tears.

I was stressed.

The food looked amazing.

And instead of the prince rescuing the princess, the asshole rescued the homeless girl.

Why did I get the messed-up story?

WHY?

"Eat," he instructed, handing me a fork. I didn't need convincing. I would eat even if he had stolen the food from a blind grandma. Hunger always won out with me.

Mouth full of food, I barely had time to swallow and yell, "Aren't you eating?"

He paused, his face indifferent. "I figured I'd let you eat first."

"No." I shook my head and stared guiltily down at the food. "I mean, that's fine—we can eat together."

As if on cue, because the universe hated me, his cell buzzed on the counter, right next to where I was sitting.

Molly.

The food threatened to come right back up.

"Aren't you going to answer that?" Tears filled my eyes as I pointed at the stupid phone.

"No," he whispered. "I'm not."

"But you will."

"No."

"Thorn . . ."

"Avery Bug . . ."

Stupid tears. The harder I tried to suck them in, the more they threatened to fall.

"I love you, you know." Lucas's words were a direct hit to my heart and my already waning sanity.

"Is it enough?" I asked, more to myself than to him.

"Damn, I sure hope so." And then he was gone, softly shutting his bedroom door behind him.

Chapter Forty-Five

Lucas

She was too exhausted to talk. I knew women. Nothing good ever came from a conversation with a woman when she was so mentally and emotionally exhausted that she almost fell into her pad Thai.

Which meant.

I slept like complete shit.

And eventually moved to the couch in a stupidly vain attempt to hear Avery breathe.

Yes. I wanted to hear her breathe.

I would even have welcomed a snore at this point.

I stared wide-eyed up at the ceiling.

It was Sunday—which was usually my sister's day.

And my mom, naturally, hadn't stopped calling about the engagement party to ask why my best friend had decided to bring his drama to such a happy occasion. When she asked how Avery was and why she had to leave, I ignored the question and told her to let us deal with everything on our own—and for once my mom respected my wishes.

I apologized and refused to answer any more phone calls.

But today was about Avery.

At eight, I woke up and made coffee.

At nine, she finally shuffled out of her room, looking the way I felt. Dark circles spread beneath her eyes, and her face was pale.

"That." Avery pointed at the mug in my hands. Rolling my eyes, I handed the coffee over. Some things never change, no matter how angry you are with a person.

"You're welcome," I said in a smooth voice.

She grunted, peering over the rim of the mug with irritation.

"Sorry, I forgot, no talking in the morning."

Avery nodded and then yawned.

"So, I figured we could go to the market today."

Still no talking.

"To buy . . . food for tonight."

Her eyes narrowed.

"And the rest of the week."

Her mouth dropped open.

"I figured it could be a new thing, fresh groceries for Monday, Tuesday, Wednesday—"

She held up her hand. "I know the days of the week, Thorn."

I smirked. "I had a really good plan, you know, a really well thought-out speech." I sighed. "But, Avery, I can't take you seriously when you're wearing a Star Trek T-shirt with bright pink shorts."

She looked down; her cheeks blushed.

"Is that, uh, my shirt?" I pointed.

"Maybe . . ."

"Hmm . . ."

"What were you saying about the days of the week?"

"Why are you wearing my shirt?"

"I stole it."

"I was saying the days of the week because I figured I should be really, really clear about my intentions. Why did you steal my shirt?"

She shrugged. "And just what are your intentions, Thorn? The shirt's comfortable, if you must know, and it smells like jackass." She grinned behind the mug, and I barked out a laugh.

"My intentions are bad, very bad." I swayed toward her. "On Mondays I plan on licking my way up and down your body—you know, as an extraspecial hello. And what exactly does jackass smell like?"

"What about Tuesday?" She gulped. "A jackass smells like Lucas Thorn—they're one and the same . . ."

"Tuesdays are naked days. No clothes allowed. Sorry, champ, but no more stealing my shirts. And thanks for the compliment about my scent."

Avery set the coffee on the bar and crossed her arms. "What if I don't want to be naked?"

"I voted, and you already lost. You missed the entire meeting, so you don't get a damn say."

She took a cautious step toward me. "Do you have plans for every day then? Is that what this is about?"

"I fixed my schedule." I locked eyes with her. "Wrote you in on every day, with marker nonetheless—and you know how I hate crossing things out."

"Because you're a freak."

"Yes."

"Every day, you said?"

I swallowed my nervousness. "Night and day."

"OH WOW—I get nights too? This is surprising, since nobody is normally allowed in Lucas Thorn's bed. Gonna move me out of the guest room, are ya?"

"I made an exception," I whispered. "And that one exception ruined me for all other days—all other women."

"Good." Tears filled her eyes. "I'm glad."

"Me too."

I don't think I could ever prepare myself for Avery Black's kiss, which was proven yet again when she launched herself into my arms and molded her mouth to mine, only to break apart and slap me across the face and whisper, "Hurt me again, and I'm slashing the tires to your car."

"Oookaaay," I said slowly. "Why do I get the feeling you still want to do that just so you can say you've done it?"

She cocked her head to the side and gave me an evil grin. "Just one tire?"

"Hell no! There will be no slitting tires in this relationship." I fused my mouth with hers. She tasted like coffee. She tasted like she was mine.

She broke off the kiss. "What about Thatch's tires?"

I thought about it for a minute. "He did just buy a new Audi . . ."

Her grin widened.

"For Austin, of course, not because we have some sick fascination with slitting tires or anything." I kissed her mouth.

She laughed against my lips. "Right, because that would be weird."

"Right."

Our gazes locked. Avery slid her hand up my neck and then snaked it around my head, pulling our mouths together again and again. I tried different angles, hungry for her, needing to prove myself not just with my words but also with my body. "Maybe," she said between kisses, "we have naked Saturdays, and then we go slit his tires."

"You read my mind," I said gruffly. She wiggled against my body, making me lose every ounce of damn patience I'd built up over the course of the night. Every hour I wanted to break down her door. And every hour I told myself that it would be a bad idea—giving her the wrong idea that I only wanted her for her body when I wanted her for everything.

"No more cheating." She took my lower lip between her lips and bit down.

I hissed out a curse. "No more cheating. Mainly because you terrify me and you did just offer to slit my best friend's tires, then followed up by biting me, not to mention the scratching of your crazy long nails across my neck."

"Oops," she mouthed. "Sorry, I was distracted."

"By what?"

"This." She jabbed her finger in the cleft of my chin. "I so wish I could call you butt chin." With a sigh, she trailed that same finger down my neck and dipped it into the collar of my T-shirt. "But it's sexy."

"And this makes you sad?"

"Humans need flaws, remember, Thorn?"

"I think I'm one of the most flawed men you'll ever encounter . . . I did fall in love with my fiancée's little sister and contemplate seducing her the night before my wedding."

She seemed to think about this a minute, then said, "Well, for the record, I was weak enough to probably let you."

"It would have ruined us."

Avery nodded.

"Instead, it ruined me."

Another nod. "Me too."

Sighing, I leaned forward, our foreheads touching. "I'm so damn sorry, Avery Bug."

Her eyes filled with tears. "I want you to burn your phone. No, scratch that—I want you to toss that phone into a barrel, set it on fire, and chant a curse around it. Something like, 'If I ever call any of these women again or cheat, let my balls be lit on fire and my penis just fall off.'"

I frowned. "Thought about this, have you?"

"Only a dozen or so times, but I can never get the curse right."

"Unfortunate." I choked out a laugh.

"I know." She actually pouted.

And this was why I loved her.

"Come on." I bent over and lifted her in my arms, then charged like a mad man into my bedroom before tossing her onto the bed and pulling off my clothes at an alarming speed.

When she did nothing but stare at me with her mouth open, I clapped my hands to gain her attention.

She jumped.

"Less staring, more stripping, Avery Bug."

"Am I your girlfriend?" She grinned.

"Are we doing this now? Because there are so many other things I'd rather be doing with my mouth."

"Thorn."

I stalked her, slowly, putting one foot in front of the other before grabbing her leg and jerking her down the front of the bed and pulling her shorts down and her shirt up over her head.

"Cute socks," I muttered.

"Thorn!"

"Yes." I cleared every stitch of clothing away from her perfect body and settled myself between her thighs. "You're my girlfriend."

"And one day you'll marry me." She tipped her chin up.

"One day . . ." I inched inside her, and the tension left me immediately. "Very soon . . . I'll marry you."

"Soon?" she asked on a moan as her head fell back against the bed.

"Soon," I swore.

Chapter Forty-Six

AVERY

He was pissed.

Because I was asking for a transfer to work with one of the other vice presidents. Something felt wrong about being Lucas's private *sexretary*—it had been just one full day back at work, and he was a giant grumpy bear.

Every time I brought him papers to sign, he pouted.

Like a child.

Twice he texted me to come into his office and lock the door.

And twice I gave him a sweet no with a smiley face.

Lucas: Dying. You're actually killing me. Remember that whole scenario where my penis falls off?

Me: You'll make it.

Lucas: Is this punishment for the calendar?

Me: Yes. That's what this is.

Lucas: I'm in hell.

I grinned and set my phone down, then went about sending in the next girl. "Molly?" I called her name. "Lucas Thorn will see you now."

She glared at me.

And I nearly skipped toward the door after her. "Lucas, your next appointment is here."

"Thanks," he said through clenched teeth.

I waved and then went back to the desk and grabbed a piece of gummy candy just as the elevator doors opened and the flight attendants walked in.

"You guys are early, but if you'll just take a seat right over there, Lucas will be right with you."

They eyed me warily.

And they should have.

Because I was cleaning house. Lucas thought all he needed to do was call the girls and let them know he was settling down. But I knew girls, and I didn't want him having that temptation in his life. So not only did he get a new phone with a new number, but he also set up meetings with each of the girls he had cheated with.

And apologized.

Ladies and gentlemen, Lucas Thorn—cheater of the year, man whore of the month—has found his heart! How about a round of applause?

"Why are you clapping?" one of the two girls asked. "Why is she clapping?"

"Sorry." I grinned. "I just have a lot of company spirit, and it's Secretary Appreciation Day." Lie, total lie, but whatever. Let them stare down the other woman.

The one who singlehandedly stole Lucas Thorn's heart.

And refused to give it back.

And just because I was feeling awesome, I offered them candy.

Naturally, they declined because, calories, which just meant more for me and my new spirit-animal bobblehead panda—compliments of my boyfriend.

I patted the head; it bobbled at me.

I had told Lucas I would quit being his intern, and naturally I said he should request a nice old lady to assist him. Someone who was bored with retirement—not that I didn't trust him. I just knew the effect he had on women.

Really, it was like his superpower.

The door to his office opened. Molly left a sobbing mess. I held out the box of tissues while Lucas yelled from his desk, "Next!"

The flight attendants didn't look happy.

Then again, who would be happy about being dumped?

I couldn't wipe the grin from my face, and it would have probably stayed there had Austin not texted me.

Austin: He's a monster!

Me: Who?

Austin: THATCH! A cheating, low life, ball-sucking bastard, and if I have to see him one more time, I'm going to strangle him alive.

Me: Drinks later?

Austin: No. Class. Sorry.

I sighed and dropped my phone. Stupid Thatch and his stupid cheating and inability to keep his pecker in his pants.

The door to Lucas's office burst open, and out walked the flight attendants. They were classy. No tears. Instead, they looked at me, each with a respectful smile.

Lucas leaned his muscled frame against the side of my desk. Slowly, I raised my eyes to his. "Yes, sir?"

He grinned. "It's done."

"All of the girls? Even the substitutes?"

"Do you realize if you smiled any bigger, your face would actually crack near your ears?"

"Smile? What smile?"

He tipped my chin toward him. "I love you, Avery Black."

"I love you too."

He was just about to kiss me when I rolled my chair backward. "What?"

"Do you love me enough to find out why the hell Thatch would break Austin's heart and cheat on her?"

"He did what?" Lucas said, and then let out a heavy sigh. "Thatch may be a player, but he doesn't cheat."

"He did. On her."

"On purpose?" Lucas had the balls to ask.

"YOU DON'T CHEAT BY ACCIDENT!"

"Whoa." He held up his hands and backed away slowly. "Yes, whatever you say. Look, I'll call him, order you some lunch, make sure to draw you a bubble bath back at home, and let you have remote time."

The door to his office closed.

What just happened?

My phone went off.

Lucas: I love you. When you love someone, you let them win—not every battle but at least the ones that matter. Calling Thatch now. There has to be a reason, not that I'm defending what he did or didn't do. Now, your only job—if you choose to accept it—is to make reservations for dinner tonight, for our first real date.

I grinned down at my phone.

Me: I say where it all started.

Lucas: I couldn't agree more.

Acknowledgments

This is the hard part.

Trying to thank everyone who helped put this book together. I think with the more books I write, the harder it gets, and the last thing I want is for this section to become habitual—because I truly mean a huge, giant, epic thank-you to all the people in my life who make writing possible.

I'm so thankful to God that I'm allowed to do what I love, and my husband for being so supportive when I have to put in long hours—for taking Thor for a walk when I just need that quiet time when I can play with the characters in my head (wow—that sounds weird, yet is oddly true).

Thank you to Erica, my amazing agent. I'm pretty sure she has no idea how fantastic she is, or how much I love her. One of these days I'm just going to force her to adopt me so she has no choice but to claim me as a blood relation—too far? ☺

Thanks to everyone at Skyscape for being willing to put your faith and trust in me yet again with another book series, hands down one of the best publishers I've ever worked with. It's an honor to be one of your authors, and I hope I can continue to write books for you!

Jill! My amazing assistant and "family"! Thanks for always being ready and willing to take over the world on my behalf. I would be lost without you!

Ah, I'm missing people! See, the longer these acknowledgments get, the more people I miss! Readers, I adore you guys—it's because of you that I'm able to do what I do.

The same goes for bloggers. I so appreciate the constant support you give me. I know most of you have thankless jobs and don't get paid to do what you do, so the fact that you take time out of your schedule to help support me means more than you'll ever know!

To the Rockin Readers—yeah, you guys are basically like the best fan group ever! (If you want to join, go to Rachel's New Rockin Readers on Facebook).

To everyone who read *Cheater*—I hope it wasn't what you expected; I hope you smiled, laughed, got angry, and were entertained. I hope it made you feel good and crave more. ;) Because, good news! Thatch's story is next, and I can't wait for you to see what I have in store for him!

As always, you can follow me on Facebook, Rachel Van Dyken; Instagram, @RachVD; and Twitter, @RachVD!

HUGS . . .

RVD

About the Author

Photo © 2014 Lauren Watson Perry, Perrywinkle Photography

A master of lighthearted love stories, Rachel Van Dyken is the author of several novels that have appeared on national bestseller lists, including the *New York Times*, the *Wall Street Journal*, and *USA Today*. A devoted lover of Starbucks, Swedish Fish, and *The Bachelor*, Rachel lives in Idaho with her husband, son, and two boxers. Follow her writing journey at www.RachelVanDykenAuthor.com and www.facebook.com/rachelvandyken.